Her husband was dead, and now she and her daughter were in danger. Who could she trust?

A light flickered in the distance. She watched it. It came closer, two lights now. *The headlights of a car moving toward this house.* Her breath came faster. Margaret felt her brain shift into a gear she didn't know she had, some kind of primal, instinctive place where the word "go" inspired instant movement.

"Melissa," she said, standing rooted to the spot. "Melissa, wake up. Get your shoes on. Your jacket. Melissa," she was almost shouting now, if you could shout when all you could do was barely whisper.

The car pulled up to the house, practically under the window where she was standing. Two men got out. They were carrying guns. Big guns. Margaret whirled around, took three long strides to her child in bed, and shook her.

"Melissa, get up now."

Melissa opened her green eyes and looked at her mother. She was instantly awake.

"Shoes," Margaret said as she heard the first shot. "Jacket," she said as she heard the solid front door of the house slam back against the wall downstairs. She heard running and another shot. She went back to the window and cranked open both sides of the casement. This bedroom was on the second floor. Her fear of heights hit her hard. Just thinking of what she was going to do, she could hardly breathe.

"Go out the window," Margaret ordered Melissa. "Climb up onto the hip of the roof and then up to the top. Lie flat. Wait for me there."

Melissa had slipped on her backpack. Whatever was in there, the kid thought it was worth her life. For a second, Margaret thought she should do the same, gather those precious documents together and keep them with her. But there wasn't time. Clay's letter was in her hand. She stuffed it into her pants pocket. Shots downstairs reverberated in her ears. She locked the bedroom door, pulled the sheet off the bed Melissa had been sleeping in, tied it to the foot of the bed, dragged the bed toward the window, and threw the sheet out the window. She grabbed the jacket Agent Erol had loaned her, threw her arms into it, and climbed out the window after her daughter.

Margaret scrambled along the slippery roof, getting snow in her mouth and eyes, scraping her chin, holding onto each shingled edge of the old slate tiled roof that she could find with her freezing fingers. Her toes clutched the edges of roof tiles beneath her. She saw Melissa above her, lying flat along the roofline, holding her hand out for her mother, her eyes encouraging. Margaret panted, trying not to sob. Finally, she reached Melissa's hand and scrambled up onto the rim of the roof. They heard more shots.

Margaret closed her eyes for a minute. *Those poor men.*

A DC conspiracy novel of grand proportions…

Washington, DC, housewife Margaret Turnbull's world literally blows up after her husband, FBI agent Clay Turnbull, is falsely arrested and killed by agents working for an international drug cartel.

Unbeknownst to Margaret, her enemy's tentacles reach all the way to the White House and control senior personnel. Their powerful enterprise in jeopardy, the assassins will stop at nothing to cover their tracks. With cutting-edge surveillance—CIA, FBI, and NSA technology—there is nowhere to hide, no one to trust. No one is safe—anywhere.

KUDOS for *No End of Bad*

In *No End of Bad* by Ginny Fite, FBI Special Agent Clayton Turnbull is suddenly arrested on his way back from lunch and charged with being a spy. Shortly thereafter he is murdered, and his wife Margaret and teenage daughter Melissa are devastated. But Margaret and Melissa don't have much time to grieve. Soon they are on the run for their own lives, trying to stay ahead of assassins out to tie up all lose ends, who don't care who they have to kill to do it. Well written, fast paced, and full of surprises, this one will grab you by the throat and hang on all the way through—a first-class thriller you won't be able to put down. ~ *Taylor Jones, The Review Team of Taylor Jones & Regan Murphy*

No End of Bad by Ginny Fite is the story of a good man trying to do the right thing. Special Agent Clay Turnbull of the FBI is working on an international drug cartel case and getting too close to the truth. In order to stop his investigation, powerful people in the government have him arrested and falsely accused of being a Russian spy. To make matters worse, they murder him and tell the press he died of a heart attack during interrogation. But not everyone believes it, especially when Clay's wife and daughter become the targets of assassins. Barely escaping their home with their lives, the women go into hiding, but even there, they aren't safe. With law enforcement officials and politicians on the payroll of the drug cartel, the criminals have a very long reach, and they are determined to leave no one alive who might have any evidence against them. I was both surprised and delighted by *No End of Bad*—a very different book from Fite's charming and somewhat laid-back mystery series, much more thrilling and intense. Extremely well written, with a solid plot, endearing characters, plenty of suspense, and an intriguing mystery, this one will keep glued to your seat, biting your nails from beginning to end. I loved it! ~ *Regan Murphy, The Review Team of Taylor Jones & Regan Murphy*

ACKNOWLEDGMENTS

Many thanks to the people who read this manuscript in its several versions and encouraged me to believe in it: Carolyn Bross, Patricia Perry, K.P. Robbins, Zach Davis, and, of course, my husband, David Fite, one of the good guys who loved books where something happens. To my agent, Jeanie Loiacono and the grand folks at Black Opal Books, a hat tip for once again making a book out of my nightmares and daydreams.

No End of Bad

Ginny Fite

A Black Opal Books Publication

GENRE: THRILLER/ESPIONAGE/SUSPENSE

This is a work of fiction. Names, places, characters and incidents are either the product of the author's imagination or are used fictitiously, and any resemblance to any actual persons, living or dead, businesses, organizations, events or locales is entirely coincidental. All trademarks, service marks, registered trademarks, and registered service marks are the property of their respective owners and are used herein for identification purposes only. The publisher does not have any control over or assume any responsibility for author or third-party websites or their contents.

For My Sons

Prologue

B ULLETINS

WASHINGTON POST
Thursday, July 19, 2001, Page A01
DEA Shielded Tainted Informant
AGENCY PAID SOURCE FOR 16 YEARS DESPITE ARRESTS, PERJURY
A confidential informant for the Drug Enforcement Administration compromised dozens of prosecutions across the United States by falsely testifying under oath and concealing his own arrest record, but the DEA continued to employ him for sixteen years despite detailed knowledge of his wrongdoing, according to interviews, court records, and an internal report by the agency.

NEWS 10, ALBANY, NEW YORK
Posted: Sep 27, 2011 3:10 AM EDT
Updated: Sep 27, 2011 1:02 PM EDT
AP SOURCES: OFFICIAL RESIGNS OVER ALLEGED SPY RING
By Kimberly Dozier, AP Intelligence Writer

WASHINGTON (AP) ~ A man accused of running an illegal contractor spy ring in Afghanistan has resigned from the air force, and still maintains his innocence after facing possible criminal charges.

Air force civilian employee, Michael Furlong, together with his boss, Mark Johnson, resigned in July after the air force inspector general told the men they'd face official censure for how they ran an information gathering network in Afghanistan.

Inquiries continue by the US Air Force Office of Special Investigations and the Pentagon's Defense Criminal Investigative Service.

SECRECY NEWS
July 29th, 2011
HANDLING OF DRAKE LEAK CASE WAS "UN-CONSCIONABLE," COURT SAID
By Steven Aftergood

The government's treatment of former National Security Agency official Thomas Drake was abusive and akin to acts of British tyranny in pre-Revolutionary War days, said Judge Richard D. Bennett at the July 15 sentencing hearing, which concluded the Drake case, one of the current administration's record number of "anti-leak" prosecutions.

Mr. Drake was originally suspected of leaking classified information to a reporter and had been charged with ten felony counts, all of which he denied. The prosecution was unable to sustain any of those charges, and the case was settled after

Mr. Drake pleaded guilty to a misdemeanor charge of exceeding authorized use of a government computer. He was sentenced at the hearing to a year of probation and 240 hours of community service.

COURTHOUSE NEWS SERVICE
Tuesday, July 31, 2012, Last Update: 10:43 AM PST
EX-NSA OVERSEER ACCUSES US OF RETALIA-
TORY RAIDS
(CNS) - A former member of the House committee,
charged with overseeing National Security Agency operations, claims the FBI raided her property and seized electronic equipment and papers after falsely suspecting her
of leaking classified information about the government's
warrantless wiretap program to the media... in retaliation "for her whistleblower activities and execution of
her congressional oversight responsibilities that revealed
inefficiency, contract fraud, the persistent waste of billions of dollars on a single, ill-conceived program that
was never built," plus illegal and unconstitutional operations.

US COAST GUARD NEWSROOM
April 16, 2015
News Release
US, CANADA ANNOUNCE RECORD DRUG SEI-
ZURE RATES
SAN DIEGO ~ Officials from the US and Canada
welcomed back a US Coast Guard cutter with more than
28,000 pounds of cocaine Thursday as allied forces set
record drug seizure rates in the Eastern Pacific Ocean.
Coast Guard, US Navy, and Royal Canadian Navy
ships have seized more cocaine in the last six months
than in all of fiscal year 2014. US and allied forces operating in the Eastern Pacific Ocean, near Central and
South America, have seized more than 56,000 pounds of
cocaine worth more than $848 million and apprehended
more than 101 suspected smugglers.

Fiscal year 2015, which runs from Oct. 1 to Sept. 30, is already the most successful year in US counter drug operations in the Eastern Pacific since 2009.

DAY ONE

Chapter 1

U ntil he was eyeballing glass fragments embedded in the asphalt walk winding from the Washington Monument toward Constitution Avenue in the nation's capital, Special Agent Clayton Turnbull thought it was a beautiful day for making plans about the future.

He finished his brown-bag lunch, stuffed all the refuse back into the paper bag, pocketed the note that came inside the bag, rolled up the top of the bag, and tossed it in a nearby garbage can. He hated it when tourists left their fast-food wrappers lying around on the ground. He judged a man and his family by their neatness, by their willingness to step five feet out of their way to do what was right. One day's litter could destroy the beauty of the park. He'd always thought those protest packs that came to DC by the hordes were a bunch of hypocrites, yelling about jobs, peace, justice, or God, or whatever the most recent cause was, and leaving the area totally trashed when they got on their buses to go back to wherever they lived.

A man of habit, who enshrined his habits as good things in the way a philosopher elevated his thoughts to truth, Turnbull started walking back toward his office in the FBI building on Pennsylvania Avenue along the same path he took every day. About fifty feet away from the bench where he always sat for lunch, he noticed a discarded manila envelope that must have blown across the mall to the ground near the base of a cherry tree. He muttered, reached down to get it, and opened it to see what was inside.

The next few seconds were a blur. From all around him, men who appeared to be bored federal workers or casual tourists were running toward him, guns pulled, yelling instructions. In a split second, he was face down on the asphalt with a knee jammed between his shoulders, a gun butt had nicked his head, and his hands were yoked together by plastic cuffs. A burly man in a suit yanked him up and frisked him, confiscating his badge, cell phone, wallet, and his wife Margaret's note. One of the guys picked the envelope up from the ground where Turnbull dropped it when they rushed him. Someone else retrieved his lunch bag from the garbage can. He was being read his rights like a radio ad, fast. They weren't giving him time to think or react. They were doing it by the book.

But what the hell was the charge? He noticed the black SUV parked on the grass, the camera, and the cameraman. *How did I fail to notice them before?* Two more suits got out of the vehicle and walked briskly to him. The men weren't from his department, he never recalled seeing them in the FBI building. *They must be from some special unit.*

This is not good, in anybody's definition of the word. They wouldn't have moved this way unless they thought they had evidence. It wasn't on impulse. They must have been watching me for months. What have I been doing that would cause this kind of response? He re-ran his activities for the last year, where he'd been, who he had talked to. Then it hit him. *The stuff about Larry Roland and his drug syndicate. That had to be it. They couldn't possibly think I was involved in that. There is nothing to connect me to that dirty business but casual interviews I documented in the Bureau's normal way. This doesn't make any sense.*

"Clayton Turnbull," said one of the suits as they dragged him to his feet, "you're being charged with espionage and treason." They shoved him into the back seat of the vehicle.

☙☙☙

Margaret Turnbull approached her own kitchen door with the joy children normally reserve for Christmas morning. She loved her home, enjoyed returning to it from every expedition away, relished being in it. With her husband Clay and daughter Melissa, her home was the center of her life.

"Melissa! Melissa!" Margaret called from the kitchen door. "Come and help me with the bags, honey!"

She lugged in two recyclable shopping bags from the car parked in the driveway, nearly dropped them onto the round oak table in the breakfast nook, and called her daughter again. She looked around her kitchen with satisfaction. This room with its lemon yellow walls and kiwi colored quartz counter tops made her blissful.

"Just a little elegance," she'd said to Clay when he raised his eyebrows over the price and the color. Solid oak cabinets with leaded glass door fronts, a wide expanse of windows over the sink, a large bay window by the kitchen table in its little nook, and the wide-planked oak floors all made her feel she was standing in something solid, something that would last forever. This house was as different from the apartment in Newark, New Jersey, where she grew up, as light was from dark. She was safe here.

For her, although she would never tell Clay this, this kitchen stood for their marriage. Every inch of it represented some kind of compromise that, in the making, looked to her like a disaster but finished was a triumph. Every morning, she sat in her sturdy wicker chair, holding her cup of tea, and gazed out the window at the old oaks and maples surrounding the house. Even in winter, their branches seemed to hold out the promise of spring. She never wanted to leave here.

Margaret unwound the long purple wool scarf from her neck and put it over a peg on the coat rack near the kitchen door. She unzipped her red wool jacket, slipped it off, hanging it over the scarf, and called to her daughter again. She shook her shoulder-length auburn hair loose from the collar of her turtleneck and turned back to unpack the bags she had lugged in, pulling out the red-tipped lettuce, the long crusty baguette, a sweet onion the color of her scarf, and a red pepper. She looked at them lying on the green countertop and thought about the composition as a painting. Her eyes framed the vegetables and bread for a second, enough time for the exposure to develop in her mind, and then she called Melissa again. *Where is that kid?* She was tempted to call her daughter on her cell phone, or text her. Maybe then the girl would answer.

She could hear the TV on in Melissa's bedroom, went to the doorway between the kitchen and the hallway, and called again, louder this time. Of course, she could carry all the packages in by herself, but she thought her daughter should help her. She'd been trying to instill the idea of a team, of working together, right now, before Melissa made it one step further into adolescence. She was a pretty good fifteen-year-old. Margaret had to give her that. But sixteen could be the bone-crusher year, and they were on the cusp. Margaret wanted to lay down a foundation for living together that might hold during the inevitable parental reactions to rebellion. She imagined tattoos, pierced belly button, blue hair—*Oh God, blue over that luscious red hair would probably wind up being burgundy*—multi-partner sexual exploits, known as orgies in her day, drug experimentation with pills she'd never heard of, and who knows what else.

"Melissa!" she called again. Still no answer from her daughter. Frustrated, she climbed the stairs, lightly holding onto the oak railing, calling her daughter's name. Melissa's paneled oak bedroom door was closed. Margaret opened it without knocking and saw Melissa lying face down on the purple quilt on her bed with a pillow held tightly on top of her head. The rest of Melissa's long body encased in jeans, a T-shirt, and loose gray sweater was still, as if she had been shot. Not a nerve twitched. She had the news tuned-in on the TV, an odd choice for a teenager who didn't know there was a world outside her school and friends.

"Melissa, what's going on?" Margaret sat down on the bed. She stroked her daughter's back and looked around the room. Nothing seemed out of the ordinary. It was the usual mess of clothes left lying where her daughter had taken them off, shoes turned on their sides, magazines lying open, school books spread out on the desk next to the iMac, a notebook with some quickly scribbled lines written in it, and her phone was on the night stand next to the bed. Melissa lifted her tear-stained face.

"Oh, Mom, oh God, didn't you hear? It's all over the news. Katie called me to tell me, and I've been watching every station. My God, Mom, it can't be true." And then the child started to sob again.

"What's true, what are you talking about?"

Margaret wondered if some rock star had been shot or committed suicide. She had felt a small tremor when Kurt Cobain had died at twenty-seven, felt some shock that talent could not see a future worth living, but certainly nothing to sob about. Kids were so dramatic these days. She'd been an adult, years older than the teen idol, when he died. Perhaps she didn't remember what it was to be a teenager. Today, she had been engrossed in her errands: running to the bank, the bookstore, and a brief stop in the local craft shop looking for the right-sized canvas for whatever project was nagging at the back of her mind. On her drive back from Whole Foods, she had been thinking about how the vaulted ceiling of trees looked in the winter, curving over the streets of her neighborhood forming an abstract of the sky. She hadn't turned on the car radio. Looking at Melissa's beautiful face, now splotchy from crying, she saw the girl's thick, red lashes had clotted from her torrent of tears.

"Tell me what you're talking about." Margaret's practiced motherhood strategy was to instill calm.

"It's Dad. God, Mom, do you live on Mars? It's Dad!" Melissa whispered between sobs, "The FBI arrested him. They said all over the news that he's a spy and that he's been doing it for years. They said he had money hidden in overseas banks." She began to wail.

Margaret turned to the television, grabbed the remote, and flipped the station to CNN. Sure enough, there were some talking heads discussing her husband, Clayton Turnbull, the FBI brief against him, and how solid their information was. *This can't be real. This can't be. There has to be a mistake.*

"All right, honey, try to calm down. Crying isn't going to help. We have to think. We have to act normally. Come down stairs and help me get the bags in from the car and put the food away."

She stood up, gently pulling on Melissa's hand, and realized she was trembling from head to toe. If any of this were true, there'd be agents watching the house. Someone would come to interrogate them; to see what they knew or didn't know. She remembered hearing through the FBI wives' grapevine about a CIA agent who'd been arrested for spying. His family had been harassed for two years until finally the FBI had shrugged and said, "Oops, never mind. Wrong guy." Her phone would be tapped. They may have already searched the house. Someone had been in her house without her even knowing it—had been looking through their email and bills, listening in on her phone calls, searching through their trash, opening all their drawers, looking through the laundry bin, and God knows what all. *How had I not noticed?* She felt violated, shamed, infuriated. *I haven't done anything! None of us has done anything! Why is this happening?*

Margaret stopped moving for a minute as the idea of someone peering into every crevice of her life wound its way down from her mind to her gut. She put her hand there, as if to stop its movement. *What am I supposed to do, anyway? Should I call a lawyer? Will Clay be able to call me? He must be able to call me. Doesn't he get a call?*

There were too many questions. She had to do one thing at a time. Empty the shopping bags first, then make dinner, if they could swallow anything, and after that, wait and see what comes next. She turned off the television, put her arm around her daughter, pulled her off the bed, and walked with her out of the bedroom. "Let's put a cold cloth on that beautiful face."

She knew at least one thing: they would have no comment for the press. She would let the answering machine get the calls. The silence surrounding her house struck her. *Why hadn't the press besieged them? Wasn't that their usual protocol? Maybe the Bureau somehow prevented that from happening. Were they afraid of what I might say? Unlikely. What could I say?* Anyway, her mother and sister, her friends, would be calling. She needed to think of an answer for them. Maybe in this case, suddenly weary, she thought the best response would be the truth: she knew nothing about anything.

Margaret and Melissa went down the staircase with their arms around each other. If they let go, they would be alone to face their doubts. Margaret was thinking about all the times Clay was away, all the times she had no idea what he was doing or where he was. She had trusted him. It was the foundation of their relationship. She had always assumed that what he told her was the truth. He slept soundly. He didn't pace or stare off into space when he was home, nor did he drink or go for long walks alone. He was always simply home, there for them, completely present. *How could he have done something like this? How could he have done it without me knowing? Not possible! No, it simply is not possible!* She would just hold onto that—her only lifeline in a sea of thoughts that threatened to sink her.

"Daddy couldn't be guilty, Mom, could he?" Melissa was the first to say it out loud.

"No, sweetheart, he couldn't be guilty." Margaret hoped she sounded convinced, wondered if that was possible when her lips were quivering. "No way, not in a million years," she said, as much to reaffirm it for herself as her daughter. "Not him."

Chapter 2

Seated in the back seat of the black SUV, hands cuffed uncomfortably behind his back, black cloth hood over his head, helpless to do anything until he could assess his situation, Clayton Turnbull thought through his activities for the last year and tried to get his bearings. He could tell by the steady rotation of the tires on asphalt that they were on a highway, but which highway going in what direction, he couldn't tell. *The destination certainly isn't FBI headquarters. We have already been driving too long for that...*

It had been a beautiful February day when he started out to eat lunch on his favorite bench. A cloudless sky—a blue iris on the lens of God's eye—hung over the city. Just as he did on all beautiful days, he had put on his trench coat and carried his customary brown bag lunch out to the park on the edge of the Potomac River that marked the boundary between the nation's capital and Virginia, completely unaware that life could go any way but the way he planned.

He'd looked across to the Jefferson Memorial slowly sinking into the tidal basin, no matter what the Corps of Engineers did to shore it up. The river was a broad palm spread out to be read by adepts who could see the power line intersected by hidden cross currents. With all its carefully wrought beauty—sloping lawns, the intricate branches of trees swaying in the light wind, the gleaming monuments—underneath, forces no one could deter were working their will on a city built on a swamp.

Still fit in his late fifties, Clayton always walked briskly from his desk in the FBI building on Pennsylvania Avenue in the nation's capital, across the open mall, spot-checking the spike of the Washington Monument sur-rounded by scaffolding like a child's strange erector set. He liked the human scale of the capital city, the white buildings, the wide boulevards, and pedestrian-friendly sidewalks. The trees and sufficient sky, the sense of monuments and history, even with the now ubiquitous massive cement barriers blocking access to icons of American history, made him proud to be an American.

He thought about his wife, Margaret, who always packed his lunch with loving care. The bottom line on women was that you never knew what they were think-ing. They had, in his judgment, multi-track minds and seemed to be able to think several things simultaneously. It never failed to amaze him when they were talking about, say, world politics, his wife would suddenly re-mind him to replace the filters on the air conditioning system. He couldn't follow the logic in how she got from one topic to the next. Women, it seemed, thought in con-centric circles rather than straight lines, with some kind of teleportation device that got them from one circle to another and back in the blink of an eye...

The vehicle jolted. They were now off-road, the tires lumbering over what must be frozen ruts in a dirt lane. Clayton returned to rerunning his movements until the moment of his arrest...

Few tourists walked on the national park grounds this time of year. The only inhabitants of the park were health-conscious, or unbelievably bored federal employees who ambled along the asphalt paths. Boredom was a fact of life in the federal service. Clayton sometimes wondered if the jobs were too minutely parceled out. Friends of his in the IRS would look only at the returns of some small portion of the population, the limits of their interest defined by income measures and some suspicious aberration on the form. Day in and day out, they did the same thing. He wondered if they dreamed of numbers on lined pieces of paper. Thank God he had not gone that route.

The FBI had allowed him to develop his intense nosiness, his willingness to talk to strangers about any old thing until he got to the trick questions and the subjects were so involved in spilling their guts that they would tell him what he needed to know. He thought these new spying devices—remote electronic listening and watching—could never get at the facts. Sure, they would collect a Mt. Everest of data, but how would they know what bits were important? He also held definitely negative opinions about what was called enhanced interrogation. You had to put the life-size puzzle of people's stories together before you knew what was going on, what was at the core of the event. Then you had to get the physical evidence, as much as you could, that proved the perpetrators had done the deed. His way took longer but made for more prosecutable cases. He was proud of the work he had done at the Bureau...

The car stopped. They had gone about a mile in from the road. The vehicle had jolted across rutted ground and then crunched over gravel. *Must be an old Virginia farmhouse south of DC.* Someone opened the rear door, grabbed his arm, yanked him out of the vehicle and onto his feet. The ground was uneven but grassy. Long, frozen grass snapped as they stepped on it. Two men, one on either side of him, gripped his arms and nearly dragged him up one, two, three wooden steps and then across what must be a porch from the sound of their footsteps snapping against wood. They were definitely at a house, not a government facility. A door creaked open. No one said anything to him.

"Hey," Clayton said, struggling to loosen their grip on him. "Check my ID. I'm FBI Special Agent Clayton Turnbull."

"We know exactly who you are, Turnbull."

"What the hell are you doing? Get this bag off my head."

"You don't call the shots here, buddy."

They dragged Clayton up one flight, turned, another flight. *Wooden floor.* One of the men punched him in the stomach. When he doubled over, they shoved him onto a metal chair and cuffed him to it. Then they removed the hood. Clayton looked at them. They were complete strangers. He looked around the room: a makeshift interrogation room in what must be a two-century old house, based on the flooring and wrought-iron heating grate in the floor. The windows were boarded up. The chair was bolted to the floor. *This is not good.* The men left the room, locking the door behind them. Clayton went back to his assessment of what got him in this miserable situation...

Certain information he had been collecting nagged at him, irritating him—an eyelash he couldn't extract from his eyeball. When it had finally dawned on the Departments of Justice and Homeland Security that terrorism didn't just come in foreign packages, nor necessarily from well-known hate groups all over the country, their task had been to find and follow the small cells of angry people before they went ballistic and started loading up on fertilizer, manure, plastic explosives or high-firepower weapons that shot armor piercing bullets. About a year ago, in the course of the ongoing investigation about who might be the next active homegrown terrorists, he had stumbled onto breadcrumbs that disturbed him. Being who he was, he followed them as far as he could.

The agency had been stung by its failure to anticipate and stop the Oklahoma City bomber, the September eleventh terrorists, the Boston marathon backpack bombers— the list was long. They wanted to get even. Clayton often thought they weren't paying attention to the right clues.

His role in this counterterrorism puzzle meant that he traveled a lot. He would follow the trail of the odd piece of information, driving a battered old Chevy wagon around the country, talking to people who might know people who might know something else. Sometimes it struck him that he was a human hound dog, sniffing other people's droppings, and then following that smell until he was up their asses. But he didn't think that way a lot, just often enough to laugh at himself.

This particular trail had led him all over the country, and he'd often lost the scent. First, it was the evasions that made him notice something was going on. That was sort of normal. People always had some secret they thought could get them in trouble. Underneath anyone's seemingly normal exterior lurked the angry soul of a latent saboteur. When a person tapped into that angry loner zeitgeist, anything could happen. In that frame of mind, people did things, criminal things—say murder—and were somehow able to justify them.

And now that disgruntled rebels could travel overseas and be trained to kill innocent civilians, it was even more important to spot them before they acted. It was his job to identify the members of this group, whoever they were, watch them, and hopefully stop them.

A year ago a source had tipped Clayton to a guy named Larry Roland who was socking away weapons, using cash to buy them at gun shows where background checks weren't required, even while Transportation Security Administration clerks were forcing ninety-five-year-old grandmothers with cancer to remove their adult diapers before they could board a plane.

Checking out Roland hadn't been difficult. The man lived a falling-down kind of life in the basement apartment of someone's aging townhouse in Inglewood, California. He seemed to be a loner. His parents were dead, two marriages had ended in divorce, and he was out of touch with his sister, who worked a fairly high-profile job in DC. That alone put Roland, even at sixty-five, within the profile spectrum of someone to watch.

Roland was a former Marine stationed in Okinawa during the Vietnam conflict, working on repairing, loading, and fueling the planes that ran the transPac missions from Okinawa to Vietnam. Those planes also went to Guam, Johnson Atoll, and sometimes all the way to El Toro in California and back with supplies or weapons. Honorably discharged after six years, Roland wandered from job to job for more than three decades—one of the thousands of psychologically wounded warriors who had difficulty finding their footing after that war—before he hooked into this flea market gig. Roland had never been arrested for anything, according to the FBI's database. He didn't even have a speeding ticket from the last three years. He was just one of the anonymous millions of people who lived in this country, seemingly minding his own business.

Roland's most recent entrepreneurial effort was collecting other people's discarded objects, often from dumpsters or trash left by the road, and selling them at flea markets across California's inland towns. He'd been doing it for about seven years. That explained the cash. It didn't explain the guns. He wasn't your usual gun collector. Maybe he was planning to sell them for a profit, a little back-of-the-van gun sale at a flea market happened all the time. Aside from his flea market gig, once a month Roland took a ride out to the San Gabriel Mountains on his Hog and camped out overnight alone. His Harley was an old bike, something he picked up in the late 1970s, according to registration records, and kept in good repair.

Clayton hadn't observed Roland doing anything unusual on these camping trips, except that he stayed within a mile of the public, and very disgusting, toilet. The guy just set out his campsite, put up his tent, gathered wood, and at night, made a fire, cooked some food, ate it, then went to sleep. The next day, he hiked a bit and then lit out. He didn't even appear to be a druggie or heavy drinker. Yet, every other weekend, Roland would set up at some flea market from the back of his van.

Clayton found that he was more intrigued by the guy's flea market buyers than by Roland. Some of them looked like they could have shopped on Rodeo Drive, the famed glam Beverly Hills shopping strip. The sharp dressers, as Turnbull had come to think of them, bought old postcards and posters from Roland. Collectors, you just couldn't explain them.

Clayton watched Roland on and off for months, whenever he was in California. Then it clicked. Follow the buyers. Something was written on those postcards and posters. He followed one long-haired guy dressed in yellow linen pants, a black silk T-shirt, and crocodile tassel loafers who drove a Jag from the San Diego flea market to Temecula. The clothes alone, not to mention the Jaguar, were suspicious at a flea market, unless the guy was

some true weirdo collector. Temecula, tucked away behind the Santa Rosa Mountain, had been found by the
upwardly mobile willing to commute two hours north to
Los Angeles or one hour south on the packed freeway to
San Diego to get away from the smog at night and sleep
in an affordable, two-thousand-square-foot house with a
red tile roof indistinguishable from its neighbors. *No, this
doesn't seem to be Mr. Linen Slacks' normal destination.*

In ten years, Temecula's population had gone from
4,500 to 45,000, but these new folks were mostly white-
collar, upwardly mobile, non-terrorist types. At least,
that's how Clayton saw it. Slacks, who Clayton would
have normally placed as a Mulholland Drive baby, got off
the freeway, took a few turns toward the vineyard region,
which fit him more accurately, and wound up at a retirement park of well-turned-out doublewides on permanent
foundations. Slacks pulled into the driveway of a home
that had more cement statues of squirrels, rabbits, and
gnomes laid out on its Astroturf yard than a highway
stand, opened the kitchen door with a key, went inside for
a few moments, and came back out with a cardboard
moving box usually used for books. In fact, on the side in
big red letters, was the word *"BOOKS."* Slacks packed a
few of these boxes of books into his car and drove off,
totally clueless to being tailed.

From there, Clayton followed Slacks to a hotel in
Palm Springs.

Basically, Clay felt he had wasted his time. The ride
to Temecula and Palm Springs seemed to have nothing to
do with whatever was going on at the flea market and Roland. He had nothing to show for the miles, and he was
way off track. There was no reason to think that bomb
materials were being assembled, transported, or deployed
in this complicated way. And the players, except for Roland, didn't fit the profile.

But loners, like Roland, kept turning up in his sights. They all seemed to be doing this flea market gig. And they all had the occasional buyer who was just out of place. Clayton picked up Roland's trail whenever he was back in California. Later, as the facts began to accumulate, Clay began to get nervous. On this case, he placed tapes of his recorded notes and interviews in his bank safety deposit box. He stored his typed notes on thumb drives and put those in the safe at home. He knew trouble when he saw it. This wasn't his assignment. Roland and his counterparts did not appear to be homebred terrorists. Clayton suspected this was no one's assignment.

He had called a contact in the ATF about the guns Roland was stashing and an acquaintance at the DEA about his suspicions. He'd done about a dozen interviews and made one other call to see if he could put some of the pieces together, but that call was never returned. His buddies in related agencies had listened politely, but it seemed to him they never followed up. That was a very loud warning bell. The one call back he got from his DEA colleague was direct. "Stay out of it," his friend said.

If what he thought was true could be supported by real evidence rather than conjecture, the country had a problem at least as serious as the occasional errant lunatic with a bomb...and nobody seemed to be doing anything about it. After a while, Clayton had taken more precautions. He sent a tape of an interview with a note to his lawyer to hold onto, just in case, just to leave some breadcrumbs to follow since he'd started to look over his shoulder. Now, he realized, he had waited too long.

It wouldn't be long until the thugs who kidnapped him came back in the room. He had only a short time to consider his options. He thought of his wife again...

They'd been married twenty-five years, not without
their minor seismic tremors, but still going. As she headed into her fifties, his wife seemed to become more beautiful, at least to him. So she wouldn't turn any heads in a
youth-is-all culture, but she had a kind of steady beauty
that endured. She glowed. If he wanted to remember how
she looked when they met, he had only to look at his
daughter, who was the spitting image of her mother.

The first time he saw Margaret, he had been pulling
out of an on-street space in DC near the Ellipse when he
spotted her crossing the street. She was a knockout, the
most startlingly beautiful woman he'd ever seen. He
couldn't help himself, he had thought many times since,
looking at her across the table from him in the morning.
She had had a way of walking that seemed to declare her
ownership of the world. But that day she had been going
in the opposite direction. He felt himself pulled out of his
normal routine, jerked off course, reversed in his own
skin by the sight of her. He pulled up to the next intersec-
tion, made an illegal U-turn across traffic, and drove up
to where she was waiting on the corner of Constitution
and Fourteenth Street for the light to change. He got out
of the car, the driver behind him leaning on the horn to
signal his outrage. But he couldn't just let her walk out of
his life. He had to talk to her. The guy could go around
him. He made his move, and then the only thing he could
think to say to her was the truth.

"Miss," he had said, standing about a foot from her,
his heart pounding in his throat. "Miss?"

She had turned and looked at him, curious but wary.
"Yes?"

"Miss, I had to stop—I had to stop you," Clayton
stammered, searching his thirty-year-old brain for the
right words for this occasion. "I had to tell you that
you're the most beautiful woman I've ever seen."

She put her hand to her cheek and pushed back a stray hair. "Thank you," she said, continuing to look at him for a minute as if she were doing some test for veracity. Then turning her head, she stared across the street as if she were judging the traffic.

Clayton stared at her ear, exposed by the way her luminous red hair was swept back into a French twist at the back of her head. That ear was the mother-of-pearl interior of an abalone shell.

"I mean," Clayton said, "I couldn't just let you walk out of my life. I had to stop you."

Margaret looked back at him, looked into his gray eyes, and seemed to assess his full lips, the strong chin, broad forehead, the suit and tie. She smiled and made his life instantly better. "Now that you've stopped me, what do you intend to do, Mr..."

"Turnbull, Clayton," he said. "Clayton Turnbull, I mean." He flushed a little, thinking he had forgotten everything he knew about talking to people, but held out his hand. "You are?"

"Margaret," she said, not offering her last name, but taking his hand, grasping it, and giving it a little shake.

That seemed to work. Her hand in his confirmed what he knew. She was obviously flattered, but a little cautious. He liked her caution. *He* would normally have been cautious. She told him where she was working, Hamm and Scheller.

He took it from there, calling the law firm, talking the receptionist into telling him her last name, ordering flowers to be delivered to her that day. He called her in the late afternoon, had dinner with her that night, and three months later they were married. He always knew what he wanted, and most of the time he got it.

They bought a lovely brick house in Alexandria and had stayed in it all this time. Now it was worth a million dollars, even after the great recession blew house values apart, and it was paid for. They bought small foreign cars when their friends started buying luxury SUV gas guzzlers. He economized in other ways. They spent their leisure time with family and friends, not on fancy and expensive cruises to wonderland. The savings added up.

Clayton had never been ambitious for the big spots in the bureau. He didn't want to take on the administration of a deputy position, or even a supervisor. He liked the field, and the income was decent. As his savings started to grow, and he'd learned about the tax advantages from his IRS friends, he started putting chunks of after-tax money from his local savings account into a Swiss bank that offered better interest and greater safety. He didn't trust the stock market. It was just legalized betting, and it looked too risky to him. The house always won. He wanted to protect the little he had.

He'd never wanted to be a rich man, just comfortable. His father had been a bookkeeper. His own position in the bureau that protected democracy was high enough on the totem pole for him. He did have hopes his daughter would be a doctor or a lawyer. That was the right progression, he thought. Each generation made it one rung higher. *What, then, would his grandchildren achieve,* he wondered. That remained to be seen, *when* he had grandchildren. There was nothing like America for possibilities, or so he had thought.

Being arrested for treason had not been one of the possibilities Clayton ever contemplated. He waited, sick to his stomach, for the next gut punch.

Chapter 3

Cheryl Roland was alone in the office. That was a rare event. The point was to catch up on the pile of papers stacked on the front right corner of her five-foot wide desk. Her tuna sandwich, half-eaten by herself and perhaps lunched on by the Cannon House office building's ubiquitously large roaches while she ran around to various meetings, was pushed to the back of the desk, nearly hidden by stacks of paper.

The advent of the computer age had done nothing to help communications directors manage the volume of paper in their lives. The Internet had simply added hours of on-screen reading and keyboarding in response to emails that flew across congressional offices and across the country at practically the speed of light. And then there was Facebook and Twitter. The endless proliferation of ways to get the word out directly to constituents was mind boggling. Not only was there more work, but more people commented on everyone else's work, thoughts, and digital sniffles. There were more opportunities to screw up, to accidentally include among addressees in an email blast some reporter who should not be privy to that particular piece of information. But all those electronic digits had done nothing to get rid of paper, which was still as prolific as the roaches.

Gathering her long black hair in one hand and twisting it up off her neck, Cheryl sifted through the paper on her desk with her other hand, searching for a barrette, something to hold her hair off her shoulders. Notes on various pieces of paper—the print-out of calls taken for her by the receptionist and her callback list from her own voice mail that she faithfully transcribed into written squiggles so that no call would get lost—were scattered around the desk in what seemed to be no particular order. At least on her cell phone the list of calls was in chronological order, not that that really helped.

Jake leaned into her cubicle. "Hey, I'm back. The Member is going to have dinner with Senator Cummings. She said to tell you."

"Okay. Thanks." Cheryl looked around her desk. "I'll be here a little while longer. I've got to sort through this mess." Being the only black woman on the congresswoman's senior staff meant she had to prove herself every day. She had to be better, faster, and smarter than every other person in the same position times four-hundred and fifty. Every day, without let up. She pretended to herself that it wasn't exhausting.

Jake ambled over to his own desk and turned on the television, its low mumbling almost as distracting as having to talk to him.

Cheryl's eyes surveyed the mess on her desk. She had long ago given up trying to keep up with calls and had her own ordering system. A's were those from high level constituents—mayors and the governor's aides, legislators and contributors, movers and shakers in the district—who wanted personal answers to questions about the congresswoman's positions, or, to put it more cynically, wanted to be able to say they had told the congress-

woman what she should think. Colleagues were in the A
category also. The B list consisted of calls from reporters,
particularly those who would use the congresswoman's
name in the story. A's and B's got call-backs the same
day. C's were everyone else. Those calls rarely got returned, unless they were very persistent, went around her
back to the congresswoman, or caught Cheryl off guard.

This was her only form of poetry: order out of chaos
for the sake of sanity, not art. It had been so long since
Cheryl had paid attention to the little voice in her head
that gave her lines, so long since she'd looked and listened in the way that poetry required, that all that remained of the practice was a kind of word-by-word approach to life. Some words stayed on the page, some
were excised.

The difference between poetry and real life, she
thought, *was that you couldn't have thirty-three versions
of the same event tucked in your drawer until you decided
which one you wanted to publish. You could never polish
a real moment to perfection.* Working on Capitol Hill for
a member of Congress had also taught her there was
nothing improvisational about life. Life was the great editor, continually crossing out lines until there was only one
option remaining.

Her hand found a long bobby pin and Cheryl looped
her hair into a bun and stuck the pin through it. Her eyes
strayed for a minute to the television screen, which she
could see above this rabbit warren of desks, dividers, and
bookcases. She heard the babble of the commercials before the evening news. The Member, as they called her,
as if she were an integral part of their own bodies, was
working on her most recent deal to make herself chair-
person of a subcommittee on the Appropriations Committee from which she could deliver the goods to the voters

at home. Cheryl sighed, leaned back in her chair, and pulled the stack of papers onto her lap.

These also needed to be sorted by Cheryl's personal alpha system, with a small difference in definition. The high priority items were speeches in process—briefings, press releases in draft, etc. At the bottom were other kinds of communications efforts: proposed Facebook campaigns and web page updates, the credentials of a person who might manage their social media, mass email letters, the quarterly newsletter draft, postcard copy, and boilerplate email responses on particular issues. Sorting this way was the only thing that made the job possible. If she attacked what was stacked up on her computer, she might never get to the important stuff. She spent most of her day talking to people, or listening. Half her time seemed to be spent in hallways. Elevators were for meetings in which a decision could be made in thirty seconds. The desk was definitely just a holding pattern. She was on a jet that never landed.

She hoped to be out of here by seven-thirty tonight, with whatever she was going to work on tucked into her briefcase. Members thought you had no life other than their office. That was the price you paid for being an underpaid political hack who wanted to be in the loop. But a question haunted Cheryl more and more often: what did you get for that price? When the thrill of telling people you worked on the Hill wore off, knowing things before others did wasn't enough, particularly if what you really knew was that nothing, ever, got done here. *Maybe that wasn't particularly a bad thing, considering the kinds of things people wanted to get done. Considering who wanted to get something done.* Often, words from the Yeats poem whispered in her mind: "*...the worst are full of passionate intensity." And the best? The best, whoever they were, were left to fend for themselves. They probably* *figured out early that Congress was no place for them and left fairly quickly. And so what are you doing here?* that clear little voice in her head asked her.

The evening network news reader was saying something about a high-profile arrest of an FBI agent accused of spying for the Russians. *Shades of Tom Clancy! This can't be for real. Do we still care about the Russians?* She couldn't keep track of the bad guys du jour. Cheryl walked out of her cubicle and stood in front of the TV.

"Did she just say what I thought she said?"

"Yeah," Jake said. "There's a new spy in town."

On the screen was a photograph of a typical looking agent—clean cut, dark suit, short blonde hair, high forehead, gray eyes, strong build evident beneath the suit jacket, basically FBI anonymous. The news reader was saying the guy's name was Clayton Turnbull and that he had been spying for the Russians for fifteen years.

"Unbelievable. It certainly took them an awfully long time to figure it out."

Jake nodded, absorbed in the narrative, and turned up the volume.

This wasn't a great demonstration of competence by the agency that was supposed to be the best at getting the bad guys. Or was the truth that they were just really good at PR? Maybe what J. Edgar started was not the best national cop unit but the best public relations outfit.

"Took them a long time to nail Aldrich Ames," Jake said, his back to her, "and they lost track of the Nine/Eleven terrorists even though they knew they were in the country. They were clued into the Boston Bombers by the Russians, who are now apparently our enemies, and still couldn't stop them from blowing up innocent people at the Boston marathon. And there was that embarrassing minor massacre in San Bernardino by an

American who married a jihadi wife, about whom they'd been warned."

Cheryl had forgotten that Jake was their legislative aide for intelligence matters. Now that he was started, he could go on all night. She sighed.

"Now that the FBI can go through people's trash and emails before they commit a crime, or are even suspected of thinking about a crime, you'd think they would catch up to bad guys more quickly, but they seem to be preoccupied with arresting and charging members of their own club. They arrested agents and administrators from the NSA, CIA, and FBI and called them traitors, and completely missed Nidal Hassan, the army psychiatrist with dodgy annual reviews who shot thirty-two people, killing thirteen of them in cold blood at Fort Hood."

"Yeah, I forgot that," Cheryl said, not that she had.

She wondered how much she thought she knew about anything was shaped by the continual propaganda pumped out by government hacks. It was a scary thought that made her uneasy, not about the world but about her own tenuous grasp on reality. *What if nothing she knew was really the truth?* That was a career ending question. She turned her back on it.

Cheryl was listening for the word alleged somewhere in the newscast, thinking about the last time the press jumped the gun on that poor schnook during the Olympics in Atlanta, branding him a mad bomber based on an FBI leak. Or what about that NSA guy, Drake, who had been branded an enemy of the state for talking to a reporter about a billion-dollar fraud at the top-secret agency? At least a judge ruled that the government had no case against Drake and dismissed the charges.

Now the show had jumped to a video of a press conference held by the FBI director, who claimed that they had boxes of information incriminating this guy and was congratulating his team for being able to get the spy on videotape making his connection. They were saying this was the other spy they'd been looking for. *Is it possible there were really only two? Surely the Russians, since they were suddenly relevant in the espionage world, had been more successful in recruiting agents than that.*

"This sounds kind of cheesy, don't you think?" Jake turned to look at her.

Cheryl rubbed her forehead with her fingertips and wondered about the repercussions of such a prominent announcement. Obviously, they weren't worried about letting the Russians know they'd gotten their spy, or alerting them that he might give away his contacts under interrogation. *That's odd. Doesn't the Bureau want to arrest Turnbull's contacts as well?* She'd love to get a copy of the flight manifest out of Reagan National to Russia or even Prague or Amsterdam over the next couple days. *What about what Turnbull had been working on in his other life, in his real job? He was in counter-terrorism. Why was no one worried about how this play had tipped off those bad guys?*

It seemed to her the Bureau had lost its center, the core of what they were about. They were supposed to investigate and catch the bad guys so that they could be prosecuted in court. That was another piece of this news business that disturbed her. Their way of announcing his arrest seemed to have another purpose other than just patting themselves on the back. The guy was being publicly black-balled, the same way Robert Hanssen had been. It wasn't just that he had been tried and convicted by the media in a front-page, *Washington Post*, single-anonymous-source story and then forgotten in a matter of a week, well before any trial. It was the very public nature of the arrest. The way the agency was handling it all reminded her of how the press had been invited to come along to the Waco debacle. She worried about actions taken for the benefit of the cameras rather than in support of the law.

Politics was performance art, but government, she used to think, was not. Certainly in the country where the rule of law was a core belief politics wouldn't trump justice. Yet, here it was, and it wasn't appealing. The brief provided by the FBI and Turnbull's face would be on every talk show, along with the inevitable pundits talking authoritatively about what they couldn't possibly know. She could imagine producers all over the country scrambling this afternoon, after the well-timed press conference announcement, to find experts on the subject who could drop everything and expound on their shows. Getting a little face time with American viewers was part of the expert game. Enough face time, and you got a book contract.

"Better watch that attitude, Cheryl," the congresswoman had said. "You're cynical."

"Not cynicism," Cheryl had retorted, "healthy realism." And, with this at the top of the news, anything the congresswoman's office had to offer would fall off the news plate. *Now that's cynical.* She smiled to herself.

Walking back to her desk, while the news droned on, something nagged her. Turnbull's name was too familiar. *Why do I know that name?* Ah, there it is! *He had called me.* Cheryl put her hands in her hair as if she were holding down the top of her head. *God, why would he do that?* She didn't know him from Adam, they didn't have any committee assignments directly related to the FBI. *Where had he gotten my name?* Hands shaking, she sifted through the call-back notes on her desk and found the one with his name and phone number. *Well, he probably won't be taking any calls for a while. He'll be sequestered somewhere, interrogated.* She wondered if he'd be able to call his family. Her mind shifted points of view. *How awful for them to get this news from the television.*

Then she realized his phone records would show the call to her. For sure, she didn't want to be testifying in court or before some committee about something she had no knowledge of nor was involved in. She could be destroyed just by this minor association with Turnbull, without ever having had a conversation. She crumbled up the note and was about to throw it in the trash, then changed her mind, and tucked it into her pocket. *I'll burn it in the fireplace at home...But phone records, they'll have the phone records.* It was time to go home.

Cindy was back in the office, and Cheryl called out to let her know she was leaving for the night. "I'll be at home if the congresswoman wants to talk about anything, and of course," she waggled her cell phone in the air, "she can always get me on my cell."

She pulled her suit jacket off the back of her chair, grabbed her purse, and headed out the huge wooden door to the office reception area. The only thing she could imagine the member wanting to talk about this evening was why Cheryl couldn't get her the same amount of airtime that Turnbull was getting. It would take some discipline not to say, "Get arrested for spying."

"Yeah, okay," Cindy said, snapping her gum and pushing her luxuriant brunette hair behind her ear to accommodate the phone clip.

Cheryl wound through the various hallways to the elevator, her heels clacking on the marble floors, and then down the several escalators that took her to the garage where her car was parked. At least the job provided indoor parking. She'd had to fight for that, though. In-office politics was sometimes more brutal than what was going on in the House cloakroom. She might as well be on that TV show, *Survivor*, never knowing if she'd be

voted out or tricked into breaking her own heart when she
found herself saying the words that would eliminate
someone else. Folks who managed a long career as staffers in the United States Congress had balls of steel, or, in
her case, ovaries. *Best not to think this way, dearie,* she
counseled herself. *Just stay on the lookout for an opportunity to do a little good.* Those moments came up from
time to time, usually one constituent or one decent vote at
a time.

Keith was coming over for dinner tonight, sometime
around nine. He would know more about Turnbull. Now
that it was announced, surely he could give her the
straight scoop. There had to be some benefits from dating
the Chief of Staff of the Senate Intelligence Committee,
though it irked her that he must have known for a while
that the arrest was coming. *How could someone you sleep
with be so tight-lipped?* She'd bet Keith was fielding a
dozen calls for backgrounders from the press. She
pressed the unlock button on her car key, tucked her long
legs into the Civic, and turned on the radio. On the drive
home, she'd listen to how the Turnbull arrest played on
National Public Radio.

Chapter 4

Jimmy Jones had been mayor of Frederick forever, that is, sixteen years. He had a lock on it, could have this job as long as he wanted it. His short, stout body always draped in a well-cut, black, pin-striped suit, white shirt, and red tie was topped by a florid face and a thick crop of silver hair he kept well-pomaded and swept suavely to the left side.

He was proud of his hair. Most men his age had lost, or were losing, theirs. He was proud of his town of more than sixty-thousand folks. Mostly, he was proud of himself. He had come up the hard way, the son of a single woman with nothing. Men had had other words for that situation during his growing up years, but his success had somehow redeemed his mother's reputation, as if you could go backward in time and change the way things were.

The richer Jimmy got, the more respectable his mother, now dead, became. He had built a trucking empire, and then a political one, all with something less than a high school degree. He had done the time—several years on the council, many years of cardboard chicken dinners at party functions. You couldn't really eat those

meals, he discovered very quickly. His best use of those
events was going around from table to table, slapping
folks on the back, flattering the women. The whole thing
had come naturally to him. Politics was in his blood. He
wouldn't be surprised if, when some historian did his ge-
nealogy, they discovered he was related to one of those
Confederate leaders who was trying to protect the ways
of the South during the War of Secession.

Whether or not he had a long southern pedigree,
Jimmy Jones owned this town now. That was a supreme
pleasure, even better than bopping the occasional secretary or female attorney in the back room behind his office. He believed in bootstrap democracy. That is, you
pulled yourself up by your own bootstraps. He did it.
Others could do it. He hated handouts and do-good agencies always whining for funding every year at budget
time. He knew he had to cave once in a while, particularly if the proponents of some group were well-connected.

He always wondered why rich people gave a damn
about those street bums and welfare mothers. Those Kennedy boys with their sob-sister act about the poor in Ap-
palachia and the Southern blacks had made him sick.
There were jobs out there. Those folks just didn't want to
work. He could think of several dishwashing jobs right
off the top of his head. There was still cotton to pick,
wasn't there? And if Congress hadn't raised the minimum
wage so high and over-regulated businesses, there'd be
more jobs, he was sure of that. It was an outrage that he
had to pay more than seven bucks an hour to the guy who
swept the floors and cleaned the bathrooms at his company's offices.

But that was another subject. He figured he'd never
win that one. It was just a question of keeping the load
down. Tonight, the game was to get the council to agree
to close down that flea market. The thing was an eyesore,

taking up an entire five acres of the fairgrounds every damn weekend. He could never figure out why people wanted to buy someone else's trash. The stuff he'd seen on those tables, it was unbelievable. You could buy everything from someone's old postcards to discarded toilets, for Pete's sake. For some of those vendors, this was a full time job. They had elaborate caravans with shelving, and they'd set up tents so that rain or shine, there they were every Saturday and Sunday selling their stuff.

There was another reason he wanted to get rid of the flea market. That corner of the fairgrounds was the right place for a new road that would open up the property behind it that he and a few friends had bought for cheap about ten years back. It was a good spot for an office park, or multi-family housing, whichever a developer would pay more for. By his estimate, they would net more than twenty million on the deal, if he moved now while building costs were low. But he wouldn't mention that tonight. The point was to get the council members all embroiled in discussing how seedy the flea market was and how it brought in all these undesirable types. The flea market wasn't, in his estimation, good for tourism. Folks were coming in from three states to see a historic town. Flea markets were not historic, in his opinion, and they drew people away from downtown where the actual taxpayers had their shops. It was the town's job to support the people who paid their taxes. That would be the line he'd use tonight, and he might get away with it if that pesky reporter wasn't in her usual seat in the front.

Jimmy fiddled with the black pens on his large, shiny, completely uncluttered desk. The pens were largely for looks, emblazoned with a tiny replica of the city's seal and his name: Jimmy Jones, Mayor. The fact was, he never wrote anything down. Just kept it all between his ears, where it couldn't be subpoenaed or requested under

some federal law that gave common folks access to public documents they had no business seeing. Behind him,
the long, yellow satin brocade drapes framing the fifteen-
foot-high mullioned windows were tied back, making
him appear to be an actor sitting center stage in his black
leather chair. This refurbished eighteenth century building, in the most historic center of his historic city, was the
perfect backdrop for him. It was classy, exactly as he de-
served.

From this command center, he could make plans for
real progress as he twirled the pen in his fingers. But he
wasn't. He had finished his exploration of options for development of his land and was now thinking about the
reporter he loved to hate. *Man, that girl is a pain in the
ass.* She'd sit there at the meetings taking notes, then
she'd hop up and corner someone who was trying to get
out the door, then she'd be back asking questions that the
members or the regular citizens who attended these week-
ly meetings hadn't thought about. He had tried to be nice
to her when she started, put his arm around her and tried
to walk her around introducing her to council members,
but she had shrugged off his arm and given him a really
cold stare with those blue eyes of hers. Natural blondes
had no business being reporters. With those looks, she
could be doing a lot better.

Once he figured out that she wasn't going to write
down what he said without question, as her predecessor
on the city beat had done, he decided he didn't like her.
But when the paper started publishing those stories about
his business interests and sole-source contracts the town
made with those companies, he decided he really hated
her. He had tried everything to get her out of city hall. He
set up a pass system where the person she wanted to see
would get a call before she showed up in his office. When
that didn't stop her, he made all reporters go first to his

executive assistant for community relations. That didn't work. She'd just talk to her sources at their homes. Then he'd issued a decree that no one employed by the town could talk to the press without his permission, and that included copying any of them on email.

All the papers reported that maneuver, even those socialist national rags down the road in DC, and all hell broke loose locally. So he'd just lambasted her at his next press conference, saying that people who didn't have the best interests of the town at heart shouldn't be writing about it. She knew he was talking about her. She'd turned beet red, the kind of red only blondes can do, but stayed in her seat and took notes while he was talking. All the papers had reported that one also, and her paper had written an editorial that brought the state party chair down on his neck. *I don't need all this trouble.*

What is the big deal? It is my town. They hadn't spent all the time he had building it up. They didn't take any pride in the fact that it was now the second largest city in Maryland, after Baltimore. *Okay, so Baltimore has ten times the number of people in it and a few buildings over four stories. We'll get there if they'd just leave me alone.* Most of these reporters didn't even grow up here. They came in as the town grew and became more prosperous. He thought this first amendment thing was way overdone, anyway. But if this one got wind that his real objection to the flea market was that he wanted a road in its place, she'd be all over it, digging up property records in the court house, seeing who owned what, analyzing what its current market value was, and on and on. *Not that I'm doing anything wrong—nope—just using my position to help the town grow a little more, increase the tax base. And if that so happens to benefit me and my friends, where's the harm in it?*

Jimmy, wrapped in his own thoughts, brought his fist down hard on his desk, startling the young woman who had just walked into his office.

"Mr. Mayor, here's your packet for tonight." Molly had interrupted his thinking.

He scowled at her for a minute. She was cute, but he thought she was too smart to be a clerk. That could be trouble. She'd been okay so far, no complaints. You just wanted to watch how many smart women you had on the payroll. When they got on the rag, they could do some damage.

"Okay, Molly, thanks. Just put it on the desk there. Anyone here yet?"

"A couple of the council members have taken their seats and Colonel Bosner, you know, that retired military guy who comes to all the meetings, he's already here." Molly looked out of the window, her face neutral. "He's talking to Lenore Cavanaugh, that reporter you hate."

"Goddammit," Jimmy sputtered. "Just what I didn't want to happen."

Molly looked at him strangely, yet didn't say anything, then turned around and walked out of his office. While he admired the gentle swaying of her ass, he wondered for a minute if she was one of that damn reporter's sources. But he wouldn't ask. He'd find out soon enough, though. *And if she is, she's out of here in a New York minute, that's for sure.* Right now, he had business to take care of. He'd just get out there and start the ball rolling in his direction. By the time anyone figured anything out, he'd have the road project funded and the ORI permits in place. He'd bet his buttons on it.

Chapter 5

From his corner window on the top floor in the FBI building, Director John Reese had a view of the Capitol, the monuments on the mall and the White House, and ornaments that lit up in the dark night sky during the holidays. He leaned back in his leather chair, loosened his red tie, pushed his glasses up higher on his aquiline nose, and stared at the view. He enjoyed the view.

He enjoyed all the perks of this position, knowing what was going on everywhere, with everyone, including whatever nitwit was currently residing in that overblown mansion on Pennsylvania Avenue. Information was power, and he had plenty of information. That was the good part of the job. The difficult part of the job was knowing what to do with that information, who to share it with, and of course, fighting to keep it from others in the powerful national security slots. Often, doing nothing was the right course of action. Just having the information in your pocket and letting the right person know you had it, could get you what you needed or wanted, especially if what you wanted was a greatly expanded empire of an agency with hundreds of billions of dollars annually, operations all over the world, and people to do your bidding. Secret renditions had gone a long way to increasing his budget. A few wars and a super-secret counter-terrorism budget didn't hurt, either. Money and power weren't the root of all evil. They were everything that mattered.

He'd been watching the news on several televisions simultaneously all evening and thought the Bureau had come off okay. His Twitter feed showed that the first take away was that the Agency had done well. After all the mess ups in previous decades, at last, he had a victory, especially when compared to his predecessors, who had the Waco, Ruby Ridge, and Nine/Eleven disasters. At least that was the way he positioned this arrest.

The media were just lapping this up. No reporter would get out of him what he really thought, that, once again, they'd dropped the ball. He had worked the Senate committee that oversaw the Bureau well enough that they would buy his version of events. The last thing he needed was being hauled before a committee and having all the agency's snafus aired in front of the cameras, day after day, in real time on television.

There was a reason the director's term was ten years. That was to protect the office from political pressure. But nobody, and particularly not John Reese, was fooled by that. The job was political, in the most naked sense. It was about power, about maintaining control for whoever was in power, and keeping the status quo by limiting the power of any upstart, individual, or group. Power was scarce, as was any valuable commodity. And if some members of Congress wanted to score a little more pow-er, they'd take it from him, by force if he didn't acquiesce or make a deal.

When Harold Lessing brought him the information about Turnbull a month ago, Reese was aghast. That's how he put it to himself. He himself had commended

Clayton Turnbull for his work. He'd felt he'd been slimed. The guy must have been laughing all the way to the bank. He'd also been unnerved that Lessing had been working the case without his prior approval, but at the stage where they'd finally given him the brief, the only obvious course of action was to go along with Lessing's plan. He had picked Lessing for the deputy director slot because the guy was good at administration, the best. He had to believe that the man's good judgment and management skills were still operating at a high level.

"One small problem," he'd said to Lessing, "you don't have any real proof that Turnbull's the spy. You only have hearsay, conjecture, and speculation. It won't hold up in court."

Lessing said, "No problem, sir, we can get it."

Within the next week, Lessing brought him a videotape of a Russian defector naming Turnbull as the spy who sold the names of US agents operating in the old Soviet Union, some of whom were still in place. Reese was stunned. He'd never seen or heard of this Colonel Borysenko before. He asked when this defection had taken place and why didn't he know about it the minute it happened. Lessing explained that CIA and the state department kept the Russian under wraps until now, allowing the FBI agents to interview him only the week before.

"Who interviewed him? And why wasn't I informed then?" Reese asked.

"Paul Perkins, sir," Lessing said.

"Perkins? That doesn't make any sense. He's the head of drug interdiction."

"Well, sir, it goes like this: Borysenko was first picked up by our guys for heroin smuggling coming through from Armenia and Turkmenistan to the US. That's Perkins's unit that did the investigation. They arrested the Russian in New York on the smuggling charges, and then he said he wanted to defect and gave them the Turnbull information as part of his deal. He has other information, too, that CI is interested in."

Reese exploded. "Why the hell didn't I know about this before? You know the rules. I get first reports on everything."

Lessing lowered his head and looked appropriately contrite. "Heat of the moment, sir. Maybe we got a little carried away." He hung his overlarge crew cut head a little more and leaned forward, a dog on the losing end of a fight.

Reese controlled his fury. He was not going to play dominant dog with this guy. Somehow he had to spin gold out of this pile of shit. Displaying anger in front of his deputy might give Lessing an edge. The guy was probably already lobbying for his job. This was a fuck-up from start to finish. It didn't matter that Turnbull had been spying through the terms of two other directors, the news would come out on his watch. He had to find a way to spin this in his direction, make the agency look good instead of blind and dumb.

"From now on, you tell me everything before it happens. Do you understand?"

"Yes, sir." The deputy smiled slightly and stood up as if at attention, pulling his suit jacket straight by the labels.

Since then, Lessing had kept Reese in the loop, deferring to him about the timing of the arrest. Reese insisted on more evidence, and Lessing had turned up boxes of photocopied material. Infuriated by the tone of the documents, Reese rapidly fell in line with his deputy's assessment. But there was still the issue of no real proof, beyond some defector's account, which could be a ruse to avoid drug smuggling charges…although naming Turnbull seemed to be pretty conclusive. After all, where would the Russian have gotten Turnbull's name and his method for dropping the data if he didn't know him? But Reese wanted more.

Lessing brought it, in the form of a small plastic baggy with Turnbull's fingerprints on it. Lessing said Turnbull had placed his most recent thumb drive inside the baggy for a drop two weeks before, although apparently, he used gloves on the stick so they had no prints on that. *Odd that he would forget to keep the gloves on when he put the stick in the baggie*, Reese thought, but he supposed someone could make a mistake when they were hurried or complacent. They had Turnbull on a videotape making the drop. The automatic dating on the video was from three weeks ago. He could see for himself that Turnbull had put a baggie in the trash bin in the park and then picked up a large envelope from the ground some yards away. That was enough for Reese. He'd ordered the arrest. Now it was history.

He was hoping prosecutors at the Justice Department would ask for enough consecutive prison terms to equal death. It would send a signal to whoever was left out there selling US secrets that when the Bureau found them, they'd be dust. He had to be satisfied with that, wouldn't think about how long the spying had been going on right under his nose. He would focus on the fact that they had the spy, they would convict him, and John Reese would be a hero for finally getting the guy after so many others had failed. When his term was over, it was possible he'd be named to the Supreme Court. He'd already let the right people inside the White House know of his interest in a seat on the bench. And he'd be satisfied with that, too.

Reese swiveled around in his chair and picked up his cell phone from his desk to call his wife and say he was on his way home.

Chapter 6

Cheryl was tearing Romaine lettuce into small pieces for the salad when Keith walked into the kitchen of her townhouse through the back door from the garage, put his arms around her from behind, and nuzzled her neck. She squirmed. She liked that, but she wanted to talk first, not try to get something out of him when he was passing out after dinner and a slow fuck.

"Hey," she said and smiled as she turned around to kiss him. "You've been holding out on me."

He looked bewildered. *How could such a smart guy with a steel-trap mind look bewildered about anything?* That look was part of his charm, though, this perpetual Clark Kent routine he played. *Those limpid blue eyes could get away with anything,* she thought. *Not to mention those soft, full lips on her neck, or his warm breath. Whoa, girl, slow down, ask your questions,* she reminded herself.

"You know what I'm talking about, Mr. Intelligence Committee Chief of Staff. This was a big day for you guys, wasn't it?"

"Oh, you mean the Turnbull thing," Keith said and shrugged. "We didn't know anything about that until minutes before the press conference. I probably know as much as you do."

"You're kidding me. Aren't the intelligence agencies supposed to keep your committee informed?"

"In cases like this, where they're trying to prevent the suspect from getting wind of anything, they have some leeway," Keith said. "They think the senators will leak the info to the press to look important. They might be right about that."

He didn't sound very convinced himself, though. There was doubt, or perplexity, in his voice, or maybe it was extreme caution. He was weighing each word he was saying to her, holding back something important.

"Come on. Don't give me the party line, tell me the straight scoop." There were usually limits to how hard she could press him, but the information was in the public domain now. Why would he hold back?

"Well," Keith hedged, picking a cherry tomato out of the salad bowl, popping it into his mouth and crunching down on it.

Cheryl figured he was slowing down time while he strategized about out how to respond to her probe. She knew he loved that first spurt of tomato juice, sweet and tangy. He had told her that, in what he thought of as a prior life, he had grown his own tomatoes in a patch behind his townhouse. That was when, as a lawyer, he'd only worked twelve-hour days and no Sundays. Now he hardly had time to go outside at all. He said it seemed to him that he'd forgotten how the world looked in daylight.

Keith looked over at Cheryl. She could see him thinking she was a long drink of water, that's what he liked to say to her, enough to quench his thirst for a long time. She knew that in her jeans, T-shirt, and bare feet she looked so different from her professional presentation in her perpetual black pants suit at work that it always turned him on. It was almost as if she was naked.

He reached out to stroke her cheek with his cherry picking hand. She squealed and jumped backward.

"Talk first," she demanded.

"Okay, but you probably know as much as I do about this." He was stalling.

Cheryl shook her head slowly, no. Her shiny hair swung across her shoulders when she did that. She knew he found that alluring also. *A girl had to use what she had.*

"The news is reporting most of what's in the documents against this guy," Keith was still hedging, waiting to see if she'd let him off the hook. He pulled a cucumber slice out of the salad bowl and munched on it.

They had always agreed it was usually best to go slowly when divulging information. Usually, you didn't have to give people too much of it. They were satisfied with very little, actually, particularly the press. Four facts and they were off to find another source to verify the very same data. Only a few reporters asked the hard questions, as they liked to say. The days of Woodward and Bernstein were well over. And if there was an editor left in any newsroom willing to give his reporters the time to develop a story, his own corporate bosses were stomping on him for even considering, neither of them had seen any evidence of it lately.

"How come the arrest was so public?" Cheryl nudged.

"They wanted to make a statement that the bureau could still do its job of protecting Americans from the dreaded Russians."

"After fifteen years of successful spying? It makes the Bureau sound totally lame. And since when are we worried about the Russians? I thought they were enfeebled, ruled by billionaire oligarchs and a corrupt ex-KGB guy who likes to ride horses without a shirt on." It was Cheryl's turn to sound bewildered.

"Well, maybe there's a little ego and positioning going on," Keith explained. "That wouldn't be unusual. The director's a holdover from a previous administration, and he wants to make sure he's a household name so he can't be shown the backdoor."

"Sorry, that can't be it." Cheryl turned her back to him and continued putting the salad together. It was code between them for disappointment. "There's something else going on here. Where'd they get all that paper on him?"

"That I don't know." Keith put his hands in his pockets, another gesture Cheryl interpreted as hiding something. "They're protecting that source. Maybe it's some Russian spy they turned, or someone defected, maybe Turnbull's contact. They've got stacks of letters. But here's the thing that's bothering me," Keith took one hand out of his pocket and laid it flat on the counter. "None of those letters have his name on them, or anything identifying him as the spy. We don't have the originals. They're only photocopies. No fingerprints. And the amount of money Turnbull's got stashed away doesn't begin to add up to fifteen years of getting paid for spying. The financials on him pretty much show he's been living within the income he got from the bureau. He's got less than a quarter-mil in the Swiss bank account, although on the news that number seems to have been inflated."

Cheryl turned around and looked at Keith. He was telling her the truth, she could see from the honest confusion on his own face. "What did they get him on, then?"

"The only things they've got that lead to him are a plastic baggy and a manila envelope that's not addressed to him but with his fingerprints on it, and they could have

gotten that stuff from anywhere on his desk or at his office or home." Keith ran his hands through his hair and
leaned back against the kitchen counter. "Someone had to
have fingered him, told them his routine—the drop off
and pick up. And, it has to be someone who turned up
recently. It's obvious, since it took them all these years to
catch him. On top of that, they're not telling us who that
source is."

"What about his family? Were they detained?" Cheryl knew she had gotten as much from him as he would
allow. It was time to change the subject.

"No. The family's not involved." Keith put both
arms around her, as if to head off an emotional outburst.
"The bureau made that clear. It's not the Ames situation
where his wife was also charged. She'd been a CIA free-
lancer. They knew she knew the drill and they had to get
her inside. The Turnbull family's in the clear."

"Did anyone warn them, his family, that he was going to be arrested?" Cheryl's voice was a little on the icy
side.

"I don't think so." Keith's voice flattened. "The bureau wouldn't have. The wife would have contacted
Turnbull and messed up the arrest. But they probably had
an agent with the family when the news broke."

Cheryl looked at him and smiled. *That's my man.*
But she wondered how a woman could live with a man
all her life, sleep with him, pick up his clothes, clean his
pee off the bathroom floor, listen to his breathing at night
and the frightened cries of his nightmares, and not know
he was spying for a foreign power? Women knew if their
husbands had a beer at lunch and didn't tell them. The
antennae were always out, always taking in information,
assessing it, putting it together, adding it to the story of
who their husbands were and how that affected them and
their children.

"There's still something about this that doesn't fit, that doesn't go together," she said. "Why would this Turnbull guy call me?"

The color drained out of Keith's face. "What? What did you say?"

For a minute, he looked to Cheryl as if he had gone into one of those guy zones where anything, or nothing, could be happening in his brain.

"He called me, Clayton Turnbull did, about three weeks ago. I never returned his call because I didn't know who he was. He didn't say in the message that he was FBI. He fell into the C category." Cheryl shrugged slightly, as if to add that maybe she had dropped the ball.

"God, Cheryl, they'll have that call," Keith said. "Did anyone identifying themselves as from the bureau call you or come to interview you?"

"No. No one. Don't you think that's strange, too?"

She watched Keith become very still. It was as if he was internally going through long corridors where the doors had been closed. He had to walk up to each door, recall what was behind it and how the doorknob worked, turn it, and go through. This could take a while.

She stepped away from him, took a measuring cup down from the cupboard, measured out a teaspoon of Dijon mustard, then put the entire spoon in the cup. She opened another cupboard and took out the box of salt, poured some into her cupped palm and tossed that on top of the mustard-filled spoon, then she added some wine vinegar, carefully watching the liquid until it measured a quarter cup. She dissolved the mustard and salt in the vinegar and added the olive oil. While she did this, she was wondering if she should tell Keith that tonight she had called the number Turnbull left and got the answering machine at his home. She had hung up immediately wondering what in God's name had made her call in the first place. She whisked the dressing with a fork and suddenly realized she usually put the olive oil in the cup first, and that her hands were trembling.

Keith wrapped his arms around her again. Cheryl's whole body was shaking. She didn't spook easily. She was not high-strung. "Okay, honey. I'll look into it," he said. "But don't talk to anyone about this."

Cheryl stood still against him. Inside, all the bells and whistles alerting her to danger were going off. She knew Keith couldn't tell her the whole story.

"Don't talk to anyone, not your mother or your long-lost brother or anyone about this," he said. "It's very dangerous for anyone to connect you to Turnbull."

Cheryl knew she wouldn't be able to let it alone, even if she had to be surreptitious. She had her own ways of finding things out.

Chapter 7

Margaret sat with her knees drawn up under her chin in the corner of her cream-colored, down-stuffed sofa holding one of the bronze-colored, silk throw pillows against her cheek. The light was on in the kitchen and the stairs, but the living room was dark, soothing. Melissa was sleeping, finally. It had taken a promise that she didn't have to go to school the next day and could wait at home for word from her father to calm her. Margaret had waited for her daughter to be asleep until she checked the messages on her machine. She had turned off her cell phone completely. No point in upsetting the kid anymore than she was. Who knew what kind of loony tune might leave a little piece of hate voice mail?

The call Margaret thought was the most ironic was from the realtor at the beach. It must have come in before the news broke. Margaret didn't think they'd be buying any beach houses this year. She'd have to call back tomorrow and tell her never mind. She wouldn't have to explain, the news had been everywhere. She'd be surprised if the realtor even took her call. She was pretty sure they'd be pariahs now, at least until people forgot their last name. Maybe that wouldn't take too long. *Oh, who am I kidding?*

Even her mother had sobbed on the phone as if the news about Clay had been the truth. All Margaret could say over and over when she returned the call was, "It's not true, Mom, it's not true." But she had wound up crying herself. Her sister had been calmer, had asked how Margaret was doing, but not about Clay. That was an easier conversation because, obviously, she was wrecked and Liz was the only one she could say that to.

"I feel like shit," she told Liz. She could almost see her sister nodding sagely on the other end of the phone. Regardless, she'd turned down the offer to go up to New Jersey and hide out in her sister's home.

"This is my place," Margaret said, "I'm waiting here for Clay to come home."

Liz, wisely, didn't try to talk her out of it, just said, "I love you. Call me if you want to talk. Let me know when to come down."

With a jolt, Margaret wondered if she'd have access to their bank accounts, whether they'd been frozen. If that was the case, what the hell was she supposed to do to live? She'd never make enough money on her own to keep them going. *Oh, I can't go there right now. What was that Scarlet O'Hara used to say? "Tomorrow is another day."* Suddenly she understood that character in a way she never had before.

She'd been waiting all night for the knock at the door, for the interview. Nothing. How could they be so sure she wasn't involved? How could she think, even for a second, that there was something to be involved with? They had the wrong man, that was all. They'd interrogate him, and when he didn't break, when there was nothing to break him about, they'd have to let him plead not guilty, make bail, and come home. Or maybe they wouldn't allow bail. He'd have to wait for his trial in jail. But at least then she'd be able to see him, wouldn't she? They hadn't arraigned him yet. Maybe they'd just let him come home. For sure, he didn't have anything to tell them. He loved his country. He'd never do anything to hurt the government...or did, and wouldn't have, before this. She couldn't imagine what this arrest was doing to him. She didn't want to imagine. Even if he were acquitted, his life, their life was destroyed.

Her mind was whirling from subject to subject as if she were caught in a revolving door. At each opening, another mural full of intricate lines of thought splashed across the canvas. She had to stop this. She had to focus. She had to talk to a lawyer and find out what she could do for Clay. He had to have a right to a lawyer. Even being arrested for spying didn't take away your rights, did it? How could you get to be fifty years old and not know anything about these kinds of things?

She wished, and not for the first time, that she'd gone to law school right out of college. She had wanted to be a constitutional lawyer, for the love of that document, for the love of the almost genetic nature of the law. Everything that governed how they lived in this country was coded into that tight language, a few words on a page—the strands of DNA that formed the rules for how to build a republic—determined what the country would be, even as it grew. But the fact was, she knew squat. She hadn't studied the law, she wasn't a lawyer, and she didn't know anything.

Focus, come on Maggie, focus, she scolded herself. The time on the VCR said eleven-thirty p.m. She wondered if it was too late to call Bob Rosen. She wondered why Bob hadn't called her. Maybe this scandal would even drive away their family lawyer. But maybe he knew she wouldn't answer the phone. She'd have to try to call him. Who cared if agents were listening? She had rights. She unrolled herself from the sofa and walked into the kitchen. *I'll make a cup of tea and then call him.* She walked toward the stove then stopped. *No, I'm calling right now.* Walking over to the desk in the kitchen, she turned her phone back on and dialed Bob's number from the list on the cork bulletin board on the wall.

He answered on the first ring.

"Bob, it's Maggie." She caught the sob in her throat, struggling to control herself, to stay calm.

"Hi, Maggie, I've been waiting for you to call. What the hell's going on? How are you doing?"

Amazing, he's on my side. Margaret closed her eyes and leaned against the wall. He was going to talk to her. Relief made her weak. "I don't know what's going on." She realized she was really angry. "I don't know what to do. I need some help here."

"I'll come over. Stay put." Bob clicked off.

She wondered where he thought she might go that he needed to tell her to stay where she was, then she realized he didn't want to talk on the phone, and probably thought he couldn't make the first contact. Everyone would be cautious. *The house had to be bugged, didn't it? They'd know everything I said and did.*

She had noticed a gray Chevy parked across the street that hadn't moved since she got home. It didn't belong on this street. Hadn't the agency figured out that everyone on this block knew everyone else, and their cars? By this time, one of her neighbors would have phoned in a suspicious vehicle to the police. That would be funny. She imagined the black and white police car rolling up to check out the occupants of the gray car carrying FBI agents. She was getting a little hysterical. Well, they'd surely make a note of Bob pulling up into her driveway at midnight. Mr. Rosen was braver than she'd given him credit for.

She looked around the kitchen. She'd managed to clean up after the dinner they didn't eat...and had forgotten doing it. No tea, she went back into the living room she'd been so proud of. Three deeply comfortable love seats were grouped around the brick fireplace. There was a cozy nook with a deep chair for reading, and a round mahogany table for playing games or where Melissa could do her homework when she wanted to be near them. And lots of space left open, so she could hear herself think, she used to tell Clay.

She had always loved this house, had never wanted to leave, even when it began to be clear they could make a bundle on it. "Wait," Clay had said, "we'll sell when we can take half a million in profit without paying the capital gains tax." He was good with money, her Clay. She had never questioned him about such things. *The Swiss bank account,* she realized suddenly, *couldn't be frozen by the feds, could it?* She would have money to live on. *Had he thought about that in advance?* No, she didn't want to go there. That had to be a coincidence.

There was a quiet knock at the door. She looked through the window panel and recognized Bob from the back. He was looking straight at the Chevy, as if daring them to take his picture. She let him in, suddenly realizing just how short he was, that he was starting to lose hair at the top of his head. *God, what am I thinking?*

"No media," he said instead of hello.

"No," she said. "Strange, isn't it?"

Chapter 8

Deputy FBI Director Harold Lessing and Special Agent Paul Perkins sat comfortably ensconced in the booth they preferred in an out of the way, somewhat trendy bar in Fairfax, Virginia. Raucous sounds from the young professionals, employed at outposts of entrepreneurial capitalism and beltway banditry twenty-five miles south of the country's political capital, surged around them—a tide of words, arrogance, and emphasis swelled by alcohol consumed at a rate consistent with heady salaries.

This was the spot where geek met nerd, where the war of brains versus beauty had come down on the side of those who could think circles around the prom queen and the high school football hero. The government agents liked being among all that youth—so much enthusiasm, so much absolute conviction. It was contagious, but they were talking quietly. In this environment, nothing they said would be detectable by any kind of listening device.

Perkins wagged his finger in Lessing's face. "Turnbull is a royal pain in the ass."

Lessing nodded and took a swallow of his drink.

"He has totally screwed up our lives. The director has made too a big deal out of his arrest. We should never have brought him into it."

Lessing put his drink on the table and leaned forward. "There is one way out of this. We take care of this problem and any related problems. No one—and I mean lawyers, judges, juries, prison guards, family, the director—can talk to Turnbull."

"Yeah, that's clear." Perkins pointed his finger at Lessing again. "No one can talk to anyone who talked to Turnbull, either. This whole arrest idea, your idea, was a mistake. We should have just taken Turnbull out in the line of duty. He could have been a hero, and we'd be off the hook. The arrest was a *significant* error in judgment. Now we'll have to correct it by doing what we should have done in the first place."

"Reese only knows what we tell him." Lessing leaned backward, large hand engulfing his glass of Jameson whiskey neat. "He's not in the field anymore. He gets all his information from us. He doesn't know the difference between fact and fiction, between whether it happened or we say it happened. As long as we dot the i's, we're fine." Lessing swirled the amber liquid in the glass and took a long swallow.

Perkins nodded. He had long ago figured out supervisors, the men who tell you what to do, only know what you told them. It was a fact he had used to his benefit for thirty-five years. The higher you were, the less contact you had with what was happening on the ground. And the less you knew for sure. You depended on the truth from other people. You had to trust that it was real. In the Bureau, they called what they served up evidence. But the man at the top didn't do the interviews, wasn't there when events happened. He got the picture from others, from the evidence they gave him, from multiple layers of information filtered through multiple agendas. There was only paper, digits, audio, video, and witness testimony—evidence which could be easily manipulated to one's personal advantage.

"In a way," Perkins said, "we're really artists, like that guy who threw paint on canvas. People see what they want to see."

"Tell them," Lessing ordered.

He didn't want it to be his voice on the phone giving the kill order. It annoyed him that Perkins seemed so calm. He vaguely remembered that the gray-haired, slender man sitting across from him wearing the far-too-expensive suit for a Bureau head of section had seen fire as a lieutenant in Vietnam years before he'd joined the Bureau. Nothing flustered the guy.

Perkins wondered for a minute about when Lessing got to be in charge. He stared at the large, well-built younger man whose goal in life was to be director of the Bureau. This operation wasn't Lessing's baby—he hadn't taken any risks, hadn't set it up—but they eventually had needed him for cover, and that gave him the juice.

Perkins woke up his cell phone, pushed a single button, and waited. Two seconds passed, then he said, "Do it," and disconnected. To Lessing, he said, "In an hour, have that guy in public relations, Turner, leak it to the *Post*. You can tell the director."

He felt a little better now that he had given Lessing an order. Their enterprise had made this numb nut rich. He'd better do what they told him to do.

Chapter 9

Clayton Turnbull sat completely still in the upright metal chair in the middle of the room they had thrown him into hours before. It was impossible to tell what time it was or how long he had been there. He was not in the usual set of interrogation rooms. Instead, he seemed to be in some kind of safe house, well away from downtown DC. He thought he might be near Quantico. They had traveled for almost an hour. When they crossed the Potomac going south on 395, he could hear the airplane traffic sounds increase to his left, then overhead, then decrease. After that, they were stopping at traffic lights so they must have been on Route 50 going south toward Mt. Vernon. When they got off the main road, though, he'd been lost. He had seen only the two agents who put him in the SUV. Nobody else seemed to be around, and no one had talked to him since the arrest—not in the vehicle, nor since they'd put him in this room, removed the hood and handcuffs, and walked out. Not one question, nothing, zippo, nada.

He'd already investigated the room as well as he could by looking around it. There was no two-way mirror, but a small camera in the ceiling kept its eye on him.

The chair, table, cot, and toilet meant this wasn't a make-shift operation. Planning was obvious here. The room was clean, though, and there was heat. Good thing, because they had taken his jacket and raincoat and of course his phone, wallet, belt, shoes, and watch. He wasn't uncomfortable, just hungry. He figured it had been twelve hours since they had taken him from the mall, probably midnight. He hadn't been offered a phone call, but they hadn't interrogated him either. Maybe they realized they had made a mistake and were trying to figure out how to get themselves out of this mess without too much egg on their faces.

Get a brain, Clay, he advised himself. *That last scenario's not going to happen.*

His arrest had been carefully choreographed. As far as he could tell, his career was over. Even if he could prove their allegations were false, his reputation was probably gone, and his cover for his own work was blown all over North America. He would be a target for any of the people he'd been investigating. If he got out of here, he'd have to take his family to live outside the United States.

Boy, that would go over big.

He could imagine Melissa's tantrum, having to leave her school and friends. *Face it, they've screwed up my whole life and everything I've worked so hard for.* He felt a small pang, a metal worm twisting through his guts, then groaned quietly and put his hands over his face. Never had he felt so helpless. The thought of Margaret and Melissa enduring this news without him there to comfort him, to tell them it wasn't true, made his throat hurt. *Had they taken them somewhere, sequestered and questioned them?* His heart raced, the thought too horrible. He shook his head slowly, knowing the suits were watching him on the closed-circuit television. He had had enough. He couldn't just let his family flounder around alone out there.

"I want a telephone," he said to the camera. "I want to call my family and my attorney, and I want it now."

There was no response.

"Just for the record," Clayton said to the camera, "this is bullshit. You know I didn't do anything. I'm not a spy. This is a frame job, and you know it."

He stopped. That should be enough to get them in the room. He was thinking about what he did know, making a list of the facts he'd been learning, trying to find a match for the charge against him. He'd written down a list of what he did know a few days before and put it in the house safe with his and Margaret's other important papers. It was a just in case move. He could never have anticipated being arrested. Being arrested by his colleagues for spying was unthinkable. For a moment, his heart ached with what his unexplained absence must be doing to Margaret. He'd thought at the time he made his list that he was being compulsive.

It was what he didn't know that would fill a three-hundred-page briefing book. As much as he surmised from following Roland, he didn't know how they got the drugs onto or out of the planes undiscovered and where it went after it got here or how, although he had seen a snapshot of that in Roland's little operation. How had the money changed hands? There'd been no time to find a money trail from Roland to anyone, no way to know for sure who wound up with the lion's share of the dough. Not a clue as to how the scumbags alerted their distributors that a shipment was coming in, although he had some idea that Roland's camping trips had something to do with that. Maybe they just texted? And how did the top guys hide their income and operations? The worst thing was he didn't know if anyone else in government knew about the operation besides him. If he got his day in court, how could he prove what he knew?

Of one thing he was certain: the chain of command for this international drug ring came down from someone in the FBI itself. If one of the drug operatives was high enough up in the bureau to order his arrest on trumped up charges, then they could take down 200 low-level dealers in Harlem, New York, or Fairmount, West Virginia, San Diego, or anywhere else for that matter, for heroin distribution or weapons violations, save thirty of their best dealers, and be heroes for the press in the war against drugs. They could do that in LA, Miami, New York, wherever, just doing their job, thank you, and keep the stuff flowing in.

Clayton thought it was a great irony that he had just decided not to pursue this case. He was going to let well enough alone, live his life, retire early, keep his mouth shut and his family safe. Thinking of how easy it was for kids to get heroin, of Melissa out there at parties where the stuff these guys were selling might be the new drug of choice, gave him another of those metal worm attacks.

"I want a phone," he demanded of the camera.

The door opened. *Finally*, Clayton thought.

One of the suits walked in, looked over his shoulder through the door, and walked over to Clayton, who only had time to notice the suit was wearing latex gloves. The man grabbed Clayton's arm, jabbed a needle into his vein in his left arm, and pushed the plunger. Clayton couldn't even jerk his arm away. He shoved the suit with his shoulder, knocking him off balance. The suit smiled, regained his footing, then turned around, and walked out, closing the door. But before it did, Clayton heard him say, "Put the video back on now."

Clayton sat down in the chair and rubbed his arm. It had happened too fast. In the second between seeing the needle and his mind registering what was happening, it was over. *Sodium pentothal? What would be the point in that? I've nothing to tell them about the spy charges, and they know it. Maybe they want to find out what I know about the drug syndicate?*

Now, he noticed that metal worm had wound its way up into his heart and was trying to squeeze the juice out of it. *Man, am I really that anxious?* He was very cold, suddenly, and yet he seemed to be sweating. His neck and shoulders hurt. He was short of breath. Cold sweat dripped from his forehead, and a long ribbon of pain shot through his left arm. He couldn't seem to get his breath. He realized with a shudder they had given him a shot of potassium chloride, coughed once, thought *Margaret*, and fell, bringing the chair down on its side on the floor beside him.

Chapter 10

An hour later, Lessing informed John Reese that Clayton Turnbull had died from a heart attack in custody. Then he gave Alan Turner, their press liaison, a story he knew the guy couldn't resist leaking to some young chump at the world's fastest online news outlet. He made one other call, this time to the office of the National Security Adviser to the President of the United States.

When Lawrence Edward Blackwell answered his phone, Lessing said, "We may have to cut our losses and sit back for a while."

There was silence on the other end of the line. Lessing waited. He was used to this. This smart guy took forever to think something through. But when he decided, that was it, and the operation moved forward.

Pulling Blackwell into the enterprise had been a brilliant move on his part. With Blackwell's planning, Lessing could be seen as a patriot instead of a greedy bastard. Then when the shit hit the fan, he had the most noble reason in the world for being part of it: he was running an operation that funded counter-terrorism operations that a hapless Congress couldn't pull their heads out of their asses long enough to consider. Plus, he looked like an innovator, a strategic thinker for coming up with the plan. The whole project made his future more secure.

Perkins never needed to know where a portion of his share of the money was going or who else was in the chain. There was plenty to go around. His plan protected Perkins and his crew and gave them an elaborate cover they didn't have before. If he sometimes skimmed off more than his share of the dough from the top, who was to know?

Lessing could almost see Blackwell sitting in his tufted red leather arm chair, the bulbous layers of fat settling one on top of the other, like old inner tubes stashed in the back of a garage.

೦೦೦

For his part, the Harvard-trained adviser to the president was thinking about the tiny brain in his mesomorph friend. In Blackwell's estimation, Lessing could see to the end of the block, but that was it. Of course, they would find a way to continue the operation, even if it looked as if it had ceased to anyone who cared to investigate. They were at a delicate crossroads and could not pull back now.

The money they siphoned off the top of this international drug operation kept carefully-inserted private teams of counter-terrorists in place even when Congress couldn't pass an annual budget for any federal department. And those agents made sure that the correct amount of financial support went to certain people who would make sure the trans-Asian gas pipeline construction surmounted all obstacles. But this buffoon wouldn't know that, and didn't need to know that.

"Pull the plug," Blackwell said finally. "I'll do what I have to do on my end."

The men disconnected at the same time.

Chapter 11

Sitting in her car, Lenore Cavanaugh looked over her notes from the town meeting, flipping through her notebook and marking in red the juiciest quotes or making a star next to the salient facts. Her method was to know the story so well before she wrote it down that she could just see it in her mind, which started this trick all by itself, usually on the drive back to the office or home if the meeting she had covered for the newspaper ended late at night. *Stories have an intrinsic shape, once you understand the subject.* She smiled to herself and patted her notes. But what was in her notebook from a meeting was never enough to really know what was going on. *You have to make some calls, talk to folks who weren't there who actually knew stuff. Then you had the context and could write more than a warmed-over press release.*

She had tried to explain this to the younger reporters, but they just thought she was making some kind of power play. One had even gone to the editor and complained that she had overstepped "her role." *'Her role'? What the hell was that?* She wasn't working in some corporate environment where there were rigid roles, rules, and rituals to obey before anyone could do anything. That was what she had escaped, that was why she had dived into this new career at forty-five years old without even assessing whether the water was deep or shallow, cold or warm. It had never occurred to her before this that the stylized routines in the corporate environment were just the codified versions of what happened naturally in any work group setting. Someday, if she had the time, she would write a book about this. *Corporations just put a gloss on the Lord of the Flies mentality that operated in its rawest form in small organizations.*

She would bet that meeting of the pissed off reporter with the editor included the wringing of hands and a few tears. God, she hated it when they cried. "Grow up," she wanted to scream from time to time. She wondered what effect that would have in the newsroom, could just imagine. Didn't these people understand that they were supposed to be working together to find and tell the truth to readers who otherwise wouldn't know shit from shinola?

She would watch the other reporters at public meetings, dutifully taking notes, or sometimes not taking notes, just sitting there twirling their hair. When she read their reports the next day, she could see how consummately lazy they were. They preferred being spoon-fed. That's what made newspapers today just pabulum, whether the content was printed on paper or available only online.

Politicians didn't realize they didn't need spin doctors anymore. They were still working under the assumption that reporters were looking for the truth, were intent on the public good, that they checked facts. *What incredible hooey!* Reporters were interested in seeing their byline on the front page, or the home page, or above a tweet, having their story show up as the first link in an online search, in getting that call for a talk show, or in being a celebrity even if it meant being a young cod in a small backyard pond.

She turned the key in the ignition of her red Subaru and eased out of her parking space. She wasn't sure what made her different. She loved the sleuthing—perhaps that was it—getting the quote that no one else had, knowing things no one else did. But most of all, she loved the scoop—lived for it—an experience you could only get in the news and never in the curated collection of other people's work that passed for news content in the web-only world. And if that meant she had to dig around in a little shit, well that was what had to be done. It was this frame of reference that made her hated by politicians and beloved by the community.

As a technique, it certainly worked. People called her out of the blue with tips for stories, people who knew the real dirt. One of her favorites was an old woman who had called to tell her she remembered helicopters dropping refrigerators into a huge hole in the ground over at Fort Detrick in Frederick. What was in those refrigerators—vials of anthrax, some nasty virus, mustard gas, arsenic—nobody was saying, but it was pretty clear the groundwater around the Fort was contaminated, mostly with the highly toxic solvents they used to clean up the labs where they made the bad stuff. She'd bet there were other communities around the country, as close to DC as Bethesda, where children were playing ball in backyards that had served as germ warfare dumps once upon a long ago, just after the US claimed it wasn't building up biological warfare capability.

This was one story that would take a lifetime to put together. She had put it on the back burner, but she would talk to any source who knew anything. Fort Detrick's public information office was an army operation. She couldn't penetrate their defenses but kept notes on the

story in a separate notebook, and it was in her backpack,
with her, at all times. You never knew when you'd run
into someone at a bar or in the supermarket who would
recognize you and start talking.

Tonight's planning and zoning meeting had been
endless. When those guys on the zoning board started
talking about the size of a pipe or the number of inches
for a side-yard setback waiver, you knew you were in for
a yawn the size of Texas. But buried in all the minutiae
was the topic of the flea market. The mayor wanted to get
rid of it. His reasons were odd. The thing had been there
for years, certainly as long as he was mayor. *All of a sudden it's unsightly? No that is not the reason.* There'd
never been any arrests there, or fights, or anything that
had merited the attention of the law. It was just people
selling and buying. *The bottom line on capitalism, Jimmy
should appreciate that.*

With one hand on the steering wheel, she fished in
her backpack for a pack of Camels, shook out a cigarette,
lit it, and took a long pull. She ran her hand through
blonde hair she kept short so that she wouldn't have to
think about it. *There had to be something else. Did the
flea market organizers stop paying whomever they paid
off to get that spot? Did the mayor used to get a piece of
the take and now that was over, and he was getting revenge?* Whatever else she thought about him, she didn't
think Jimmy Jones was on the take for small bucks. He
didn't need to be. He was a millionaire twice over. He
and his wife had matching Jaguars, for God's sake. *There
had to be something else.* She'd have to go over this
weekend and talk to people, see what they thought of the
flea market and the whole prospect of its not being there
anymore. *Maybe the community wanted this and had lobbied the mayor.* She'd talk to some residents on the
streets near the fairgrounds. But no one had been there

tonight to back up the mayor. *If the request was coming from the community, people would have been there to make a statement.*

What was that Colonel Bosner had said? "There's more to politics than meets the eye." No kidding. Was he trying to be diplomatic, or shut her up, or did he know something? She made a mental note to call him in the morning. Maybe he was just another pompous windbag who wanted to see his name in the paper, but she'd have to check it out.

She tossed her cigarette out of the car window just before she pulled into her driveway, glad she lived a fair distance from the town. It gave her some privacy. She grinned. Probably the last thing anyone thought about her was that she needed privacy and quiet. She was, in their opinion, the quintessential extrovert. But the part of herself that she protected, the kernel of her that no one knew, was the introvert who needed time alone to recharge, to read, to think, to play with her dogs, and all without saying a word to anyone.

Lenore unlocked the door to her split level home, hugged each of her dogs as they leaped up to be petted, and dropped her backpack on the kitchen table. She took a beer out of the fridge, yanked off the top, and turned on the television in the family room. She flipped to the nightly rerun of the News Hour at eleven p.m., sat down on the couch, put her feet up, and lit another cigarette from the pack on the coffee table. She noticed the ashtray needed emptying and put that on her mental do-later list. A dirty house just didn't bother her.

She was scratching behind Gordo's floppy red ears when Judy Woodruff introduced the spy story. She stopped scratching Gordo's ears. They were talking about the FBI guy who had been a great background source on a story she'd done on homegrown terrorism, her version of the local take on the Oklahoma bombing. *This couldn't be for real.* Turnbull had been so down to earth and straight with her. She couldn't have so wildly misread him. Her shit detector was in pretty good working order.

The whole story just didn't make sense. How come no reporters were asking specific questions at that press conference? The only footage the News Hour played was the director's statement, which, to her mind at least, was totally staged. And then they just rehashed what he said. Somebody at the *Post* had to be digging into this. She'd take a look at the byline in tomorrow's paper. Maybe she'd make a call or two.

No, better not, she cautioned herself. This was big time stuff. She didn't have that kind of hunting license. This was definitely not her beat. It was always better to remember who you were, what you could really do. And who knows what kind of bloody hell would be unleashed on her life for digging into a dunghill that was this big. Better to leave it alone, just as she did with so many good stories. At some point, self-preservation had to kick in. She knew her boundaries. Stick to the flea market, lame as it now seemed, that was her beat, and she would get that story.

But she knew she wouldn't be able to leave the Turnbull arrest alone. She was just keeping that fact from herself right now. Some people had compared her to a terrier on steroids. "Once she got your leg in her teeth, she just wouldn't let go until you gave up the goods," they said. Without her paying direct attention to fact gathering and sorting, her mind would be alert for the local angle, as remote as it seemed.

Chapter 12

Margaret lay in her king-sized bed with the quilt drawn up to her chin, her hands gripping the covers as if her life depended on it. It was midnight. No call from Clay, no visit from the Bureau. Nothing. She stared at the ceiling and listened to the house hum. The ache she felt in her heart was more than loneliness, more than missing Clay. She amused herself with the thought that she and Melissa were probably safer tonight, with that Chevy parked across the street, than they had ever been when Clay was gone on a trip.

Unless the FBI planned to break into the house when they were asleep, roust them out of their beds, and drag them to some detention spot in their pajamas. She shook her head. *Can that thought. Put a lid on it. Stuff it on the back shelf where it can gather dust.* But she was still wearing her clothes, just in case. She suspected she would never feel safe again. Never again could she could walk down the street without needing to look over her shoulder, scanning the cars parked there, or wondering if some car rolling slowly through her neighborhood was coming for them.

Clay had made her feel safe. First, it was about being in his arms, his heart beating against hers, his lips on her skin, then about the way he listened to her when she spoke, then about the way he planned their future. Safety was in how he had let her grieve after each miscarriage, and how he had held her hand during the entire labor for Melissa, her miracle baby, without blanching. Then safety was about the house, the private schools for Melissa, the time he set aside to be with her. *My perfect husband*, she decided. She had never really graded him before, because, well because, this had always been an education in progress. *And perhaps today,* she guessed with dread, *the class was over.*

"He gets an A," she whispered out loud to the walls of their bedroom. And to anybody who was listening, a little louder she said, "He gets an A, you bastards."

She reached under the covers to touch his side of the bed, as if something of him would be left there to console her, a few cells of the love he had given her left sloughed off on the sheets, enough to feel with the skin of her hand. Nothing. He wasn't there. An ache that reminded her of the emptiness in her womb after Melissa was born began in her belly and reached up and down, racking her body.

"Clay," she said out loud, "Clay." And then the sobs came.

DAY TWO

Chapter 13

Lenore Cavanaugh was looking for Bosner's number when her editor, Mike Allen, leaned against the metal support rod for her cubicle and said, "Hey."

Lenore assessed the tone. It didn't sound like she was in trouble. Trouble was sort of par for the course for her, though. If you didn't write about the pressed chicken dinner circuit politicians made before, during, and after winning elections, you were bound to get into trouble some of the time. She was probably in trouble more often than anyone else, but she also won more awards than anyone else. Her editor wasn't so bad. At least he'd stick up for you if he believed you were on to something. And then afterward, when the shit hit the fan, if he believed in the story, he'd be right there on the line with you, fighting with his boss, the executive editor, and sometimes even the publisher.

Mike was something of a hard ass himself, always asking questions you hadn't thought of. He had Tom Cruise good looks, if Tom Cruise had allowed himself to look fifty, and, Lenore judged, he had a modicum of intelligence, or at least enough that she wasn't always feeling she had to teach him his ABCs. He was the one who had lobbied the publisher for these cubicles, after all, a significant improvement over the open bull pit formation of most newsrooms and one that gave writers just enough privacy to think. But he was also tough on her. From the stories Lenore read in her own paper, "gentler, kinder" was standard operating procedure with everyone else. Somehow, the standards for her were different, more challenging. She wasn't sure that was fair. But bottom line, it made for a more interesting job.

"Yeah?" Lenore responded.

"What are you working on?"

"The flea market thing." Lenore assumed Mike would know what the "flea market thing" was since he always seemed to know everything that was going on in town.

"Is there more to it than ill-kempt long hairs lounging around the fairgrounds?"

"Yeah, I think so. The mayor's eagerness to clean it up smells fishy." Lenore thought that should be enough for a while. Mike knew she would fill him in as she got the details. In fact, sometimes she had the sneaky suspicion that he wished she didn't fill him in so thoroughly, so frequently. But Mike never said go away and just write the story. He always listened intently and asked good questions. But this time he was waiting for more. *Does he know something?*

"What do you have?" Lenore asked. She was a little miffed and could feel that competitive gorge rising in her throat. She enjoyed being the one with leads, not the other way around, and she didn't want to be tested.

"I got a call from someone who lives across from the fairgrounds in one of those boarding houses." Mike grabbed an absent reporter's chair from across the aisle, rolled it over into the cubicle, and sat down. "He's got one of the old family names around here. Might be an interesting sidebar on how he came to live in the boarding house. Anyway, he says he thinks there's drug dealing going on at the flea markets."

"Wait. Are you saying the mayor is Mr. Clean, that he's trying to get rid of an open air drug market without advertising his motives?" Lenore was stunned. *No way could Jimmy Jones know this and not want to capitalize on his omniscience. And it certainly wasn't his style to gather facts first and shoot later.*

"No," Mike seemed to be choosing his words carefully, not particularly his usual method. "The mayor's interest in getting the flea market out of there and the drug dealing might be two different stories. But if it is true, I don't mind him coming out smelling like a rose, either." He paused, his head slightly tilted, looking at her intently. "Can you follow both, or do you want me to put someone on the story with you? If we're going to go with the drug story, we have to be really sure, and I'd rather you follow that lead than someone else."

Christ, was Mike saying he didn't think I can handle two stories at once? Where did that come from? She turned in more stories, and better ones, on deadline than anyone else in the entire, damn organization. *And what was that crack about the mayor and roses?* She didn't have a vendetta against the mayor. He had one against her. She was just reporting information as it came. She could feel her face getting red. She could see Mike watching the red spreading across her cheeks.

"I can do it." Lenore realized there was no point in getting into a pissing match with him.

"Okay." Mike handed Lenore the source's name and phone number on a yellow sticky Post-It note. "Whatever you find out, we'll need several confirming sources. See if the police know anything about it, if they're setting up a sting operation. It's okay if it takes some time. I don't think any other paper is on to it."

Lenore nodded. As if she didn't know how to do this. Sometimes Mike was a broken record. Micro-manager, she muttered to herself. It was the worst she would say about him.

Mike put the chair back where it went and walked back to his office. He ran his hand over his thinning hair and pulled a little on his waistband. He walked back to his office a little unsteadily, as if he'd been near the edges of a tornado.

Lenore stuck the yellow sticky note on her computer keypad and went back to looking for Bosner's number. She wanted to go talk to the colonel on his own turf, away from town hall, where he might be less cryptic. She'd get to this guy Rittenhouse later. He was probably a druggie. That was why he knew about getting drugs at the flea market. He had firsthand knowledge. And that's probably why he was staying in that fleabag boarding house.

But if the flea market was where he was making his buy, why would he turn them in? Even if he was getting his drugs at the flea market didn't mean there was systematic, structured trading going on there. You could get drugs on just about any corner in this town, even within view of the police station. There was nothing new in that. Even the interdepartmental drug coalition couldn't stop the drug trade around here. She'd ridden along on a bust that never happened and seen how pitiful their efforts were. The guy they'd gone out to apprehend hadn't shown for hours, and when he finally did, there was nothing in his car or even in his pockets. Obviously, he'd been tipped by someone in the police department who knew about the bust. They couldn't arrest him. And that was after months of police work to net the big dealer in the area.

She'd just have to go to the flea market and observe for herself. Besides, current details would give the story color. She tucked her hair behind her ear and dialed Bosner's number. While she was waiting for someone to answer, she opened a new Word file on her computer.

"Bosner residence," Colonel Bosner said on his end of the phone.

Lenore wondered if you could tell something about a person by the first words they said on the phone. Certainly, you could tell something about their mood. He sounded pretty open.

"Hi, Colonel Bosner, this is Lenore Cavanaugh at the *News*. We were talking the other day ..." She left the subject open to see how he would respond, what he might give her. Balancing the phone receiver between her shoulder and her ear, she held her fingers above the keyboard ready to type, just in case.

"Yes, Lenore. I've been waiting for your call. Why don't you come by my house so we won't be interrupted by anyone? How's that sound?"

He was being careful, she thought, that's how it sounded. She got his address and driving instructions from him, said she would be there in half an hour, and hung up. She threw her pad, cell phone, the sticky note with Rittenhouse's number, and a couple pens in her backpack, put on her leather jacket, walked into Mike's office and said she was heading over to Bosner's house.

Mike looked up from the screen and nodded and then went back to his editing. Maybe he did trust her.

Chapter 14

Her mother was sitting in the kitchen, staring into space. That's how Melissa saw it. Her mother had left the planet. Margaret's hands were around her mug of tea, but the tea was cold, and she wasn't drinking it. She had poured it about an hour ago. Melissa felt a huge surge of anger, nothing she'd ever felt before, at her mother's helplessness. *How could she just sit there and do nothing?*

For days—well, yesterday and today—her mother hadn't called anyone, talked to anyone but her, hadn't gone anywhere. She was a damn zombie. Melissa was pretty sure her mother was wearing the same clothes she had worn the day Dad got arrested, which was yesterday, she reminded herself. The only reason Melissa wasn't really sure about the clothes was that she didn't pay a lot of attention to her mother's clothes. They were so boring. But now, yeah, she was sure, those were the exact same pants she had on yesterday, the exact same turtleneck. The difference was that her mother had added an old sweatshirt on top of the turtleneck. Had she even changed her underwear? *Gack, that was an awful thought.*

"Mom."

Margaret turned her face toward her daughter, but her eyes were blank. Melissa might as well not have been there.

"Mom, geez, do something, say something."

"Don't swear, honey."

Melissa rolled her eyes. Her mother was on automatic. *That's it. The world is falling down around our heads, Daddy's arrested or missing or whatever, and Mom's worried about my language. And besides, I didn't really swear.*

Melissa wasn't in school, and her mother didn't seem to care. Normally her mother would have dragged Melissa out of bed and made sure she got there in time. The old rule, the pre-doomsday rule, had been she could only stay home from school if she had a fever. She was never sick. That wasn't so bad. She really loved school, she just couldn't tell anyone that if she wanted to maintain her Brahmin status. If it hadn't been for Katie texting her this morning, she would go out of her mind. Katie was keeping her up on what the kids were saying in school. According to the group mind at school, Katie was a geek, but that was okay with Melissa. Behind those glasses was the smartest girl she'd ever known. Melissa, by virtue of her much-admired beauty, was part of the in-group. But her real self, the one she kept secret, was probably geekier than the kids at school would ever guess.

Most of the parents of Melissa's schoolmates worked in government somewhere, some of them at the assistant secretary level, whatever that was, and were friends with her parents, so Melissa had thought there'd be a buzz about her father's arrest. But there wasn't. It turned out that Katie might be the only teenage girl in the world who watched the news. Katie texted Melissa between classes and said no one was talking about Melissa's dad. Some of the girls had asked Katie if Melissa was sick. Katie said she had just sort of nodded and that had satisfied them. By the end of lunch break, Katie had said there was a rumor going around that Melissa had mono.

It was awesome how people could take two and two and come up with fifteen. Melissa figured in two days she would have dropped off their radar screen. That was okay. She wasn't sure she wanted to be on anyone's radar. She felt exposed enough. She wasn't sure she ever wanted to go back to that school again. Their history teacher, Mrs. Butler, had taken Katie aside and asked if Melissa was okay. Katie had said, yeah, she was fine. And that was it. Nobody else seemed to care.

"Mom, what about school?" The question was more to see if her mother could still speak than to get an answer.

"You can go back when you're ready, honey." Margaret shifted in her chair, looked up at her daughter, and put her cup on the table. "I called Mr. Pierce and said you needed a few days. He said fine."

"That's it? He didn't ask why?" Melissa's voice suddenly took off on that trajectory that meant small hysterics to follow. Even she couldn't understand how that happened. It seemed she had her own rocket pack of emotions ready to fuel small explosions without notice.

Margaret looked at her, fully conscious now. "Don't start, Melissa. Just don't start. The world, in case you haven't noticed, doesn't revolve around you."

Melissa, who would have normally taken those words and that tone as the starting point for loud conscious rebuttal, stopped. It was almost as if she could feel her cells reorganizing themselves around this thought. She wasn't the center of the universe. The world didn't revolve around her. *It's too early to have to think this,* she thought. *I'm too young for an idea like this.* She stored it away to talk to Katie about.

"Sorry, Mom." She reached across the table to pat her mother's hand.

"Oh, sweetheart, I'm sorry. I shouldn't have said that. I'm just tense."

Melissa did not want her mother to cry. That would be really gross, more awful, maybe, than the zombie routine. Melissa got up, took her mother's mug off the table, and went over to the stove, shaking the stainless steel kettle a little to see if there was still enough water in it, then put it back on the burner and turned the dial to high.

After she rinsed out the mug in the sink, took another green tea bag from the canister on the counter, and put it into the mug, she stood looking out the kitchen window, waiting for the kettle to whistle. Clouds were coming in, and it was getting colder outside. It *was* February. Heck, it might even snow. She loved their backyard, all the old trees leaning their heads toward each other to make a canopy of leaves in the summer. Her old rope swing was still attached to a stout oak limb. From time to time, even though she was too old for that sort of thing, she'd go out and swing on it.

She could still climb up the rope and perch on the branch the way birds did, looking out over the neighborhood almost as if she were ready to fly, as if she could just will wings to sprout from her back that would lift her up and out over all the houses. From the sky, she imagined she could look down at the place she had come from, and it would be small and insignificant compared to the blue vastness of the airy vault over the earth.

She was old enough now to know she had to content herself with what she could really do. That wasn't so bad. She loved the ease with which her body did physically hard things. Her father said she was a natural athlete. His comment made her feel pretty good. *Dad. Will I ever hear him say anything again?* The thought plunged her into fear.

The last time they spent quality time together, as he put it, her father took her to a gun range. It seemed really strange at the time, trying out several kinds of guns to see what felt comfortable in her hand. She was intrigued but worried that her mother would have a cow. Her dad said, "Never tell your mother." She took him at his word and had not mentioned the adventure to her.

She was fascinated by the fact that every gun had its own name. They settled on a semi-automatic pistol. He taught her how to load it, cock it, turn the safety off, and shoot it holding her right hand cupped by her left, arms straight out, knees bent. After an hour of shooting practice, she was hitting the target. At the end of the second hour, she was hitting the center mass of the body shape on the target. "A natural." His compliment made her happy. They bought ice cream cones on the way home.

Someone knocked on the kitchen door. Melissa, without thinking, walked over and opened the door. She had forgotten the new rule, look first. She froze for a minute and then realized it was Mr. Rosen, Mom's lawyer friend.

"Hi, Melissa," he said. "Can I come in?"

Well he's halfway in already, isn't he? "Sure." Melissa opened the door wider and backed away. "Mom?"

But Margaret was already on her feet, her hands gripping each other in a way that Melissa had never seen her do before. Her mother used to be so calm, so totally in control of everything.

"Melissa, would you, would you..." Her mother seemed to be at a loss for what she wanted to ask. "Let us be alone for a few minutes, honey," Margaret got out finally.

"Sure. Remember the kettle's on." *Something's up.*
Melissa loped out of the kitchen and stopped on the third
step on the stairway to her room to listen in on what the
adults were saying.

Margaret and Bob Rosen waited, standing in the
middle of the kitchen, until they heard Melissa's feet on
the stairs. Rosen put his hand on the back of the chair
Margaret had been sitting in, and she sat down again. He
sat in the chair nearest her, the one Clay always sat in.
It's odd, Margaret thought, *to see another man in that
chair.*

"Maggie, I don't have good news," Rosen said.

She liked that about Bob. He was a straight-to-the-
point kind of guy. "What is it?"

"I got through to the assistant deputy in Clay's department early this morning." He paused. He seemed to
be searching for how to tell her the rest. She hoped this
wasn't going to be a cat-got-lost story, after all.

She waited.

"There's no good way to say this. Clay's dead. He
died of a heart attack during interrogation. They're going
to release the body to you this afternoon." He stopped
and waited for her reaction.

The kettle whistled. Margaret got up from her chair,
went over to the stove, and turned the dial to off. She
picked up the kettle and tipped it over the blue mug on
the counter. A few seconds passed before she realized
there was no water coming out of the kettle because she
hadn't released the top that covered the spout. She put the
kettle back on the stove where it hummed briefly, walked
back to the chair with the empty mug in her hand, and put
it on the table. The white paper tag at the end of the string
twisted a little in the breeze created by her movement and
then was still. She looked at Bob Rosen. He seemed older
than she remembered. There was gray in his hair, dark

circles under his eyes, and lines on his face. He seemed weary.

"Clay didn't have a heart condition," she said. "Not even high blood pressure."

"Maggie—"

"I heard you. Clay's dead." Margaret didn't know if her extreme calm was because she was strong or because she was numb. It would matter later. There was more to do. If she were going to collapse into tears, this would be the time. She was on automatic pilot. "What's the drill?"

"We need to call a funeral home, get them to pick up the body, and make arrangements for a funeral. Do you have a plot at a cemetery?"

"Guess he won't be buried at Arlington, huh, even with his service record?" This time she'd found the edge of that anger she felt last night.

"No. It will need to be a private burial."

"Can I see him?" She had started to shake, trembling so hard that the wooden table her arms rested on was moving.

"Yes, once he's at the funeral home." Bob put a hand on her arm, as if that could comfort her.

"Don't let them embalm him before I see him." She was talking through clenched teeth. "I want to touch him before they turn him into hard plastic." She paused. "Do I have any money, any credit?"

Bob Rosen looked startled by the switch of subjects, but he had an answer. "I checked on this. Your accounts aren't frozen, the ones in which your name was listed as the primary account holder, and that turned out to be all but one. You're thinking of how you'll pay for the funeral?"

Margaret nodded.

"You're okay. You'll have the insurance that Clay had through a private insurer, half a million dollars. It's tax free. I've checked already. They'll pay as soon as they get the death certificate. That has to come from the state. It'll take about three weeks." He looked at her. This was too much detail. "Don't worry. I'll take care of it."

"I have to tell Melissa." Margaret stood. She bumped her hip on the table without even registering it, caught her balance by sticking out a hand against the wall, walked out of the kitchen, and staggered into the living room.

Bob waited in the kitchen until he heard the unmistakable howl of adolescent female wailing. Then he let himself out of the house by the back door. He would come back later.

Chapter 15

Colonel Robert Bosner US Marines (Retired) opened his front door and led Lenore Cavanaugh into his living room. She looked around, taking in her surroundings. Observing as much as possible in one look was her habit. The room was done in chintz, lace curtains at the windows. Not what she had expected. Must be his wife's taste.

Bosner wasn't the kind of man who apologized for his wife. He seemed entirely at home in the room. He asked if she wanted coffee or tea and then went into the kitchen. She heard a low murmur and realized he was getting his wife to put the refreshments together. If her memory served, this was his one and only marriage. That fact made him more intriguing to her. Her own marriage had ended five years before, and she was still carrying around a backpack of resentment. On cue, she could haul out the spiky ball of unpaid bills, the long metal bar of a foreclosed house, the sharp blade of a cheating spouse. She was always ready for the divorce version of *Dungeons and Dragons*. She wondered if long-married people had resentment baggage as well, or if their resentments had the same weight. When Bosner came back into the room, she'd made herself comfortable on the couch and was flipping pages in her pad to find a blank one.

"Let's talk off the record for a while," he said, settling into a large plaid wingback chair next to the sofa and pushing his horn rimmed glasses upward on his nose with his pointer finger.

Lenore said sure and realized that he had done this before. He knew the rules. She put the pad down on the couch with her pen, crossed her legs, and looked at him. He wanted to be in control of the interview, so she'd let him, at least for a while, until he got comfortable. She'd remember most of what he would say, word for word, anyway. She just couldn't quote him.

"You know I worked at the Pentagon a number of years before I retired," Bosner said. His sparsely lashed eyes blinked.

Lenore nodded. *Full bird? Pretty nice house. Would have cost a few pennies. He must have a decent pension.*

"I worked largely in procurement for the last fifteen years. I'm the guy who told Congress about those seven-hundred-dollar toilet seats." Bosner grinned and waited for some acknowledgement.

Lenore smiled back at him. He seemed to have taken pleasure in blowing the whistle on Department of Defense overpayments to sole source contractors. *That's where he would have gotten training in doing back-grounders. Obviously, the whistle blowing hadn't hurt his career. Or had it? He was about sixty, which would mean he'd spent about thirty years in the military before he retired five or so years ago. And he was probably under-stating his command. But he wasn't modest, or he wouldn't be bragging about leaking the toilet seat story.* Lenore noticed her own pun and ignored it. At any rate, he was establishing his credentials with her. This was the foreword to the real story.

"That was a good deed," she said to encourage what she hoped would be another in her direction.

"I left some good friends back there at the Pentagon," Bosner continued.

Does he really have to spoon feed everyone a little information at a time? If so, he might, instead of modest, at least be arrogant. She'd have to wait and see.

Lily Bosner walked into the living room carrying a silver tray with coffee cups, creamer and sugar, and some cookies on a plate.

Bless me, the Beav's mother! Lenore stood up and held out her hand to introduce herself. Damned if she was going to put women's lib in her back pocket. This woman wasn't a servant. "Lenore Cavanaugh from the News."

"Hi, Lenore." Lily took her hand firmly and shook it. "My husband has talked a lot about you."

Was that a smile? Lenore threw her head back and laughed out loud. "I can imagine." She grinned, looking straight into Lily's brown eyes. She got the answering, almost conspiratorial grin she wanted. *Deep down, women are all in this together, no matter what their economic or marriage status was.*

"Good to meet you. I'll let the two of you talk alone. I have some work to do." She smiled again, her eyes twinkling, and went out of the room.

Bosner, Lenore could see, was proud of his wife, her trim figure and Liz Claiborne way of dressing, and perhaps her masterful manners. She was obviously the perfect officer's wife. He smiled after her and then turned back to Lenore as he fixed his cup of coffee.

"Have a cookie," he said. "They're homemade and the best chocolate chip around."

Lenore picked one up off the plate and hoped her willingness to do this meant he'd feed her more than cookies. The cookie would go right to her hips, but it was worth the sacrifice if she got what she needed, although at this point Bosner seemed to be offering only a relationship to cultivate and not any hard facts for a story.

"You were saying you still had friends at the Pentagon," she prompted.

"Yes, we keep in touch from time to time," Bosner continued. "They're good men, the ones who came up under me. A lot of people don't think of administration as a very patriotic posting, but we're the ones who provide the grease that keeps everything running smoothly."

Lenore momentarily thought again that maybe he'd leaked information in the past because he had felt slighted in his command. But that didn't fit with everything else about him. Maybe he was just telling her something about how deep his information went, as in, down to the grease. She nodded to indicate he should keep going. Maybe he'd get around to telling her something she needed to know.

"I've got a pretty good idea about how things are supposed to be run if they're going to work well, and I can spot a boondoggle miles away."

She nodded again, waiting for him to move a little closer to home.

"I've been watching the mayor and council for two years now, and I can tell you they need a real administrator at that city hall. They don't even know how to run a meeting."

She laughed. "Tell me about it."

"You've written some good stories about the mayor's real motivation for holding political office." Bosner seemed to change tacks. His comment didn't seem to be a compliment the way he said it, just some fact he happened to know. "I'm sure you know the rule about following the money."

Lenore nodded and almost sighed. *I know he didn't bring me here just for journalism 101, did he?*

"But in this case, the flea market situation, the mayor might be in over his head and not even know it. I think he might find it a harder to get rid of that little circus than he thinks. He's going to be up against some people with more clout than he's got."

"You mean somebody more important than the mayor politically wants to keep the flea market going?" Lenore reached for her pen. "Why would that be?"

"Not someone politically connected," Bosner corrected her, "someone with real power."

Lenore felt a little lost. Maybe she was out of her league. She didn't want to guess at this and guess wrong. She wanted to be told something he knew. She wasn't playing *Who Wants to be a Millionaire* with this guy.

"Tell me more about that. Are we talking about Colombian drug lords, or—"

Bosner put his hand up in the "stop" sign, a gesture Lenore always hated, but she stopped talking. "Just follow my train of thought here," he said, a little peevishly. "What if something was going on at those flea markets that made certain people rich, not just here but all over the country?" Bosner talked as if he were just now piecing together what he knew out loud. "And what if those people were untouchable, couldn't be arrested, or, if they were arrested by some low level police officer, wouldn't ever be charged, much less convicted."

Lenore couldn't stand the speculation a minute longer. She interrupted him, hoping to jumpstart a more specific line of thought. "What does your military experience have to do with what's going on at the flea market?"

"If what I suspect is true, I may have tried to stop this scheme nearly twenty years ago."

Lenore settled back on the sofa. This was going to be a long story. Lily Bosner should have made lunch instead of cookies. She pulled her phone out of her back pack, checked the screen quickly for messages, and set it to record. The man said his comments were off the record, meaning she couldn't write them in her article, not that she couldn't record the interview. She momentarily chided herself for her ethical flexibility, but there were limits to her memory, and to her patience. If this story didn't wind up with some lead in the present, she would have wasted her time here. But listening to people's stories was one of her strong suits, particularly if it netted her a story in the paper at the end, and it was part of the job. "Shoot," she said.

Chapter 16

L awrence Edward Blackwell had his usual eleven o'clock appointment with the man who occupied the White House oval office. Lawrence refrained from thinking of this man as "The President," although he dutifully called him by his title as required in his presence. Lawrence loathed the man's chumminess with the voters, his casual air, his way of seeming to care about the person he was talking to and forgetting who they were in the next breath. He loathed the President's very appearance, his demeanor, and what he considered the man's innate stupidity.

In Blackwell's estimation, the man was preposterous as the leader of the free world. If it weren't for Lawrence Blackwell, and others in the close circle around the president, the country would be up to its eyeballs in manure...and the nitwit didn't even know that. Not that he, Blackwell, would ever say anything of this sort to anyone. But his private thoughts were a breeding ground for contempt.

"Mr. President?" Blackwell said, addressing the short, balding, slender man who was sitting on a sofa, scratching behind his dog's ear.

President Calvin Blythe Werner looked up at his national security adviser. He had forgotten this guy was coming today. He did remember that Carrie had reminded him of the appointment. He had simply forgotten with whom. So many people came and went. He watched their mouths move and let the significance of what they were saying fade away—so much wind in his ears.

He smiled. Werner liked this big guy some of the time, and often when the man was at his most arrogant. He particularly liked to listen to Blackwell roll out his long Harvard-learned, twenty-five-dollar words in a large meeting of other advisers. The whole tone of Blackwell's speech put Werner into a pleasant coma.

He suspected it had the same effect on the rest of the staff. Werner knew what Blackwell thought of him. It was written in every sag and waggle of the man's overly large face. Werner's position on his adviser's personality was basically "so what?" Blackwell served his purpose. He looked serious. He had a string of degrees indicating expertise, but, more importantly, his presence at the Cabinet table signaled the president's high regard for expertise.

Perception, after all, was everything. He frequently reminded himself that Blackwell could be dismissed at any time. He served at the president's pleasure. *What a lovely phrase. Any high level appointee might always need to spend more time with his family at the drop of a hat.* Werner was president, elected by a majority of forty percent of the people in this country who bothered to vote. His kindly manner and handsome face would get him another term, too. As for Blackwell, if he turned out to be too annoying, he was expendable.

"Yes…uh…Lawrence, what do you have for me today?"

"Sir, you recall our operation in the former Soviet republics?" Blackwell sat down on the opposite sofa, hitched up the leg of his trousers, crossed his right ankle over his left knee revealing argyle socks, and waited for some sign of recognition.

The president watched the maneuver, amazed that the man could raise his leg that high.

Receiving no verbal response, Blackwell enumerated, "Armenia, Azerbaijan, Georgia, the Ukraine, Tajikistan, Turkmenistan, Uzbekistan, you know, central Asia?"

"Oh, yes, yes," Werner said. "What about it?" He noticed Lawrence had left out a few of the touchier central Asian countries through which they were trying to get oil and gas pipelines put in place for their good friends and contributors, those affable men at the multinational energy companies.

"You recall the point of that operation was to create relationships, secure access, and build a pipeline from rich oil and gas fields that will assure our nation's energy security without having to cozy up to the Arabs?"

Blackwell always told him what he already knew, Werner noticed, and now he realized that Blackwell's statements always ended with a question, as if he were quizzing him. Blackwell's deep voice, coming out of those flabby, flapping lips, lilted up at the end of everything he said. And Werner was sure this questioning tone was really intended as some kind of adaptation for Blackwell's real condescension, his natural arrogance. *How annoying*, Werner thought.

"Sir," Blackwell continued, "you recall the way we were financing that security operation, with a small allocation from the counter-terrorism budget?"

"Nope," Werner said. "Know nothing about it." The president went back to scratching Buffy's ear. The dog practically groaned with pleasure.

Blackwell sighed. He took another approach. "Mr. President? You remember that state has set up an Internet communications system via satellite to link the countries and keep us informed of progress and other developments?"

The president said nothing, unless cooing to his dog could be considered speech.

Blackwell, now totally frustrated, to the president's great amusement, continued. "I just wanted to inform you that we are going to temporarily suspend the program until we work out some difficulties which have recently arisen?"

President Werner nodded. "I have to go to the bathroom." He understood perfectly that this meeting would give him plausible deniability, a wonderful term, since he had clearly not known anything about the suspect project. He also understood that the project would continue. It was far too late in the game to pull out now.

Werner had never asked how the project was funded and truly wasn't interested. He knew from time to time that he had to make speeches about protecting democracy with a capital D and then drop bombs or send drones to kill people to show they meant business. That was low-level stuff, delegated to people who would come up with and execute appropriate plans. After all, what was he paying all those guys in the Pentagon for? The point was, his big contributors in the oil industry seemed pleased with the general direction of the plan, and that was all that mattered to him.

Even if they extracted the oil, the US would be deep into an energy crisis by 2030 since profits required that the product be sold to the highest bidder, very likely China. This project was a stopgap measure that worked for now: lots of American tax dollars going to non-American contractors to make his big donors happy. The only thing that mattered to Werner right now was the possible eight years of his possible two terms, the two paragraphs in the history books, and the book deal at the end of his term. The details of everything else could be managed by someone else. The president got up from the sofa, walked to his private bathroom, and shut the door. The dog looked expectantly at Lawrence, wagging his tail.

Lawrence Blackwell stood there in the oval office for a minute, wanting to kick the damn dog, looking yearningly at the big desk. He should be sitting there, but that would never happen. He wasn't, as some consultant had said to him, photogenic. And that was that. The presidential election was at its essence a beauty contest. But he had the next best thing to the desk, he had control of the man who had the right to sit behind that desk. Better yet, he had a relationship with the big boys who really ran the world, and his offshore bank account was all the better for it. Lawrence Blackwell left the office to make his next set of calls and meetings.

Chapter 17

Cheryl was flipping quickly through the back pages of the *Washington Post*. Sometimes that was the place she found the real news, the stuff that some reporter had slaved over, asking the right questions, checking all the facts, getting more than one source, and putting it all together in a story you could see had been cut to eight inches.

These stories wound up on the back pages due to their lack of importance. They were second-day stories, not today's news. To find these stories online, you'd have to search by reporter's name, guess at the headline, or stumble on the correct search term. Back page stories weren't replicated in other newspapers. No other major paper would have exactly the same story with exactly the same quotes from the actual named sources.

Mainstream media outlets would follow the well-worn path of recasting anonymous, inside-source, press releases quoting what she thought of as the highly-mythical, well-placed nameless, administration sources—that is, the assistant to the assistant of the assistant big shot. The first five pages of the majors always looked the same. It was just a question of whether the story played in the right column or left, above the fold or below, or online in the scroll order top to bottom, boldface or italics. No wonder people scanned, it was all canned news.

Her habit was to read the leads of back page stories and see if they were follow-ups on major stories that had long ago, as in a week, left the A section. Apparently the reading public, at least according to editors, didn't care what happened next...but she did.

And there it was, the follow up she was looking for, on page C-32 in the bottom left column, six inches with the headline.

She leaned forward in her chair, almost not breathing. The two-deck, two-column headline was almost longer than the story.

FBI AGENT TURNED ALLEGED SPY FOR RUSSIANS
DIES IN CUSTODY DURING INTERROGATION

Clayton Turnbull, 55, arrested yesterday on charges of espionage, died of a massive heart attack while being held by the FBI awaiting an arraignment hearing.

FBI Director John Reese, in a special press conference on Feb. 11th, announced the arrest of Turnbull, a field agent with the FBI for two decades who'd been assigned to the agency's crack counter-terrorism unit.

Turnbull is said to have spied for the then-Soviet Union and now Russia for 15 years, amassing over $1 million hidden in a Swiss bank account. FBI sources claim the information he provided the Russians is responsible for the deaths of more than four agents.

Sources close to the investigation say that he was identified by a recent defector whose name is not being disclosed.

Turnbull, whose service in the Marines during Operation Desert Storm earned him a Bronze Star, and whose career in the FBI netted him several commendations, had allegedly begun the relationship with Russian embassy officers on his own initiative.

Colleagues in his unit at the Bureau say they are stunned by the arrest and that they had not been aware of his spy activities. Deputy Director Harold Lessing refused to comment on the arrest or on Turnbull's career.

The story ended there, but Cheryl thought there must have been more. *Dead. My God, he's dead! There won't be a trial. All those boxes of evidence will go into a warehouse somewhere.* But the arrest was not without repercussions. The state department today had issued a statement saying it was expelling forty Russian diplomats. That was on the front page. There would be the inevitable retaliation from the Russians. The ripples from this thrown stone would go a long way.

Cheryl's mind went into overdrive. *How had they not known about his heart condition? Didn't these guys have to stay in pretty good shape? God, his poor wife. How would she be coping with this—first he's arrested, and now he's suddenly dead. No time for final words, for a last touch, no opportunity to say that he was sorry or tell her that he was innocent. No, what? What was it people said to each other before death? Wasn't it, I love you?* For a minute Cheryl felt as if a metal plate had lodged sideways in her throat. She couldn't get her breath. She must be feeling his wife's pain. *Ridiculous, I don't even know the woman, except for the sound of her voice on the Turnbull answering machine. Why's this bothering me so much? Was it just that he'd tried to reach me—to ask something, tell me something?* She had blown him off and never returned his call. There were no accidents.

She closed the paper, folded it in half, and then in half again and placed it in her large purse, the bag Keith said she could live out of for two weeks. She'd look at the story again tonight and check with Keith. At least half the story seemed to be missing, probably edited out for space by a lay-out editor. The headline would have been written from the whole story. *How in the world had they gotten it so fast? Obviously a leak, right around deadline?*

Right now she had a meeting with The Member who wanted to know Cheryl's long-term strategy for getting her more airtime on television and the radio. As it happened, she had such a strategy, but it would involve the congresswoman actually taking stands on issues the way she used to do, and that might not be what The Member was looking for.

I should go to that funeral, Cheryl thought walking toward the member's office. *I should find out when it is and go. I have to know why he called me. But more than that, there's something about the wife that's important to me.*

"Congresswoman?" she said leaning into the office from the doorway. "Are you ready for me?"

Chapter 18

Margaret was at the funeral home with Bob Rosen quietly talking about coffins and ceremonies when the hearse arrived with Clay's body. An assistant had obsequiously passed a note to the funeral director, who informed them that Mr. Turnbull had arrived. It was almost as if he were a butler informing the mistress of the house that the master was home for dinner.

"Give us a few minutes, Mrs. Turnbull, while we bring him in and lay him out for you," he said, slightly bowing before he left the room.

Margaret noticed the change in the use of the verb. *Alive you lie, dead you lay.* Dead *you're an inanimate object.* It was okay with her if she occupied herself with these verbal hi-jinks. It was better than staring at the somber landscapes on the walls or down at the plush gray carpet. Bob had chosen well. The place was subtle and elegant, no frou-frou. Even the potted plants were kept to a minimum. The reception area the funeral director showed them appeared to be a well-furnished living room rather than a place where final words were said for the dead.

She waited, her hands in her lap, feeling the same kind of anticipatory dread she'd felt before her college freshman year meeting with the dean. Only this dread couldn't be the same. She was kidding herself, setting up a false comparison to protect herself from the shock. You couldn't just strip off the gloves at the end of the interview and go to the bookstore to collect the texts for classes. She had nothing to compare it with. This meeting would reorient her entire life. This would be the only time she waited to see her husband's dead body.

"We're ready for you now, Mrs. Turnbull." The funeral director stood in the doorway with his hand held out the way Vanna White pointed to the board on the television show *Wheel of Fortune*. She wondered vaguely if they had the same kind of training. *Can I buy a vowel and make it all okay?*

Margaret and Bob Rosen followed the funeral director into another room where the body was installed in the coffin she had chosen. She was still hoping that somehow this was a mistake; that it would be another man, not her husband; that somehow identities had been confused; and the FBI had gotten the names wrong. *Maybe he'd gone off on some very deep cover operation that he couldn't tell me about.*

From the door, she could see the mahogany casket, striped gray and white silk inside, brass handrails, and just the curve of a chest, the jut of a chin. *Deep cover*, she reminded herself, stunned that her mind could joke with her. As she insisted, they had not yet touched the body, the funeral director was warning her. She walked closer. It was Clay. He was wearing the suit she'd last seen him in. She inched closer to the coffin, not knowing what to expect. She noticed first that his face was gray, then that it was contorted as if he had been angry and trying to yell something, then that his eyes, those wonderful blue eyes, were closed. She would never see them again.

She touched his hand. *He had been in pain.* She thought she could feel the residue of the pain in his hand. She touched his face, first with her fingertips, then with her palm. She leaned over the casket and kissed his lips. She ran her fingers through his short hair, the only part of him that still felt human. She couldn't bring herself to say anything. It was as if all words had been obliterated from her mind. She stood there, her hand over his heart, almost as if she could will life back into him.

She stood like that for what seemed like her whole life and then turned around and said to Bob and the funeral director, "All right. You'll need to fix him for Melissa. You'll need another suit. Bob, would you..." And then her voice trailed off.

"Yes, Maggie." Bob calling her by the name she used when they were all young seemed to be a strange insider's joke. "Whatever needs to be done, I'll do it."

He took her by the elbow and led her out of the room, out of the building, across the veranda with its row of high white columns, down the wide white steps, opened his car door and steadied her as she got into the car.

She was still dry-eyed and silent as he parked the car in her driveway.

"You're home, Maggie." Bob turned off the engine and opened his door.

"Home." The word was part of some foreign language she was trying to learn.

He walked her into the house, using the kitchen door. Melissa pounded down the steps and met her mother in the living room. Bob watched as the two women came together, arms wrapping tightly around each other, heads tucked into the crook of each other's necks, sobbing, rocking back and forth, back and forth.

He took Clay's suit, still in its dry cleaning bag, off the coat rack where Maggie had forgotten it on their way to the funeral home, put it over his arm as if he were placing an infant there, and let himself out.

Chapter 19

Fucking bastards," Bob muttered as he got into his car, "fucking bastards. Lousy sonofabitch Nazis." He had a mind to go over to that damn Chevy, still there for two days now, and tell them to go fuck themselves. *What the hell do they think they're doing? Do they think Maggie or Melissa will cause any trouble for them?* The whole thing stunk to high heaven.

When he talked to Clay's boss, Steven Turner, the guy had been in shock, a robot just going through the motions. For sure, he had nothing to do with this arrest, hadn't even known about it until it happened. He'd probably heard about it on the news just as everyone else had. The guy was even apologetic when he met Bob at the morgue where they'd stashed Clay's body.

What Margaret had been spared was seeing Clay's body in a bag, tagged. But they sure hadn't spared her anything else. At the very least, they could pick up the tab for the damn funeral. That should be on the Bureau. He'd see if he could finagle that much. He'd try for the pension also, but he didn't think he'd get that out of them. *Then there were the papers Clay had sent him that he hadn't opened yet. Maybe there is more I can get for*

Margaret. She'll be okay, financially at least. He was going to try and talk her into selling the house and moving.
Her life had been Clay. With no other ties here, she
should go out to California where her mother lived or to
New Jersey to be near her sister. Melissa was young
enough to adapt. He could imagine the fight Maggie
might have with her. Or maybe not, the kid seemed ma-
ture for her age.

Bob couldn't remember when he'd been so angry.
Maybe when he'd been a kid out in the playground where
some young punks had called him a kike. He had been so
young, five he thought now, and they had been so big.
But he'd lit into them, running head down into the stomach of one of those twelve-year-olds, knocking him over.
He had swung his arms like windmills, tears and snot and
outrage dripping from his chin as they battered back.
They'd gotten the best of him, bloodying his nose, bruis-
ing his face, kicking him in the ribs when he finally fell
down on the asphalt patch that was supposed to be a play
yard in the middle of the projects where he lived with his
mother. From the ground, the three-story buildings
seemed to rear up higher and sway through the prism of
his tears. When the young punks got tired of beating him
up, they ran. Then some adult who had been watching the
entire time came over and took him home. His mother
cried when she saw him, yet he never told her why he had
gotten in the fight.

He never went to that playground again.

There were enough episodes in life similar to that
one. At his first interview at a law firm, the hiring administrator, a tall, dignified man with stylishly-cut silver hair
and a thousand-dollar suit, didn't exactly say they didn't
hire Jews to represent their WASP clients. But he set the
bar so high that having made Law Review or clerked for
a Supreme Court judge hadn't gotten Bob an associate's

chair. Whatever the US had fought World War II for, he'd always thought, it hadn't been to avenge the atrocities committed by the Germans against the Jews. Scratch a WASP and you got a whiff of anti-Semitism, no matter what part of the country they lived in.

It was ironic that, in this case, he was trying to protect a family that was clearly WASP from the prejudices of their own kind. You could do a lot of bad things, maybe even evil things, if you were part of the white, good-old-boy system and you'd never be censured. It was being caught, being publicly flayed that would get you excommunicated. *Clay*, he reminded himself, *was not that way*. Sure, Clay was a poster boy for the FBI, clean cut, physically powerful, well trained, but he had come up the hard way, by working rather than connections. He had made something out of his life, something solid that had turned to jelly under the heat of this accusation.

Bob didn't know if the charge was true or false, but he knew there was something funny about the way the arrest and subsequent death had transpired. Maggie was right. There wasn't anything in Clay's personnel record that indicated a health problem of any kind. The results of his most recent physical, not six months ago, were right there in the file Turner had handed him. Clay had a clean bill of health. "In better physical shape than most men his age," the physician had written.

He wondered why Turner had given him the file. He didn't have to do that. Then it hit him. They hadn't done an autopsy. Certainly, Maggie hadn't asked for one. They didn't really know what Clay died of. There hadn't been time. They had just taken the Bureau's word for it. Clay's boss had simply handed Bob the death certificate with the coroner's signature. Cause of death was listed as heart failure. He had been amazed at their efficiency. And right now, the body was being embalmed, probably already was, and any clue about what happened was, literally, going down the drain.

Bob closed his eyes and shook his head. *Maybe it's best to just let it lie. What would we do if we really knew? Sue the Bureau? Does Maggie have the stamina for that? Do I?* The fight at age five had been his last head-on assault against bastards. Since then, he'd gone around the enemy, getting where he wanted to go by a circuitous route that took longer but was more likely to succeed. He had his own firm, hired who he wanted to hire, took on the clients he wanted to represent and measured his worth not in net, but gross, terms. Had he done any good? The answer, each year at Yom Kippur, was yes. That was enough.

Bob backed his car out of the Turnbull driveway, turned so that he had to pass the Chevy driver's side to driver's side, stared right into the eyes of the agent watching the house, and then drove away slowly. His defiance made his heart beat harder. *Watch it, Bobby,* he warned himself. *You're going to get your face bashed in again.*

He had Maggie's address book in his pocket. He would call whoever he thought it right to call about the funeral from his office in old town. Whoever was coming had only two days to get there, and he needed to tell them soon. It occurred to him that he was putting his own life on hold while he managed this whole mess for Maggie. He'd take a few minutes to talk to his partners, keep them in the loop. He didn't expect any hassle from them.

After dropping the suit off at the funeral home, he drove his car to the parking garage, directly to his reserved space, then walked to his office. With gentle authority, he asked his admin to order him a chicken Caesar salad and an ice tea, then settled into his chair to make the calls. He had gotten to the R's when he saw a name he didn't recognize at all written in red ink, not Maggie's usual blue, and not in Maggie's hand. *Cheryl Roland?* She had a DC phone number. *Probably not a friend, maybe a chance acquaintance.* Maggie made friends easily, her charm simply enveloping you until you thought you might be her best friend, intimately known and cared for, in only one meeting. *Maybe this Roland person had written her own name down in Maggie's book.* No, *that didn't make sense. All the other entries were in Maggie's handwriting. Well, he'd call her anyway. The more, the merrier.* Grimly, he dialed the number.

"Cheryl Roland," said a pleasant voice on the other end.

"Hello, Ms. Roland, this is Bob Rosen, Maggie Turnbull's friend." Bob heard an intake of breath on the other side of the line.

"Yes?" was the cautious response.

Perhaps she didn't know Maggie well, or that Clay was dead. Or perhaps she knew what everyone knew, what the news had reported, and didn't want to be associated with the Turnbulls. He'd gotten a few cold receptions so far, people who had invented other important events or had appointments to have their hair done that would keep them from attending the funeral. It was to be expected.

"I'm calling to tell you about the funeral arrangements for Clay Turnbull, if you want to come," Bob continued.

"Yes, I want to come," Cheryl said. "When is it, and where?"

It sounded to him as if she were trying to keep her voice noncommittal. He could hear other conversations around her. *She must be in an open area in an office.*

"In two days, at ten a.m., at Stevenson's on Duke Street in Alexandria."

"Thank you. I'll be there."

Bob put down the receiver. Her response was no odder than many of the others. He would try to remember to ask Maggie who she was, though. *Well, maybe not. The last thing Maggie needed to worry about was who was coming to this funeral.* It would make no difference whether the woman showed or not.

Chapter 20

Larry Roland's gear was ready. He made one more check of the bike to make sure it was in working order, not that he hadn't done this the night before, not that he hadn't worked on the bike all week as if it was the prayer part of some religion. He didn't really need much going out, just a sleeping bag, some food, a weapon, and the two large leather saddlebags. But he was nothing if not thorough. Check and double check, just the way they taught him in the Marines. He had already wired the money.

It wasn't a bad day at all for a ride out into the San Gabriels—no flash floods, no raging forest fires. Of course, you never knew about earthquakes. He'd have a nice weekend. And now that the Turnbull guy wasn't following him anymore—and wouldn't be following anyone ever again, Larry had made sure of that—he could relax on the trip. Coming back, it would be easy enough to leave the product in the new places he had picked.

This was the only tricky part—selecting new sites, places that were just enough off the beaten track that no one would suspect what they were being used for, and transporting the stuff. Places he could rent for one month and then disappear were the best. California was big enough that he'd been able to find locations for years. In a pinch, he could rent storage lockers, mail boxes, trailers. He kept a color coded map—locations marked in blue—so that he didn't go back into the same locale twice. All anyone would have figured out from his map was that he got around on his bike. The map was marked BTDT: Been there, done that.

When Perkins first recruited him for this gig, he'd thought the whole operation was nuts. They would never get away with it. But they obviously had it planned down to the smallest detail. Every year, the big guys changed the distribution method and the bank accounts. He had only one point of contact. He didn't know the names of any of the other players, and he'd never gotten caught. Half of his reason for doing this, he knew, was a big up-yours to the government that had nearly tossed him in the brig for selling marijuana when he was in the service. If he dwelled, he'd feel that old bitterness against the officers who were always half drunk out of their minds but who had gotten promoted during that fucking war. But he didn't let himself notice. Those alcoholic bastards were in charge now, running the whole damn country, and nobody seemed to know. He just laughed when he saw senators on the TV news saying they would do what the generals said they should do. The generals, he knew first hand, were a bunch of burned out bozos. It turned out that he'd had the last laugh.

The other reason Larry did this was it gave him enough money to live life on his own terms. It had taken him long enough to figure out he didn't want the hassle of a wife and kids—who he'd abandoned in New Jersey right after his youngest daughter was born—and all their demands and expectations. He preferred living by himself, with his own mess, doing it the way he wanted to do it. Getting out of this racket might be tricky, and he could see a time not too long down the road that he'd want to get out. *Maybe this year, in fact.* This thought was so covert that he didn't let himself think about when, as if the guys in charge could hear his thoughts. He had a little cottage in South Bimini waiting for him where he could sit all day on his small stone patio and watch the infinite array of blues where sky met sea. He kept his thirty-nine-footer docked at Weech's. They were the cheapest marina around and had the fewest slips, which was what he wanted. The less contact he had with people, the better. He had no interest in people.

On Bimini, he had a whole different identity. He was John Keating, marlin fisher. He was some eccentric richy, as far as the locals were concerned. He only went into Alice Town if he had to. When he retired, he planned to fish the rest of his life away, taking out an occasional group for fun, but not often. He would get a charter airline to bring in supplies he couldn't get locally. But he shouldn't dwell on this now. It would make him hungry to get there, and he still hadn't completely figured out his exit.

He didn't know how many guys were doing this gig around the country. It wasn't as if they held annual conferences and workshops. Face-to-ace transactions were limited. The less anyone knew about anyone else, the better. Brief instructions came by email, from someone in Turkmenistan, on some email server put up by the US State Department's Bureau of Educational and Cultural Affairs. Larry wondered sometimes if the state department knew what its Internet server was being used for.

The guys who ran this operation were high up in the government. He could see how much control they had by the way they'd dealt with Turnbull. All it had taken was a few words from Larry on the back of a photograph sold to the right buyer at a San Diego flea market saying "get this guy off my back," and, a few months later, Turnbull was dead. He'd learned his name was Turnbull from the television, which flashed the agent's photo on every news show last night. *Man, they broke that big time.* But you'd only know Turnbull was dead if you read the back pages of the paper today, and Larry was an inveterate back page reader. Real life, he figured, got written up just about the time the ink was running out.

He had no feelings about Turnbull one way or another. Turnbull had been tailing him, jeopardizing his operation. It wasn't too hard to pick him out after the second or third time. The guy didn't blend, even in a T-shirt or flannel. There was nothing you could do to disguise those straight-arrow looks, that candid eyeballing that folks who had nothing to hide seemed to do without knowing they were doing it. Somebody must have been watching Turnbull or they wouldn't have known what Larry's note meant. He realized that their efficiency could easily be directed at him, in much the same way but without the high profile public relations effort. Regardless of the implied threat, Larry thought they'd done a neat job of it.

If they went after him, the job would be simpler. He was nobody, a gnat that could be squashed between the tips of their fingers. That, after all, was why they had picked him. That was probably how they picked all their distributors. The anonymous, almost non-existent men who could give a flying crap about the law and a sanctimonious government. He wanted to be sitting on his little veranda, staring off at the ocean, when he learned that somebody had finally figured out what was going on. For the time being, he was gathering a few weapons that he hoped would handle the first assault if they decided to clean house. He had them staged in various locations in his home. If they sent one guy at a time, or even two, he'd be good. He was no match for a squad. That much he had learned in the service, and he'd also learned to run, and hide, and maybe that would serve him better in the end.

Meanwhile, he kept an eye out. What they didn't know wouldn't hurt him. Just in case though, he had wire-transferred the bulk of his cash to his bank in the Cayman Islands. If necessary, he could bike down to Mexico City and take a flight from there to George Town where he would blend with the other tourists who had nothing better to do than dive and sit in the sun. He kept his guns in a golf bag stashed in a locker at a club nearby where he was known as Eric Walters, a man who had gotten rich early in the import-export business and retired.

Larry went back into the apartment for a second check around, looking for anything that might catch the eye of any law enforcement type. Nothing. It was clean, but not too clean, the way it would look if he was coming home any minute with things left to do. A cup in the sink, a pair of dirty socks on the floor near the worn out sofa, a pile of junk mail on the small wooden table in the hallway, his bed sort of half made. *Perfect. Time to go.*

He went back out to the driveway and checked again to make sure his van was locked and that nothing that lent itself to itchy fingers was showing. Then he tied his blue bandana around his head, slipped on his helmet, hitched up his jeans to sling a lean leg over the seat, and rode out.

Chapter 21

Well, Jimmy Jones. We haven't seen you in the shop for a dog's life. What the hell are you up to?" Martin leaned over to shake the mayor's hand, his balding head shining with sweat from moving boxes from basement storage to shelves.

"Just doing my rounds." Mayor Jimmy Jones grinned his vote-winning smile back at the shopkeeper and staunch contributor and held out his hand. "Just checking in with constituents to see how everything's going."

"Been a good year so far, but of course we're only into the second month. Usually, it slows up a bit after Valentine's Day, but those ads we've been running on the News web site seem to be bringing people in from all over. I put my chocolate diet in the ad. There's even still some street traffic during the week."

Martin stopped talking. He knew better. The mayor could care less about how the store was doing, although Jimmy did help him get commercial zoning where there had only been residences this high up on Market Street. That had worked out fine for Martin and his wife, his second, who had been happily spending a fortune making the two floors above the shop into a showplace for god-knows-who to admire. If Jimmy Jones was walking Market Street, he wanted something from the people for whom he'd done such small favors. *Well, shoot, that's fine with me. You scratch my back, I'll scratch yours.* "Come on, Jimmy, what's really on your mind," he said.

"Well, I've got this concern about the flea market down there at the fairgrounds every damn week. I think we could do better with that space." Jimmy looked sheepish, his second best gambit after looking candid. He shoved his hands into his pants pockets and leaned back, looking at Martin.

Martin knew that look. The mayor could arrange his face in the manner needed for any occasion.

The mayor now made his face admiring. "You have lost weight," he said. "That chocolate diet of yours must really work."

Martin wasn't fooled by this approach either. *Flattering people was the first step to getting them to do what you wanted. It was one of the mayor's smoother talents,* he thought. Jimmy had these faces down, knew which ones to trot out for which people. *He must practice in the bathroom mirror while shaving.* The only look Martin figured the mayor didn't have to practice was being mad. That one was natural, and very effective.

"Come to think of it, I thought I saw something about that in the paper," Martin said, turning the conversation back to the flea market. "Seems there's some ne'er-do-wells hanging out over there, or something."

Martin pretty much thought that what he read in the paper or saw on the TV news was the truth, not an idea, or conjecture, or notion, or just one of the facts about something. He had no idea that, if you really had all the information, a completely different picture might emerge.

"Yeah, I was talking about it at the council meeting the other night," the mayor said. "I'm real concerned

about the types of people it brings into town. But the reason I'm here is that I wanted to know if any of them flea
market shoppers ever stop by when they're in town. I
mean, do you see any benefit from them coming into
town?"

Martin picked a handkerchief out of his back pocket
and wiped the sweat off his forehead and neck, giving
himself time to figure out where Jimmy was going with
this. *How the hell would I know if customers were coming
from the flea market or the damn movies?* He certainly
didn't ask them. Jimmy knew that. What he was really
asking was, would he, Martin, support him in his effort to
get rid of the flea market? He reached under the counter
and pulled a box of rich looking chocolate truffles out,
offering one to the mayor. The mayor held up his hand,
palm out, the gesture for stop.

"Gotta watch my waistline, you know," Jimmy said,
patting his belly fondly, "but I'll take a box back to the
office for the girls."

"So you think the flea market is drawing people
away from downtown on the weekends?" Martin asked
while he was placing the box of expensive candies in a
small clear plastic bag with the store's logo on it. Martin
really didn't believe this and didn't think that Jimmy believed it. He pulled a length of gold ribbon from the spool
on the counter, cut it with the scissors, and wrapped it
around the bag handle, making a perfect bow. There was
some other reason Jimmy had started this oddball cru-
sade.

"What I think is that solid business people like you
shouldn't have to be competing for the customer's dollar
with a bunch of junk salesmen," Jimmy sputtered. He
seemed genuinely steamed about the whole idea.

"I'm not sure they hurt my business, Jimmy," Martin
said, watching the mayor's face. "I mean, folks who'll

pay fifteen dollars for a box of ten chocolates are not exactly running to the flea market to buy their furniture. See what I mean?"

"All right, I can see I really need to give you the lowdown on this," Jimmy said in his most conspiratorial voice. "There might be an opportunity for you to expand if that ground could be used for something else."

Martin looked at him hard. The mayor was way off base. He wasn't interested in expanding, and if he was, he'd be shopping for space where the foot traffic was, not off in some remote part of town where no one went if they didn't have a specific thing they wanted. After three years here, he was just getting out of hock. It wasn't time to invest in any expansion. But he *was* curious. The mayor's way of asking for campaign contributions was pretty direct. He normally said, "How much are you going to give me this year?" This time, he was using some back door approach that didn't suit him.

"So, are you saying there's a mall going in there?" Martin asked. "I don't think the owners along Market and Patrick would be very happy with that. It's taken ten years to get people back into downtown. We are just starting to see lunch-time shoppers."

Jimmy backpedaled. "No, no, nothing like that. But maybe some space for a lot of folks with high-paying jobs to work, people who would have a few bucks to spend on luxuries."

"What, in those five acres?"

"Just thinking out loud, Marty," the mayor said. "Just thinking what else could be done with that land if we didn't have a contract with the flea market organizers, is all. I think the council's probably going to come down on my side of this. Just wanted to give you a heads up."

He smiled, took the beribboned package off the counter, waved goodbye, and walked out the door.

Martin stood at the counter, looking through the glass door as the mayor walked up the street. He shook his head. He was a sheep that had been nipped and nudged into line by a sheep dog. It wasn't even necessary. By his own measure, he was a go-along-to-get-along sort of guy. The mayor didn't need to trot out all his tricks to persuade him to do something in his own interest.

"The guy's always thinking, I gotta give him that, even if what he's thinking is sometimes truly ridiculous," Martin said out loud to his chocolates.

Chapter 22

When Lenore got back into her car after her interview with Bosner, she pulled the yellow sticky note off her pad and entered Rittenhouse's phone number into her cell phone. If he was available, Mike's source on the flea market boondoggle was next on her to-do list.

She sighed. She didn't know what to make of what Bosner told her. She could sling conspiracies theories with the best of them, but right now she thought Bosner was pretty crazy, paranoid even, and all of it hidden behind that straight and narrow old soldier routine. *Who did he think he was talking to?* She wasn't the *Washington Post*, and there weren't seventeen reporters behind her ready to research the stuff he had given her. In fact, there was just her, and what he said made her nervous.

The conversation reminded her of the scientist who used to work at Fort Detrick who told her that fluoridating water was a government conspiracy to give children attention deficit disorder and old people Alzheimer's. "It was," he said, "an experiment to see how toxic fluoride really was if it were administered to large groups of people over a long time." He'd showed her his numbers, how the incidence of those health problems had increased since fluoridation started. He had already tried the *Times* and the *Post*. They had strung him along for a while and then dropped the idea of doing a story.

That was just what Mike told her to do, after he'd laughed his head off. "We don't have the resources to prove or disprove the science," he said, "and the guy sounds crazy, as in with paranoid delusions."

She'd been annoyed and a little embarrassed. The scientist was very convincing and local. But she'd dropped it as instructed.

The older she got, the more careful she was. That was probably a fault, not a virtue, but it's the way it was. To follow what Bosner had given her, she'd have to have sources that just didn't exist. The whole conversation had been off the record, even the part about Turnbull coming to interview Bosner about a man who had been under his command back in Vietnam. After an hour, her head was spinning. At two hours, she was sure she was inside a Kurt Vonnegut novel. He wasn't giving her anything she could use. Another blind alley, as far as she was concerned. Right now, it was better to stick to something closer to home. That would be Rittenhouse.

"Yeah," a woman's voice said at the other end of the phone connection.

"William Rittenhouse, please," Lenore said.

"Wait a min, hon," the woman said.

Lenore waited. She hadn't realized this wouldn't be his phone, in his room. They must have a pay phone in the common area of the boarding house.

"Yes, this is William Rittenhouse," said a pleasant, educated man's voice.

"Hi, Mr. Rittenhouse, this is Lenore Cavanaugh from the News. You called my editor?"

"Oh. Yes, I did." Rittenhouse lowered his voice. "I thought he'd want to know some facts about what's going on at the flea market."

"Well, we would. Mike passed your number on to me, and I was hoping I could come by in about half an hour and talk to you."

"That's fine. I'm at the Hilt'N Hotel on Patrick right across from the fairgrounds. I'll wait on the porch for you. Maybe we could go up the street to the Chat 'N Chew for a coffee while we talk."

Wants a free meal. Lenore smirked and tilted her head. *Well, that's better than talking in his room. The tab's on the paper.* "Great. I'll be there in about thirty minutes, maybe less."

Lenore took out a cigarette and lit it, maneuvering her car out of Bosner's driveway and onto the main road out of the little neighborhood where he lived, and then back onto Interstate 70 going west. The city had expanded its limits to include this upscale neighborhood, and the best way in and out was the highway, on the edge of which the community perched, a huge bird of prey waiting for road-kill. She took a long drag on the cigarette and went back to thinking about Bosner's story while she drove. It was a doozy...

In ROTC in college, Bosner had already made captain in the army when he was shipped over to Okinawa to oversee military transport there during the end of the Vietnam War. Okinawa wasn't a bad posting, given where he could have been. "It was far from the killing and maiming," as he put it. His command involved "making sure planes were ready to go, that shipments came in and went out on time, and that in-air refueling operations were done with only acceptable casualties." She had been amazed at how easily those words came out of his mouth. An acceptable casualty rate was only one plane shot down a week, only fifteen men dropping out of the sky. It made her wonder if he had some equally convenient equation for regular life, his life, as in, if you had five kids it was okay if one didn't make it. She wouldn't bet on it, though. Acceptable losses only referred to other people's kids.

Anyway, by 1972, when everything was going to hell in a hand basket, troops seemed to be falling apart. Drug use was rampant. If a soldier didn't turn up for duty stoned or drunk, he was sure to be out of it by the end of his shift. There were so many guys buying, selling, and using heroin and marijuana that Bosner didn't know from one day to another whether he'd have a full squad to do the work. In the middle of this chaos, he'd noticed he had two lieutenants who were keeping their heads.

They may have gotten roaring drunk off duty, but on their duty rounds, they were in command of their men and efficient. He had given these men high ratings. They were getting the job done, and they seemed to have the loyalty of their own men. He also noticed that they stood by their troops if their boys were picked up by the MPs. Given how easy it was to get potent, mind-altering, war-erasing drugs, the temptation level was way beyond the ability of these young boys to resist.

"They aren't bad boys," Lieutenant Perkins said to him when Bosner wanted to come down hard on the troops, "they are just scared and tired and far from home." Bosner let Paul Perkins and Arnold Jawarski handle things their own way. "That was what I thought was best, then," he told her a little sadly. "Now, he said, "I wish I'd acted differently."

After a year, Bosner was posted out of Okinawa, back to the States, greatly relieved that he was not there for the bombing of Cambodia. He washed his hands of the war and forgot about it. But he kept track of his lieutenant, Perkins, from time to time, checking on his progress. He'd noticed with some sadness that Perkins had resigned from the Marines after his six years were up but had stayed in a service dedicated to protecting their country. Perkins went into the FBI. His other lieutenant, Jawarski, had gone into the CIA. "It wasn't easy for the military to keep good men," Bosner told her, "there were so few spots at the top, and really the income wasn't great compared to what you could make in other parts of government service."

Lenore had wondered at this point if he was talking about himself, about giving his whole life to military service and winding up only with a colonel's rank. That didn't fit, though, with his almost smug demeanor, or his lifestyle. He seemed to have no rancor about it. It was just another fact on the spreadsheet of life. He had perhaps gone as high as he could see himself going, had not imagined anything more, not even a brigadier general's rank. *He might,* Lenore conjectured, *just be a uniformed pencil pusher content to move paper from one side of his desk to another.* She felt her mind drifting during part of his recitation, her attention captured by the fine detail of a dogwood branch and its sleeping mauve-colored buds that she could see from Bosner's living room window.

She was jolted back to attention by hearing that Turnbull had thought Bosner knew something important to some investigation he was doing. Turnbull had come to interview him about a guy in California who had been under Bosner's command in Vietnam and was now turning up at flea markets selling drugs. Bosner apparently had unburdened himself to the Special Agent, but now that Turnbull seemed to have turned spy, he still felt the need to tell someone else, someone who might tell the story to a larger audience. Lenore didn't think her audience was large enough for this story, if any of it was true.

She was already on Patrick Street. She'd have to put aside these thoughts to have a clear mind for whatever Rittenhouse was going to tell her. She made a U-turn at the light and pulled up in front of the Hilt'N Hotel. At some point in time, this huge house with its columned veranda and front-facing balcony must have been a wealthy family home on what had then been the outskirts of town. Now it was just one of several places with chipped paint and mismatched adults sitting out on the porch.

One of those people stood up and walked over to her car. He was tall and thin, with sandy-blonde hair almost down to his shoulders. When he leaned in the window she rolled down, she noticed he had gray eyes, clear. No stubble, no trembling hands, and he was wearing what she thought of as prep school, alumni clothes that looked as if he'd bought them new, not that they were flashy, but they seemed to have belonged to only one owner. He wasn't shopping at the Rescue Mission store. She wondered if his clothes kept him apart from the others in the boarding house, and if that was on purpose.

"Bill Rittenhouse?"

"Yes, that's me. Lenore?"

"Yep. Get in."

She watched the traffic for a second and then made another U-turn against traffic that had Rittenhouse gripping the armrest.

"You're a risk taker," Rittenhouse said. "That's good."

Chapter 23

Melissa was flipping through the clothes in her closet. Several different outfits in shades of black were tossed on her bed. Shoes were scattered across the old Scan black and white geometric shag wool rug that had once graced her parents' living room floor in their first apartment.

She threw herself down on the bed on top of the clothes and yelled, "Mom, I don't have anything to wear for the funeral."

From her room, Margaret yelled back, "It doesn't matter. Wear anything. Wear your jeans. I don't care."

Margaret thought of the attire fight she had with her grandmother when her own father died years ago. On the morning of the funeral, she came down the stairs of her mother's house wearing her jeans and a blue denim shirt, tail out.

Her grandmother stood at the bottom of the stairs. Her face was stern, her tone indignant. "Stop right there, Margaret. The way you're dressed is disrespectful to the dead."

"Grandma, who cares what I'm wearing?"

"You can't dress that way for a funeral. Your father would care."

"He's *my* father. He's dead. He won't care now how I'm dressed," Margaret said, but in the back of her mind, she recalled his strict dress code for going downtown. "Always wear a skirt," he had commanded.

Her grandmother didn't budge. Margaret went back up the stairs and changed. After the service, one of the young boys she had hung around with as a teenager, the son of her father's best friend, had come up to her as they were getting into cars and hugged her—something he had never done before—and whispered in her ear, "You look wonderful."

It was a strange time for compliments, but then again nothing about that funeral had made sense to her. Perhaps that was the nature of funerals. Most funerals were so detached from normal life, artificial and conducted by someone who barely knew the dead, that they failed to honor the life of the person in the coffin. She had hated her father's funeral and still resented it now, almost twenty years later. This funeral she hoped, for all the artificiality of place, would be something organic, something natural to Clay—how he had lived, what he meant to do with his life. She planned to say something about him and would invite anyone who had come to say something. She would have the funeral home play his favorite funky Van Morrison songs. The last thing she wanted was to pretend that this was some classical event, some society do. If it turned out to be that, she would scream.

She walked into Melissa's room and looked at her daughter sprawled on her bed in the middle of the clothes frenzy. If she had been able to take a photograph of the room from the ceiling and slightly abstract it, it would look as if her daughter's brain had exploded. *An appro-*

priate metaphor for what we're both feeling, Margaret thought.

"It doesn't matter, honey. Wear what you're comfortable in. We're not on parade. People will think what they think anyway, and it's possible there will be no one there but us."

"Mom…" Melissa stopped and stared at her mother.

Margaret looked at herself in the mirror. She looked a hundred years old. It was scary to think you could age so quickly in two days. Melissa got up from the bed and stood in front of the mirror next to her mother. The child looked exactly the same, except for her puffy and bloodshot eyes. *My badge of courage,* Margaret thought. They looked at each other in the mirror. They used to look like sisters, everybody said. No one would make that mistake now.

"Okay, Mom. It was just a brain fart. I'll figure something out." She put her hand on her mother's arm. "Mom, what are we going to do after this?"

Margaret put her arm around her daughter and kissed her beautiful red hair. The child had her entire future ahead of her. Whatever Margaret did, she had to make sure she didn't jeopardize that. But first, she had to make sure they were safe. *Then, what was it I have to do? Oh, yeah, survive the funeral. Then what?* She had no idea. But for Melissa's sake, she had to have some plan. Life was already insecure enough.

"We'll have the funeral. We'll fly back to San Diego with grandma and stay at the Coronado Hotel. It's really fancy and right on the beach. We'll stay as long as we want. We'll go to the zoo and take walks on the beach. We'll eat a lot of avocados and strawberries. Maybe we'll take a trip down the coast to Mexico. Maybe we could go to Costa Rica? We'll wing it."

Melissa took that in. Her mother really didn't know what they were going to do. "What about school?"

"I'll talk to the dean. See if you can make up the work later. I'm sure he'll make some kind of arrangement for you." Then, on impulse, she said, "Would you be willing to move to California?" Margaret was thinking she might take back her maiden name, and change Melissa's name as well. It wasn't a betrayal of Clay, no, just protection. He would want that.

In the pause before Melissa could respond, the doorbell rang. That couldn't be Bob Rosen. He always came to the kitchen door these days. She walked down the stairs and looked through the window. It was one of the men from the gray Chevy at her door. He was looking around the front yard. She recognized his profile. Her heart thudded. *Is there time to call Bob and tell him something is happening?*

"Just a minute," she called, thinking they could just bust in. They had already violated her privacy and surely didn't have to be polite now.

Margaret walked quickly into the kitchen, found her phone, and called Bob's office number. She got his secretary. "Put me through to Bob, please," she said, hoping she didn't sound as if she was ordering the woman around.

"I'm sorry, he's out. May I take a message?"

Out where? Had they picked him up also? "Yes, tell him Margaret Turnbull called. The men in the Chevy are here. Please, tell him to come to the house immediately."

The doorbell chimed again. "Mrs. Turnbull?" the man called loudly through the door.

"Please get hold of Bob," Margaret begged and hung up.

She walked back to the door trying to calm down, almost hearing Clay say the words as he had so many

times during stressful situations in which she was about
to flip out. She opened the door about six inches, blocking it with her body, as if that could stop them if they
wanted to push their way in. One of the men who had
been in the vehicle outside her house for two days stood
politely at the door. He was wearing a suit. Margaret had
an odd thought about how uncomfortable he must be sitting in a vehicle for days in a suit.

"Mrs. Turnbull, we want you to come with us right
now. You're in danger. Would you get your daughter and
come out of the house, please?" The words had the sound
of a request, but they weren't. He was issuing a command. He put his hand on her arm and gripped it as if to
pull her out of the house. Margaret pulled her arm away
from him and stepped back.

"*You're* the danger." It was all Margaret could mus-
ter in her instant fury at him.

"Right now, please. Come right now."

He was too sincere. Her resolve buckled. "Do I have
time to grab some things?"

"No. Come with us right now."

*The guy is a goddamn broken record. And how do I
know whether he is really here for our protection, or
we're going to be taken away and never heard from
again.* She was shaking so hard, she could hardly stand
up. Margaret turned away from the door and saw a wild-
eyed Melissa at the top of the stairs.

"Get some clothes and things that are important to
you," she said to Melissa in a low, tight voice. "Right
now, Melissa. Don't argue."

Margaret ran up the stairs, hearing the man calling
and running up behind her. She ran into her room,
grabbed her purse, checkbook, snatched the few pieces of
jewelry from her dresser that she'd been considering for
the funeral and put them in her purse. She walked into her

closet and crouched down to open the safe where she kept her important papers. Her fingers were shaking so hard she could hardly open the combination lock.

She scooped all of the papers in the safe into her purse, gathering the deed to the house, her marriage certificate, birth certificates, savings and CD papers, Swiss bank account information, and some envelope she didn't remember putting in there. Thank God, she had already given Rosen the life insurance papers. If these guys wanted to know all about her life, all they'd have to do is take her purse. But she couldn't leave this information here, either. She had no good options. She had run out of options the moment Clay was arrested.

They met at the top of the stairs, Melissa with her backpack, Margaret with her purse, the man coming for them up the stairs. He got behind them and moved them down and toward the door the way a sheep dog manages its flock, pushing from behind, from the sides, to get the foolish animals to head in the direction he wanted.

At the foot of the stairs, Melissa broke away from him. "Oh, wait, I forgot something," she muttered and ran back up before the man could grab her arm. Margaret refused to leave the house without her. Melissa ran back down the stairs, her backpack over her shoulder.

The man put them in the back seat of the gray Chevy, and the vehicle took off. There were no introductions. One hundred yards down the street, Margaret, looking longingly back at her wonderful house, saw the front of it explode out in tiny pieces onto her beautifully landscaped front yard.

Chapter 24

It's the same as building a nest, Cheryl thought. *You take a tiny piece of string, a few short straws, hairs from somewhere, then more straw, some twigs, and tuck them one inside the other until they formed your life. That little object called your life was as fragile as a nest, able to be blown away, or picked apart by a larger scavenging bird that was after your eggs. When you had this fragile, tiny bowl ready, you put things in it, valuable things—your hopes, your ideas, your investment in people, your children.*

She was waiting for the congresswoman to read through her memo. Her presentation had been short, as required for an attention span akin to that of a three-year-old child. She had learned over the years that more than twenty words earned her no points. Either Representative Hannah Gittleson would start looking at other things on her desk or snap at her to get to the point.

"Cheryl." The congresswoman's barked order for her presence interrupted her reverie.

It hadn't taken long for Gittleson to look over Cheryl's written strategy. She had expected it would be a make-it-or-break-it moment. "On my way," Cheryl yelled back.

It didn't matter that Cheryl could be buzzed on the phone. The congresswoman preferred to bellow from her office. It was her way of making sure everyone knew the pecking order. *Well, she* was *the top pecker. That doesn't sound right. The top hen in this hen house. Cut it out,* Cheryl told herself. She hoped to use this meeting to actually get something done, something she cared about. She tugged at her jacket, fixed her collar, and mentally got her brain in order for the conversation with her boss.

The congresswoman's office was the same size as the outer space into which all of the staff was crammed. The huge desk behind which the elected representative's diminutive body perched was off the right wall. Under the huge windows that no one ever gazed out were a camel back sofa covered in green velvet, two club chairs in a faux needlepoint design that picked up the green in the sofa, and a rectangular mahogany tea table. A round rosewood conference table with red leather rolling chairs was at the end of the office near the hallway door. Two large oriental rugs in dominant shades of red and green covered the floor.

The congresswoman had great taste for someone who'd grown up in Highlandtown, Maryland in the apartment above her parents' grocery store. It never failed to impress Cheryl how far this woman had come on grit and brains alone. She never forgot how smart Hannah Gittleson was, how fast she learned new facts she was interested in, how quickly she synthesized existing facts into new ideas. That was the talent Cheryl had come here to serve, that and what had once been a devotion to the community the congresswoman had come from.

The question in Cheryl's mind was whether she could get the congresswoman interested in the Turnbull case. The Turnbulls weren't constituents and the FBI was not on the radar screen of any of their committees, but Cheryl was hoping the publicity angle would intrigue Gittleson. She might be making it up as she went along, yet she thought there was a plank they could walk out on that would give them a lot of air time, maybe a congressional hearing, if they played it right. Otherwise, it was a plank to walk off, right into the deepest part of the ocean.

"I've been looking at your strategy." The congresswoman started talking before Cheryl even got to the Queen Anne chair facing the desk. "I like what I see. You have some good ideas here. What did you have in mind for starters."

Cheryl took a breath. "Abuse of power."

The words hung in the air for a minute. She could almost hear the whirring of gears in the woman's head.

"Tell me exactly what you have in mind." Congresswoman Gittleson leaned back in her chair, her hands in her lap, fixing Cheryl with that X-ray look that made new staffers melt onto the floor in an anxious puddle.

Cheryl felt her throat constricting. *Why is this making me so nervous?* She'd pitched ideas to the congresswoman before that got them fabulous press and many terms in office. She was the oldest person on staff, the staffer who had been with the member the longest. She took a breath and forced herself to be logical, to speak slowly and without emotion. As she put the words together, she could almost hear the outline shaping up on the page, complete with numbers and bullets.

"Over the last several decades the FBI has had an ever increasing budget, staff, and power over the lives of American citizens with minimal congressional oversight. The disasters resulting from that increase in power include Ruby Ridge, Waco, and the Olympic bombing case. They bungled the Los Alamos spy case, were unco-

operative with Senator Danforth in the Waco investigation, withheld evidence in the McVeigh case, refused to
share information about terrorists who were in the country before September eleventh, and that's all before they
got unlimited rendition and unwarranted search powers
under the Patriot Act. There's also the Turnbull arrest and
subsequent death, and the Justice Department's position
that states don't have the right to prosecute FBI snipers
who kill the wrong target. They appear to be operating
beyond the law, in violation of constitutionally protected
rights."

Cheryl stopped. That was enough to assimilate right
now. Maybe too much, and really, that was all she had.
She had been calm and unrushed and packaged the Turnbull incident with the rest. But she was holding onto the
bottom line, what Gittleson always insisted her staff provide first. If she could get Gittleson to ask for it, Cheryl
might have the congresswoman on her side.

"What's in it for me?"

There it was. It was the obvious question, the bottom
line question, and the only question these days that
seemed to matter to Hannah Gittleson. But maybe her
ever-increasing egotism could be put to good use.

"You have an opportunity to ask for a GAO audit of
whether, or how well, the FBI has complied with the
whistle-blower ruling congress issued. You're the chair
of the House Government Reform committee. Call a
hearing when the FBI doesn't cooperate and get a lot of
press coverage for exposing their secrecy and failure to
inform Congress about their actions and methods. It
should be worth several months of national coverage that
would culminate just before we go out to campaign
again."

Cheryl knew it was a stretch. She wondered briefly if
the office was bugged. No one went up against the FBI

director. He had files on everyone. Cheryl wasn't sure what he had on Gittleson—she doubted it could be felony or treason—but personal issues could be enough for Gittleson to give up her hopes of being chosen as a vice-presidential running mate. Everyone in power knew the FBI director wasn't afraid to leak information when it served him. If that wasn't abuse of power, what was?

Cheryl watched the congresswoman's face, drew in a breath, and concluded her pitch. "Surely when the founding fathers wrote the Constitution, they hadn't envisioned a single department within a balanced tri-part government that held so much power. FBI is part of Justice, a government agency under the Executive with checks and balances carried out by the courts and Congress, and that doesn't mean just signing the check for their budget."

"What's in it for you?" Gittleson asked. The Member had leaned forward and placed her elbows on the desk. It was an important question.

It was also a new question. *Never underestimate the perspicacity of Hannah Gittleson,* Cheryl reminded herself. "I see an anti-democratic wave coming from government agencies. In their continual grasping for power, they are not working for the people. They are working against them." She leaned forward, intent on making her point. "Ultimately, the rights of every one of your constituents are in jeopardy. It's analogous to the IRS situation where you were so good at reining in their power."

That was the truth. But it wasn't idealism that had spurred her to this. She wanted someone powerful to look at the Turnbull case, if they could. She really didn't even know why she wanted this. Some part of her was calling out for help. She was a small child lost in a forest who had gone around and around in circles for days and was finally reduced to huddling by the side of a large tree, terrified, sobbing, with no hope. She couldn't be the only one who thought something was wrong with what had just happened to Clayton Turnbull. She couldn't be that different from the average American. And if she was...well, maybe this was the one time it mattered to be different.

If it took a year, or longer, somebody should figure out where that rotten smell was coming from. And from where she was standing, it might take all of Congress, a lot of press, and maybe a special investigator to dig out the truth. She couldn't do it alone. She needed Gittleson and all her power.

"What's the downside?" Gittleson asked.

"We get slammed, they play some pretty dirty tricks on us, you lose your office." In Cheryl's experience, it was best to give the worst case scenario first without any sugar coating. But she was leaving out the thought: Maybe we get killed, for real, as in deader than a doornail.

"I'll think about it. I'll talk to some people." Gittleson looked at Cheryl carefully.

Cheryl knew she was measuring how much she trusted her. Inspired by the recent anniversary of Brady jumping in front of President Reagan, Gittleson had once asked Cheryl if she'd take a bullet for her. Cheryl hadn't responded immediately, and that was sufficient answer. The answer was no, she wouldn't. The pause had made a tear in their relationship that was exploited by other women who characterized themselves as ambitiously successful, as if that were something to take pride in. Now Cheryl was asking Gittleson to put herself on the line, to maybe take a political bullet that would kill her career when all she really had to do was coast for the next twenty years.

It was a lot to ask. And in the way that things always worked here, Gittleson knew that Cheryl knew that Gittleson knew it was. Asking for this implied years of service in return, and maybe taking a metaphorical bullet. Gittleson would add whether she wanted more years of service from Cheryl into the formula that helped her to calculate whether she would take on this project. If the prospect was too risky, she might fire Cheryl for having suggested it. Frankly, Gittleson didn't need a reason to fire her. Cheryl served at the pleasure of the congresswoman and the congresswoman never let anyone forget it.

"I'll talk to you later." Gittleson shrugged off the red jacket of her suit and tossed it onto the sofa. She turned to pick up the telephone, dismissing Cheryl with a slight shooing motion of her hand.

Cheryl left the office, closing the inside door to the reception area behind her. She had pushed over the first domino. It was the best she could do, and right now she had no idea what Gittleson would do. It was up to the congresswoman and her advisers. Among whom, she reminded herself, she used to be counted. They would weigh the political liabilities against the advantages. Whatever Gittleson did, it wouldn't be because the Constitution was being violated.

Sometimes, Cheryl thought, the ends just had to justify the means. And she knew that, as with everything here, just saying something out loud made it real. Word would get out. There could be repercussions against them without them taking another action beyond this conversation. The thought made her more anxious than she had been before.

Chapter 25

Lenore leaned back in the booth and took a long drag on her cigarette. Although you weren't allowed to smoke anywhere in Maryland, this restaurant owner didn't seem to care about the law. Tables still had cheap glass ashtrays on them. The place was dark and nearly empty. These were the end of days for the Chat 'N Chew with its plastic checkered tablecloths and plastic flowers in milk glass vases.

Business folks went to Tauraso's just up the block where they could pay seven dollars for a chilled glass of white wine to go with their brick-oven-baked artichoke and Brie pizza. The few remaining farmer types went to Flohr's down past the fairgrounds on the way out of town where the service was fast and the food predictable. Construction workers picked up a sub to go at Brown's. Women worked now. There was no time for ladies' luncheons, the kind that this restaurant was built on. The place would go the way of Women's Clubs in all the little towns in this county. It would be defunct. Frederick would eventually blend into the homogenized metropolitan district, all of its individuality and quaintness erased by its own prosperity. It seemed quite a price to pay for success.

The waitress had come and gone, but not before she had leaned in toward Rittenhouse, her huge bosom nearly touching his face, her hand on his shoulder, saying "What'll it be, honey?"

Rittenhouse, acting as if the waitress was an old time friend, had cocked his head to look at her face, smiled and ordered a bowl of the Chat 'N Chew's famous vegetable soup. "You're lookin' good, Patsy," he said after ordering, giving her another smile.

Patsy, close to fifty and short on compliments, touched her hair, her other hand on her hip, and bounced a little. "Good as can be expected." She smiled at him, revealing the gap where a tooth had been pulled, and then walked away to get his order.

Lenore wondered if Patsy was going to just scoop Rittenhouse up and take him in the back for a few minutes, have her own lunch. She considered the man sitting on the other side of the table. He was eating the bowl of vegetable soup slowly, as if this were some required ritual before the confession could begin. She shrugged and took another long tug on her cigarette. It had been a weird day anyway. She might as well let him enjoy it. She wasn't in any hurry, and it didn't seem as if she was going to get anything for the flea market story today. She sipped her coffee.

Bill Rittenhouse looked up at Lenore between spoons of soup. She was older than he'd expected, maybe in her early forties. Somehow, reading her work in the paper, he'd thought she was some young twenty-something who was extremely bright. There was a huge energy in her writing. He didn't discount the extremely bright part but now he thought he understood why her stories were so insightful and thorough. She had some life experience,

some memory of what had happened in the past, some
knowledge of how things were supposed to go. That's
what gave her an edge. She was constantly comparing
what she heard to what she knew.

He was weighing what to tell her, how to tell it to
her, how to guide what she would do with it. He didn't
want to lose control of the story, at least before he could
see that it would turn out the way he intended. The purpose of this leak was to get attention paid to the problem,
but not to blow the whistle on the entire operation. That
would be too dangerous, for him and several others. They
were working carefully, all over the country, and it was
time to throw some dust in the eyes of the bad guys. If
they could synchronize this media action, they might be
able to get the attention of the big boys who could help
them blow the whole operation wide open.

"So, you're working on the flea market story," he
said, putting his spoon in the bowl, pushing the bowl
aside, folding his hands together on top of the table.

"Yes," Lenore said.

"What have you got, so far?"

"Not much. What do you have?" she asked, matching his tone and style.

"Frankly, I don't know why the mayor wants to stop
it."

"What *do* you know?"

"You live up to your reputation for being blunt," he
said. "I know one of the flea market vendors, a regular, is
a drug dealer and this is a regular distribution hub for the
region."

Lenore fished in her backpack and took out her pad
and a pen. "How do you know that?" The words "distribution hub" said "undercover cop" to her.

"Don't take any notes," Rittenhouse said. "Just listen."

Lenore sighed.

"When you get back to your office, don't put any notes on your computer and don't email anyone about what I've said," he continued. "Don't talk to anyone about talking to me but Mike and the other people whose names I give you."

"God, another off-the-record interview," Lenore muttered. "What the hell is going on?" She put her pen down on the table and drummed her fingers. Then she lit another cigarette and leaned back, letting her head rest against the high seat back. "Are you on or off the record?" Lenore asked just to hear him say it.

"Off, on deep background. No names, no attribution, not even unnamed sources."

"So you're not a down-on-your-luck druggie looking to get even with a dealer who no longer gives you a fix for free. How the hell can I write a story if I have no attributed sources?"

"I'll give you sources who'll go on the record."

"How do I know they're for real?"

"It'll be obvious."

"All right. Tell me how it works."

"This is what we know—"

"Wait a minute. Who's we?"

Rittenhouse smiled. "I was told you had a steel-trap mind."

She waved her hand as protection against flattery.

"I can't give you any identification about me that you can check. But just listen for a few minutes. Then I'll answer your questions. Okay?"

She blew smoke in his direction. He waved it away. They both took her silence as agreement.

"There are a group of guys around the country doing this flea market gig. They pick up a shipment somewhere—we haven't figured that out yet—break it down into smaller units, and place these units in various places, say trailers, lockers, mail boxes, and so on. Certain buyers at the flea markets identify themselves by wearing a particular color. It's different every week. The vendor knows who they are. These buyers pay top dollar for some odd purchases, post cards, posters, that have the address of the drop spots written on them somewhere. Their purchases are put in long poster containers or envelopes with a key. They go to the drop, pick up their shipment, and bring the product to their local distribution spots." He paused to look at her.

"If you start talking about the ruby computer that's directing everyone's minds, I'm out of here," she said, "but go on."

"Local police haven't been able to put two and two together. No drugs change hands at the flea markets, so they can't nab the vendors. The lower line distributors collect their stuff out of town, different locations all the time, so local law enforcement can't catch them. They can pick up small-time dealers till blood runs out of their eyes, but they can't connect the dots. The dealers on the street don't know where the stuff came from."

"How do you know this?"

"We've been watching the operation for some time."

"Who's we?"

"Let's wait on that. Recently we got a line on how the vendors pick up their shipments, and we're watching this local guy, Jack Vance, to see where he goes before the flea markets. He tends to go camping a lot, out to the Catoctin Mountains. We think that's where he's picking up the stuff, or at least another key to where the product is waiting for him, but that seems a little unprotected to us. If it's placed out there, anyone, a hiker or another camper, could find it. If we can spot him picking it up, we can grab him. Then maybe we've got a way into the middle of this spider web. If you write about Vance, it may make him jittery enough to make a mistake."

"How can I write about him if you don't arrest and charge him?"

"We will arrest him. We just need to be precise about the timing."

"Why don't you go to the FBI with this?"

"Not a good idea."

"Wow, that's an interesting answer. Who else knows about this, then?"

"Besides us? Nobody, we think. The one guy who stumbled onto it is dead."

"Turnbull," she said.

Rittenhouse gave her a hard look. She looked stunned at her own leap, as if she wished she could suck the syllables back into her mouth. "I see you don't just connect the dots," he said. "Or was that just a really good shot in the dark?" He looked around. The restaurant was dark. The waitress was off the floor. There were no other customers. Lenore said nothing, holding her breath. "Yes, Turnbull."

"Jesus." She stubbed out her cigarette and lit another.

Rittenhouse watched her face and knew she was wondering if her own life was in jeopardy just by talking to him. She still didn't know who he, or "we" for that matter, was. Other reporters would have left by now. She had courage.

"What does Perkins have to do with this?"

Rittenhouse held his breath. "Who have you been talking to? You couldn't pull that out of thin air. If there's somebody else who knows something, that somebody could be just as dead as Turnbull."

Lenore gave an elaborate shrug. It barely covered her jitters.

"You don't know anything about Perkins," he said. "You only know what I've told you."

Of course, saying it this way didn't discount what she'd guessed. Lenore stared at him. "How safe is his wife? Turnbull's I mean," she asked.

"She doesn't know anything. We're watching her. The funeral's tomorrow." He pushed the bowl of soup out of his way. "That's not really your concern, anyway. But now that you remind me, I'll personally check on Margaret Turnbull's safety."

"How did you see this playing out?" Lenore asked. "Is there a plan?"

"You go to the flea market," Rittenhouse said, "watch Vance for a while, see the operation. Then you talk to the undercover cop who's been working the scene for us. He'll be an unnamed source but on the record who I'll point out to you at the flea market. Then you talk to the police chief, who's in the loop and working with us. I'll also connect you with the captain at the local state troopers' barrack who's working with us. He and the chief will go on the record as named sources. Then you write the story, file it, give AP a call and let them know about the story."

"Why don't you go directly to the *Post*, or the Associated Press for that matter?"

"Too risky. No offense, but the pros will either think I'm crazy or dig too deep and publish too fast. I'll lose control of the story. Then the bad guys just take out their own distributors, hole up for a while, and start again."

"Take out? You mean they just kill them? Is that what you're saying?" Lenore put her hand across her stomach. Her face paled.

"Yes. This way, the story gets picked up all over the country from the AP wire. You get a national byline, if AP gives it to you. Other small papers where we've

planted the story also do their thing. Eventually, it will hit
the editors at the large dailies that they've missed the story and they'll put entire teams on it to catch up, looking
for the Pulitzer more than anything else. We're hoping
the result will be a lot of arrests not engineered by the
FBI. Then, we hope, the other shoe will drop during our
interviews."

"Boy, you've really got journalists and newspapers
pegged, haven't you?" Lenore stretched. "Why are you
using me as your patsy?"

"You're the gutsiest reporter in this region," Rittenhouse said.

Lenore laughed. "You would have said that to any
reporter my editor sent you." She settled back into the
seat. "Let me see if I've got this right. You want me to
write only the local angle. You don't want me to go near
the Turnbull connection or the other thing, or breathe a
word of that to anyone, is that right? And, wait, you want
the stories spread out across the country because they
can't kill all of us, at least all at once, without someone
catching on?"

"Yes."

"So, you're DEA, is that it?"

"No."

"How do I check out that you're not just some lunatic who wanted a bowl of soup for free?"

Rittenhouse smiled. "The police chief will give me a
reference. It *is* a lot to ask." He waited.

"How do I know you haven't conned him, too?"

"I'll give you another source fairly high up for background—you can't name him, of course—who will verify
what I've told you and who I am."

Lenore lit another cigarette, took two long pulls,
blew smoke above his head this time, and stubbed the
barely-smoked cigarette out in the full ashtray. "I have to

talk to my editor," she said. "Do you want a ride back to
your place?" she asked, thinking that the Hilt'N Hotel
wasn't really his place at all.

"I'll walk."

She nodded, relieved. "It might have been a bad idea
to pick you up in my car in front of so many people."

"I don't think that'll be a problem."

"What did you tell the folks at that boarding house
about meeting me?" She put on her jacket.

He grinned. "That you were my date."

She laughed, simultaneously placing a ten-dollar bill
on the table to pay for the soup and cover the tip. Standing, she waved at him, gathered up her backpack, and
headed toward her car without even a backward glance.

Shit.

In just a few minutes, she had driven the ten blocks
to the parking garage in town. Striding into the office, she
dropped her gear on her desk, then bee-lined to Mike's
office. No knock, no hello, she passed through the doorway, closed his door, took in his surprised look, and said,
"Boy, do I have a story for you."

Chapter 26

Larry Roland stopped at his usual roadhouse on Route 39 just past Azusa and before Falling Springs. He locked his bike and walked into the dark interior of the bar that always smelled like spilled beer and crushed lemons, the strange mixture of molecules escaping from fermented grains associated in his mind with fist fights and blood, with pheromones and big mistakes about women. He waved to the bartender, who was leaning over a newspaper spread out on the counter and smoking, and headed back to the bathroom. As usual, he had his leather saddlebags slung over his shoulder. He pushed opened the men's room door, checked to see if anyone was in the two stalls, and went into the one against the far wall. Locking the stall door, he pivoted and lifted the lid off the tank. No package.

He stood staring at the bottom of the grimy lid where remnants of tape glue had gathered other less easily identifiable dirt. *I have the right day. I wired the money sufficiently in advance, and there's been no word about a change in procedure.* The text to him had said only Orange. He put the lid back and went into the other stall. Same deal. No package. Now he felt as if someone had just pushed his head down into the scummy water in the toilet bowl. He was gasping for air, worried he might drown in his own fear.

Be cool, man, he advised himself. *Don't panic.* But, in the back of his mind, he knew this could only mean one of two things: He was out or the operation was shut down. If he was out, it was because of Turnbull. *Man, the guy's ghost was still making trouble.* There was one other roadhouse closer to Falling Springs to check, and then the stone outhouse in the park. He debated, standing there in the filthy stall, whether to check them or get out right now. As long as he was here, he thought, he might as well go ahead and use the damn facilities. Standing there pissing, the thought hit him. *They know my whole routine, they set me up.* Someone or something nasty would be waiting for him at one or the other locations. They expected him to keep at it, a trained rat searching a new maze for the cheese, a rat afraid to displease his keepers.

He had the Glock in the saddlebag on his chest, but it wouldn't do him any good if Perkins sent more than two men to take him out. Larry had never been that good a shot. He shook off, zipped up, buckled his belt, and walked out of the john. *Could the bartender be in on it? Naaa.* Larry stopped at the bar, bought a bottle of water in the way of thanks for the use of the facilities, and went back out to his bike.

This is it, then. Time to get out. He wouldn't be able to go back to the apartment. *What would they expect?* They would expect him to want to get the stuff, to recoup his cost. They would expect him to base all of his actions on greed, not survival. They would expect him to want to keep what he had. *Well, they're* wrong. *I only need one bell to go off.*

He had learned long ago that the most important thing to hang onto was life. Just about everything else, you could let go of. Sometimes you had to let go of everything else to survive, and that included people who you might have loved, people who were related to you, people who might care about you. There were two sides to this coin, and he had flipped it often enough that he knew the odds were even. And that was the case now. *Perkins just doesn't know who he's dealing with.*

Larry considered briefly whether he should go back through Azusa or off-road it up to Falling Springs and then head south again toward LA. *No. They're expecting me to panic, to go off-road, to do some macho, reckless thing. In their limited minds, they only have the picture of the me* they *have created.* Perkins and his henchmen had no idea who Larry Roland was except as a pawn in their game. *They'll be waiting for me somewhere in the mountains.*

He was better off going through the small towns. *I'll ditch the bike in town—man, it hurts to think of that— get a suit, haircut, rent a car, and drive down to San Diego as Eric Walters, then buy clothes again in the crowded airport, change, and get a flight to the Caymans as John Keating.* Good thing he'd remembered to bring both passports and sets of credit cards.

Calmer now that he'd figured it out, Larry chugged the water, threw the bottle into the trash can in the parking lot, mounted the bike, and drove back in the direction he'd come.

Inside the bar, the bartender was making a call. "He's been here. He's headed down Thirty-Nine going southwest."

Chapter 27

Lawrence Edward Blackwell had just completed his third obligatory call. The president's national security adviser sat back in his well-padded leather chair, his fingers with their curlicues of wiry gray hairs gripping the arms, his head lowered so that his bottom chin spread out across his white shirt collar and blue tie as if his skin was the expensive leather of a woman's designer hobo bag. He was thinking.

The leather bindings of the hundreds of books on the shelves behind him glowed in the light from the lamp on his desk. The blinds on the window opposite him, that would have given him a grand view of life on the most important street in the world, were partially closed. Lawrence wasn't interested in that view, or daylight. He thought better in closed spaces.

He didn't appreciate the man's tone on that last phone call. *Who the hell does Richard Hopkins think he is?* Obviously, Hopkins had expected Lawrence Blackwell to grovel. The man had no concept of how things worked. And threatening him, grousing about the thirty-five million dollars they had given him, *and on this phone line*—it was intolerable. The wheels in Lawrence's head were whirring so fast he could feel the synapses pinging off each other. Hopkins would be shut out. It was that simple. They didn't need him. When the deal was finally closed, Hopkins' International Oil would not be one of the players.

Lawrence wondered if there was a way to taint Hopkins, to connect him to the drug money they were using to fund the project, millions of it just rolling into the bank accounts he had set up and from which corrupt politicians in other countries could draw hefty sums at will. That was the beauty of the scheme. Lawrence never knew who withdrew what amount nor when. There were no direct payments that linked him to other officials. He was completely clean. He would let the question about what to do with Hopkins percolate a little while. The answer would arrive in its own time.

Meanwhile, he had some maneuvering to do to protect his own assets, both financial and in terms of personnel. There were some people who might get swept up in the inevitable political drama who Lawrence wanted to preserve for future use, including that twit Lessing, who would then forever-after be in Lawrence's debt. Lessing didn't have to say anything specific about why they needed to step back from the project. The only reason to do so would be that Congress was breathing down their necks, calling for a hearing, and looking for some prime television time. While Lawrence hadn't quite figured out what some congressional committee would be calling a hearing about, he realized that it was better to err on the side of caution. It was a lesson he had learned long ago from watching the Watergate and the Iran-Contra affair hearings: *Pull your fingers out of the pie before the guys on Capitol Hill decide they want a piece, and before your career is destroyed so that theirs can be expanded.* It never occurred to Lawrence that members of Congress were anything but self-serving. He judged them by his own conduct.

Lawrence turned to the computer on his desk, his pudgy fingers moving surprisingly swiftly over the keys, and accessed the Bureau of Educational and Cultural Affairs Internet server. He sent three e-mail messages. Satisfied, he pulled a large white handkerchief from his back pocket, mopped the sweat from his forehead and cheeks, and blew his nose. Everything was in place. He would now walk over to the office of the secretary of state and fill him in.

Chapter 28

Majed Faiez read the email message, which appeared on his tablet screen almost the instant Blackwell sent it. Faiez was well set up, using the latest satellite Internet and wireless hookup for his iPad. He read the message again. They would not be making any more purchases, the email said. The account would be closed. There was no signature, and the address was a complicated assortment of letters and numbers. But he knew who had sent the email, and he wasn't misreading it. They were shutting them down. He could feel his anger simmering in his stomach. He set his mouth in a thin line and willed himself to be controlled.

Slowly, deliberately, he quit the program and powered off the tablet then stood up from the small folding stool, tucking the iPad safely under his arm, and walked out of his room into the bright courtyard. Sun glinted off white walls of the surrounding buildings as he paused for a minute to let his eyes adjust. Peering around cautiously, he proceeded quickly across the courtyard, opened the iron gate, pulling it closed behind him, and went out onto the street. He had to deliver this message in person. It was also important to see Satam's face when he spoke the words and to hear the tone of his voice. *Then* Majed would know what was to happen next.

In a few minutes, he had reached the apartments he sought. Opening the street door, he briskly crossed the courtyard, found the numbered door, turned the knob without knocking, and stepped inside. Four men were sitting cross-legged on low pillows around a table. They all seemed to be talking at the same time. Their voices stopped mid-sentences. They looked up at Majed. There could be only one or two reasons for him to be here.

They waited.

"They are cutting us off," Majed said, his voice low. "The Americans will not buy any more of our product."

He stopped. That was all he knew. He did not know why and would not offer a conjecture. Although he had spent many years in the US, going to school and then working as an interpreter in the state department, he had never understood the Americans, who seemed to do nothing from a logic he could understand. At one moment they were committed to this idea or passionate about this other thing and then, suddenly, they couldn't care less. He knew the Americans were using the sale of heroin processed here to finance their dream of an oil pipeline through the region. He knew also that they didn't care about their people, or they wouldn't buy the deadly powder and ship it to their country to sell to their people. But he didn't care about that, or about their pipe dream. It would be a simple matter to disrupt the pipeline the minute it was completely built. Let them spend their billions of dollars. He and his comrades were waiting for instructions...and could wait a long time.

"Who sent the email?" Satam asked.

"Lawrence Blackwell."

"It must be a fact, then." Satam looked carefully at Majed's scowling face. "Do not worry, Majed, we have a plan. We will just carry it out a little sooner than expected. They will discover they cannot discontinue their relationship with us so easily. They have not learned from their experience with the Cubans. This time, we will teach them a lesson they will surely understand."

Majed nodded. "I volunteer," he said patriotically. His eyes blazed with the fury his heart could barely contain. The impotent, stupid giant would learn a lesson. That was all the encouragement he needed to lay down his life for the cause.

"No." Satam motioned with his hands, palms down, for the young man to be calm. "The leader has other work for you. Go back to your room. Do not come here again. You will be contacted when we need you. God is on our side."

Chapter 29

Cheryl made her way toward her car. She was going to the mall in Georgetown to pick up something to wear to the funeral tomorrow, still rattled by her conversation with Gittleson, yet the jitters didn't make any sense. *Am I really willing to put my whole career on the line, go up against an agency that no one could take on, because a man I don't even know was arrested?*

Gittleson's question rattled her. *What is my stake in this proposed strategy?* She couldn't imagine bringing down the FBI. *I'm so confused.* She had replaced marriage and kids with a career that now seemed to mean nothing. *What have I been doing all these years?*

Ten feet from her car, in the deserted garage, she heard tires squealing, rounding the sharp bend of the narrow driving lane between hundreds of parked cars. She froze, listening. *Nobody drives that way around here. It could cost you a bumper and a lot of hassle.* She looked in the direction of the sound and saw a dark blue Chrysler sedan bearing down on her, accelerating. *Nobody accelerates in a parking garage.* Still, she couldn't move. It was twenty feet away, fifteen, and she was rooted to the

spot. Finally, the screaming in her head, *GET AWAY!*
GET AWAY! connected to her limbs and she dashed between the cars nearest her.

The sedan rushed passed her and skidded to a stop. It
backed up with the same squeal of tires it had used to
zoom toward her. Again, she stood there watching it,
stunned, her mind and body disconnected. When the car
had backed up twenty feet, it began its rush at her again,
this time angled right at the cars she was standing between. Again, time slowed as she watched the car come
closer and closer. And then she moved, running in the
opposite direction, twisting between cars, as the sedan,
unable to stop this time, powered into the parked cars
where she had been standing. Metal ground on metal.

Cheryl didn't look back. She ran until she came to
the stairs and dashed up them. It was only when she was
in the stairwell that she realized they had seen where
she'd gone. They would be after her. She reached the
next level, panting, and tried the door. It didn't budge.
No, idiot, her mind was yelling, *you have to scan your ID
in the gadget by the door*. Holding out the ribboned
badge around her neck, she bent forward.

Feet thudded up the stairs.

Panicking, she ran up another flight, snatching the
ribbon off her neck as she went. She was high enough
now that there should be people in the corridor when she
got there. She presented the badge, heard the click, and
yanked on the door. It opened. She had a moment of relief and then threw herself through the opening, shoving
on the door to close it behind her.

She stood with her back against the wall in the corridor watching the constant traffic of well-dressed people
walking purposefully from place to place. Sweat ran
down her neck, soaking the collar of her silk blouse. Her
legs shook. Any minute, they would be storming the

door. *Please, God, don't let them have a key card! They must have a swipe card for the garage. Hell, they wanted to run me over!* She had to move. People would begin to stare at her if she just stood there. She'd go out the front of the building by the guard and check out the area before she went any farther, then call Keith when she got outside.

The doorknob rattled. *They don't have a pass card. What a relief. What were they going to do, anyway, whack her right here in the building with hundreds of people for witnesses? They must be amateurs. No, I'm the amateur. If these guys had wanted to kill me, I'd be dead. They wouldn't be using this car routine. They'd be using guns. They were just sending a message, a loud one. It certainly didn't take long. Who had Gittleson called? And who were the 'they'?* It had taken her only a nano-second to slip into a paranoid linguistic framework. She reminded herself grimly of the quote attributed to Henry Kissinger: "Just because you're paranoid doesn't mean someone isn't trying to kill you."

At any rate, she had seen enough movies to know she shouldn't try starting her car. Cheryl started walking, matching the stride of the others in the corridor, pretending she was still a put-together career woman. It occurred to her that beyond calling Keith, she had no idea what to do next. *I should probably call the police.* Basically, her life had just come apart. This, she supposed was the point of terrorism, to disrupt ordinary lives. Obviously, it worked.

Cheryl put her body into gear, imitating all the others in the corridor, moving quickly through the halls of power toward some purpose, known or hidden. For Cheryl, that purpose had suddenly been consolidated: it was survival. Everything else, including what the hell had happened to Turnbull was now relegated to the C pile of life.

It doesn't take much to get your priorities straight. She walked down the last flight of interior steps to the exit where the guard was on duty. Just outside the door, she called Keith on her cell phone.

"Come and get me," she said when Keith answered. "Don't stop to leave any messages or check your calendar, just come now."

"Where are you?" Keith asked. "You sound absolutely terrified."

It was a logical question. Somehow, in her terror, she had forgotten he couldn't see through walls or telepathically know her location. She did notice that he didn't ask why. "I'm in front of the building at First and C, by the guard door. I'll be the one shaking like a leaf. You can't miss me."

"Five minutes," he said and hung up.

Only after she disconnected from the call did Cheryl realize she could be spotted standing there by anyone else who was looking for her.

Chapter 30

"Okay. So now that we don't have a home—" Margaret's lips stretched tight across her teeth to keep them from trembling. "—tell me who you are and what's going on."

She addressed her command, if she could be said to have a command left in her, to the backs of male heads in the front of a vehicle speeding her away from her home of twenty-five years. One of the men, the black man who had come to the door of their home and was sitting in the passenger seat, turned around and looked at her. His face did not seem threatening, but she couldn't tell anymore who was a threat and who was a friend. He seemed calm, confident, and greatly relieved.

He could just be a really good actor, Margaret thought. She glanced at Melissa, who was hugging her backpack to her chest and shaking. Margaret had to be strong for her child, had to at least pretend to be in charge of their life.

"I want to see some ID, please."

The man reached inside his jacket, and for a moment, Margaret froze. Images of him shooting her and Melissa, of blood and brains all over the rear window, popped into her mind. He pulled out a leather wallet, flipped it open, and showed her a badge and an identification card. She almost sobbed with relief. He was Agent Carl Erol. *He looks a lot younger in his picture than he does in the flesh. The ID must be several years old.* She reached for the ID and studied the words on the badge. He was with the US Secret Service. Margaret could feel her mouth dropping open, but clamped it shut.

"We're the good guys, ma'am," Agent Erol said, smiling slightly. "We're going to take you somewhere safe and stay with you until this thing is over. This—" He pointed to the driver. "—is Agent O'Brien. We're assigned to protect you, and that's what we intend to do."

Margaret's head was whirling, a hundred thoughts and questions a minute. She tried to quiet her brain, to catch one question. She sank back in the seat, trying to control her breathing. *I should be able to do that much.*

"What happened to our house?" Melissa asked. She was glaring at Erol, her anger and disbelief on full display. "And what about the funeral for my dad tomorrow? And where are we going?"

Melissa doesn't seem to have any trouble finding the right questions, Margaret thought. Her daughter continued to surprise her.

"We'll know more about exactly what happened to your house tomorrow when other guys on our team have had a chance to inspect it," Erol said. "Right now, we think a bomb was triggered remotely. Most likely it was put in place on the day your father was arrested, while you were both out of the house. They probably made it look like a gas explosion. We're sorry we didn't know earlier, but we did get you out in time. We'll take you to the funeral and stay with you there. Our agents have already checked the funeral home. We will also pick up your grandmother and aunt from the airport. We know

their arrival times and flight numbers. You are being tak-
en to a protected location." Erol stopped and waited to
see Melissa's reaction.

Melissa was silent, her glare reduced to simply staring at Erol.

"Why the Secret Service?" Margaret asked, finding
her voice.

"We're part of a special task force that includes personnel from other agencies as well, ma'am."

Margaret noticed that he really wasn't providing a lot
of information. He answered their questions, but that was
all. "What task force?" she probed.

"Ma'am, I think that knowing that will endanger you
further. You are at risk because of what your husband
knew. I think—" Erol glanced at the driver, as if to confirm he was taking the right approach, "—that's enough
risk."

"What happened to my husband?" Margaret had to
ask, even if she got no answer. And what answer could be
good enough, anyway?

"Your husband was killed, Mrs. Turnbull. I'm sorry.
We weren't able to get to him in time." Erol passed a
hand over his face.

"He wasn't a spy?" Melissa's voice shook.

"No, Miss Turnbull, he wasn't a spy. He was a good
agent, doing his job."

Melissa turned to Margaret. "Mom?"

She burrowed her head into her mother's chest and
started to sob. Margaret felt tears running over her own
cheeks before she realized she was crying, with relief. *My
husband is not a spy.* Holding onto that thought and her
daughter for dear life, she glanced out the car window.
They were passing Mount Vernon, the home of the country's first president. She turned back to Agent Erol, who
was watching her intently.

"Thank you, Agent Erol. Thank you." Margaret buried her face in her daughter's sweet-smelling hair.

Chapter 31

Keith drove around the corner as fast as his car would maneuver in crowded city streets. He spotted Cheryl standing by the door of her office building. Dense plantings on either side of the walk framed her. She was a painting of a woman in distress. Her hair was tousled, as if she'd run through a hurricane. Dark glasses shaded her eyes, and her cupped hand hid most of her face. The collar of her black coat was pulled up. Keith smiled grimly. She stood out as starkly as if she was waving a sign. Fifty feet from her he saw a dark blue sedan with a crushed grille driving swiftly toward her from the other direction. A man's arm reached out of the passenger side window. Light glinted off the metal barrel of the gun in the man's gloved hand. He saw the kickback of the man's hand, once, twice, three times.

Keith screamed, "No!" as he slammed on brakes in the middle of the street, threw it in park, and leaped out of the car just as the blue sedan rushed by him. He ran up the cement walk toward the building, where Cheryl was lying on the cement path. He reached her in seconds, kneeled down, and touched her. The right shoulder of her coat was wet, a dark stain spreading down the sleeve. Only one of the shots had hit its mark. *She's breathing! She's alive!* His heart leaped. The shooter had missed the instant kill zones. Keith cradled her head, pulled out his cell phone, and made a call. Around him, he heard the sounds of the office building going on lockdown.

"It'll be all right, honey." Keith used a tone he hoped was soothing when what he was feeling was that he wanted to kill the shooter in the blue sedan with his own hands. "We'll get you patched up. You'll be okay."

Cheryl looked at him with half closed eyes, tears seeming to leak from under her lids. "I'm going to build a new nest."

Keith thought she was delirious.

When the guard finally ventured out of the door to see what had happened, Cheryl was unconscious. "An ambulance is on the way," Keith said. "I've got things under control. It was a specific hit. No need to put out a full alert."

The man looked dubious, pulled his walkie-talkie out of its holster, turned his back to Keith, and talked to his colleagues.

Chapter 32

Congresswoman Hannah Gittleson was so tiny she could swing her feet without touching the floor while sitting on almost any standard chair, but she was a powerhouse in the political world. Slowly but surely she had made enough alliances, enough agreements and compromises, done enough favors and learned enough secrets that little got done in the House without her sponsorship on a bill or her agreement to let it pass out of any committee to the House floor.

No one screwed with Hannah Gittleson, and that included her staff, who turned over, someone had once said, every eighteen minutes. She had laughed when she heard that, chalking the comment up to sour grapes. Those few stalwarts who had remained were there because they had proven their loyalty, and competence, over and over under fire, mostly from her. She knew her own reputation as a Gorgon among staff people. She also knew that the women who came to work for her were there as a stepping stone to more important careers, if they didn't break, that is.

She had some questions about why her communications director would now suggest that they embark on what was a politically precarious mission, but Gittleson was also intrigued by the way it would play. A hearing about FBI methods and management would put her in the spotlight, as long as she did it the right way. She would need the right allies on the committee, but she wanted to arrange it so that it was clear she was leading the charge. There was safety in numbers.

Her first two calls to other members on the committee were promising. She figured they had their staffs already researching Cheryl Roland's itemized list and determining what their position was and what they could get out of a hearing. Face time with the American people was the obvious payoff, two minutes on CNN, a quote in the New York Times, and many inches in their hometown papers. Maybe a little payback to an arrogant and overly independent agency was a secondary benefit.

She needed two more colleagues to agree, in principle, to going for a hearing, and then she could bring the subject up in committee. Even her chief of staff praised the idea, a surprise given that it had come from Cheryl, although Gittleson thought that encouragement might be more about what kind of exposure Elaine could get from the hearing than any particular interest in its outcome. That was all right with her, the staff could have their limited moments of glory. It certainly wasn't the salary that was keeping them here.

Cindy leaned into the congresswoman's office and knocked on the door simultaneously. "Senator Archer's here, Congresswoman," she said, and then backed away so that the imposing, white-haired man in an impeccably tailored gray suit with matching gray, silk tie could enter the room.

Before Senator Archer reached her desk, Gittleson had a second to wish that Cindy didn't chew gum in the office and that the young woman would do something about her extreme makeup, which suddenly seemed inappropriate for the office of a chair of a house committee. Then she hopped off her chair and stood to take Archer's hand. "Senator, to what do I owe this pleasure?"

"We've got ourselves a problem, Hannah." Archer moved to the couch and sat down, immediately changing the configuration of power in the room.

Gittleson gracefully moved to sit in one of the chairs near him. "What problem is that, Teddy?" trumping his use of her first name with his nickname.

"You need a little background on this FBI hearing you're planning, and then we need to work out how we'll do this together so that we get the right outcome," Ted Archer explained.

Hannah Gittleson knew that Senator Archer was familiar with the tricks she used to keep power and that he wasn't bothered by them. She was one of his oldest friends, if one could have friends in politics, and she knew that he knew she would do what he wanted, as long as it was to her advantage.

Word had certainly traveled quickly, probably staffer to staffer. But what surprised her was that Archer was here in person rather than by phone. He was chair of the Senate Intelligence Committee. It didn't bother her if he knew more than she did. He should know more. She also didn't want him thinking that she had been planning to usurp his lead.

He was her next call. But it bothered her that he would think she didn't know enough to even test the waters. That was Cheryl's fault, and Cheryl would hear about that later. His being there was a courtesy, and probably to prevent her from making a huge mistake. Gittleson should take it as a favor, one she would be required to return somehow.

"Fill me in, Ted."

"Over on our side," he said, referring to the fact that the Senate's offices were on the opposite side of the Capitol building, "we are about to launch our own investigation into the FBI. Did you know that?"

"No," Hannah said truthfully, wishing again that Cheryl had done her homework. Or had Cheryl known, and just not told her. Regardless, this strengthened Gittleson's case, if the Senate really wanted to get something done and members weren't just posing for cameras. "What prompted your concern?"

"We've been intensely researching the Bureau's activities for some months now, and we have many questions about their operations and their attitude toward Congress and other oversight mechanisms. In particular, we've been concerned about the department's flagrant flouting of the IG's office and their failure to cooperate with internal investigations." Archer paused. He sounded to Gittleson as if he was rehearsing his opening remarks for his own hearing.

"Well, that fits precisely with what we've been considering in the government reform committee, Ted." It didn't matter that she'd only been considering it for about two hours or that there was no we, except in the royal sense. She could feel her feathers settling down. *Cheryl hasn't hung me out to dry, after all. In fact, Cheryl has made me look absolutely brilliant. Maybe I'll give the woman a raise.* "It sounds like we can work very well together on this, in a kind of pincer movement."

The seventy-year-old man, a veteran survivor of many political battles, watched her. He placed one long arm along the back of the sofa, the large hand slightly gripping the fabric. His other hand lay on his leg, palm down. When Gittleson had finished verbally repositioning herself, identifying him as a partner, Archer raised one eyebrow. His blue eyes, often warm enough to make Gittleson's heart leap, were cold and considering.

Well, Hannah Gittleson told herself, *I'm not trying to leapfrog him. I'm simply taking advantage of the situation.* She could see that Archer was appraising her, wondering how much she knew. Probably not enough, really, in fact, just enough to gain some prominence on the issue, and she was smart enough to make pay dirt out of the mud that might be flung around or leaked to the press during a hearing. She could see him deciding that she could get some glory out of this, but he would keep control.

"I suggest we set our hearings to begin simultaneously on February fifteenth, beginning at two in the afternoon," Archer said in a tone that was more command than suggestion. "Our staffs can take care of the rest. Have your communications person—is that Cheryl Roland?—give Keith a call to work out arrangements."

Gittleson thought it was odd that he knew Cheryl's name. *Had Cheryl been fishing for a new job?* Right now, she simply nodded. She'd find out later.

"Oh, and, Hannah," Archer said as he got up from the couch and headed out the door that led to the hallway instead of the office's reception area, "don't jump the gun, leak anything to the press, or tell your big supporters, or you'll be in more trouble than you know what to do with. I say this with your best interests at heart."

He nodded to her, a kind of modern bow, went out, and closed the door behind him. Even Senator Ted Archer didn't know how much trouble he was talking about.

Hannah Gittleson sat back in the chair and wished she hadn't given up hard liquor.

Chapter 33

Jimmy Jones made two calls from his office, quick ones just to confirm the time of his two appointments, then went out of the building the back way to the small parking lot on the side of the old courthouse that now served as city hall. He got in his black Jaguar, put the car in reverse, and smoothly pulled out of his reserved spot onto Church Street. The town's one way streets meant that he had to go out of his way to travel two blocks to Doc's, but he'd get to see how the general population was doing as he drove.

There was the usual straggly group of AA members out on the sidewalk, at Church and Market, waiting to get in for their meeting. He shook his head. People who couldn't hold their liquor got no sympathy from him. He could knock back several bourbons a night and still be ready for anything that came his way. *Bunch of wimps. No backbone.* All that boohooing about hard lives. Made him sick. He drove past the group, not looking at them.

He passed the county building. *Another bunch of softies*, he smirked. It was so easy to get them to do what he wanted that it was laughable. There wasn't one person on the county commission who hadn't run for election to do something good for the county. They didn't have a clue about how to wield power, *and* they were constantly battling with each other. That was fine with him, too. Left him an open field.

He went up the alley, next to the funeral home, and turned right at Patrick Street, then was prompted to stop by the light at Market. He stared at the old McCrory's, a dead five-and-dime that a lame arts group was turning into a performing arts center. *God, that place is a mess.* They'd spent 40,000 dollars of taxpayers' money and, as far as he could tell, they'd gotten nothing for it. He'd been inside once, at the ribbon cutting, and noticed they had put linoleum on the floors and painted the walls black. The place was some hippie teenager's dream of an off-Broadway theater. Not that he'd ever been to one of those, either, but he'd heard. He wouldn't give them two cents for their performing arts center and their artsy-fartsy ideas. And he meant that literally.

The light changed and Jimmy drove past the new courthouse, then pulled into the parking lot just behind it, where Doc had his office in a small group of two-story row houses. Doc was a retired veterinarian whose real claim to fame was that he ran politics in this county. He'd been at it for nearly a half century after serving in various offices, including state delegate and senator from the area, maneuvering his chosen people into important seats, arranging pretty much who could run and who couldn't all the way to the statehouse, expecting favors in return. Jimmy was mayor because of Doc. The vet had put together a coalition of business people and old time Frederick folks to support Jimmy. The point had been to prevent that black fireball Earl Stevens from getting into the mayor's office. The thought of all of the city's money going to support the poor in town gave Jimmy Jones the willies, even now when that threat had long since passed.

Jimmy planned to reassure Doc that he was still doing the job of mayor the way Doc wanted it. Doc was, after all, one of the silent partners in the land deal. Jimmy opened the door of the shabby office without knocking and walked inside. He was expected. The reception area consisted of two weathered brown leather chairs and a beaten-up wooden table that held a lead-glass decanter of whiskey with two glasses, a box of cigars, and an ashtray.

No receptionist, no paintings or framed mementos, no autographed photographs of great men shaking hands with the office's occupant indicated to a casual visitor that this was power central in the county. In fact, the place was seedy and cheap. Doc didn't believe in spending a lot of money for no reason. What went on here required only the grease that oiled political wheels. "For that," Doc was fond of saying, "you don't need an interior decorator, fancy accessories, or receptionists." You didn't come to see Doc unless he told you to.

From the back room where Doc ran the show from a long conference table and telephone, came a deep voice, "Be there in a minute, Mr. Mayor."

Jimmy settled into one of the chairs, took a cigar out of the box, smelled the wrapper, clipped the end, lit it, and sucked hard. Blue smoke billowed around his head. Thirty seconds later, a large, bald man with a nose to match his six-foot five frame and peculiarly thin lips hobbled into the reception area and eased into the other chair. He rubbed his arthritic knees and sat back in the chair. Jimmy imagined Doc Varney sticking his arm up the backside of a cow to deliver her calf. Then the mayor noticed Doc hadn't offered him a drink.

"Been hearing you're getting yourself in a bit of trouble, boy," Doc rumbled, making it clear who was boss. "You want to watch it a little. You need a little coaching on subtlety. You can't just ram any old thing down their throats."

Jimmy was caught off-guard. He hadn't been called boy since he was a kid on the street. "W—What the hell are you talking about?" he spluttered. "Things are breaking our way. No problem."

"Not what I hear. Phone's been ringing off its cradle all damn day. You're using a bulldozer when you should be using a spoon."

"Who called you?"

"You don't need to know that. You just need to slow down. You're a bull set loose in a field of young heifers. Pick your time. You'd have been better off negotiating with those flea market folks before you went to the council, and having a little talk with the fairgrounds' board before you set out to decrease their annual income. Now, you're just going to have to back off for a time, let things settle out."

Jimmy thought about this a minute. It was really beginning to piss him off that this old bastard could tell him what to do. Doc wasn't out there taking the heat from the press. He didn't have to manage a whole herd of staff and rambunctious civil servants. And, he didn't have to make nice to contributors and would-be contributors or sit with his heart in his throat every four years hoping he'd get enough votes to stay in power. He could just sit back in that crappy office of his and field calls all day, giving orders, shielded from whatever happened. Jimmy clenched his hands into fists. His teeth clamped into the cigar. *I don't need this old man.* He got up from the chair.

"I'm the mayor, Doc, in case you've forgotten," Jimmy Jones said around the cigar still in his mouth. "I'm the one taking the shots, making the baskets. You're just sitting on the sidelines now, and don't you forget it."

With that, Jimmy strode over to the door, yanked it open, and walked out without closing it.

Doc Varney sat in the chair stroking his large face with one hand, feeling the spots on his cheeks where he hadn't gotten close enough with the razor. *Boy's outgrown his britches. May be time to get a young stud in office, someone who can still be controlled.* He got up, closed the door, and went back into his office to make a call.

ഐ

Jimmy Jones got back in his Jaguar, rammed the gearshift into reverse, backed out of the space and sped out onto Patrick without looking to see if there was oncoming traffic. He was pissed. He was more than pissed. He could buy and sell that vet seven times without looking. He was so pissed he missed his turn onto Jefferson Street and had to go around the block to get back on track. He hated it when anyone messed up his routine. *Who the hell did that fat bag of lard think he was talking to?* Doc would be very surprised when a slate of candidates he hadn't chosen turned up to run in the next election. Jimmy had his people, too. It was time for a change in leadership.

The mayor wound his way over to Route 355 and pulled into the Jag service area. He locked the car, tossed the cigar, and then walked about one hundred yards to a pre-fab, one-story building with the sign "Frederick Spa" hand-lettered on the door. This time he knocked.

Vanessa, as she was called, opened the door. She was wearing the outfit he liked: black corset that pushed up her tits with just a little nipple showing, black lace garter belt with black stockings, no panties, and red stiletto high heels. Her red lipstick and nails matched the shoes.

"Hello, lamby-pie." Vanessa leaned over and gave him a kiss. "You're right on time. Come on in."

The mayor stepped into the darkened room, walked over to a deep chair layered with velvet draping, dropped himself into it and undid his tie. This was the one place he could relax. Vanessa went to the small table in the corner where she kept her calendar, leaned over, and marked something down. Jimmy Jones admired her ass.

"Do it for me, baby," he said, unbuckling his belt. "I've had a rough day. I need a good massage."

Vanessa walked slowly over to him, leaned obligingly forward, brushing his face with her breasts, and unzipped his pants.

છબળ

Across town, Chief of Police Warren Spats was listening to Doc Varney explain what he wanted. Spats nodded, taking some notes on a pad on his desk. It seemed to him it was bad timing for this, what with everything else that was about to happen. But if Doc wanted it, Doc got it. Spats owed his prominent position in the police department to the vet. He didn't tell Varney about Operation Clean Sweep, as he had come to think of it. That was none of Doc's business. He said okay and pushed two buttons on the phone, one to disconnect from Varney and the other to call Captain Taylor.

"You're gonna raid that whorehouse out on Old Frederick Road today, Taylor," Spats said. "You know the one. You're gonna do it right now."

He paused, listening to his captain's objections. "And take a camera. Photograph whoever's in there when you break the door down. No matter who it is. No matter what they're doin'. Take the photo of the exact way they look when you bust through that door. You got me? Arrest all the johns. Let me know when it's done and you're back in the office."

Spats put down the receiver and turned up the sound on his scanner so he could hear whatever was said in the cars as his officers drove out to the Frederick Spa. This would be a little bit touchy. He knew at least five important guys who got their massages from that gal a few times a week. Once the bust was done, he was supposed to leak the information to that reporter Lenore Cavanaugh, the gal Bill Rittenhouse had said was going to call him later today about the other matter. "There are too damn many balls in the air." That's all he could say about this whole mess.

Chapter 34

At four o'clock, Lenore emerged from Mike's office. Office chatter died immediately. She had been in there for over an hour with the door closed. Some reporters were hoping she'd been fired; or at least shot down; at a minimum, taken down a peg or two. Those reporters whose cubicles gave them a view of the aisle between desks stole glances at Lenore's face and the way she was walking.

Hopes were dashed. Lenore's color was normal, and she was sauntering, in that particularly annoying way she had, as if she owned the world. Glenda got up from her desk and walked back toward the kitchen area, her hands twitching as if she wanted to wring someone's neck. In a minute, Valerie emerged from behind her partition and walked back to the kitchen. Lenore could hear the murmur of voices all the way to her desk.

After she had filled Mike in about the story, he'd just sat there at his desk leaning back in his chair looking at her. She could tell he was trying to decide if she was as crazy as the people she had talked to today, because of course, she had told Mike everything that Bosner told her, as well as the story from Rittenhouse. Mike didn't say anything for a while. She sat there watching him, her hands in her lap, wishing she could smoke in the office. Finally, Mike had picked up the phone and called the publisher and filled him in. Lenore looked around the office: photos of Mike's family, a few framed awards, stacks of journalism magazines, some framed cartoon originals, piles of newspapers on the credenza behind him and more on the floor. Mike definitely lived his job.

There was a long silence on Mike's side of the phone while the man on the other end of that connection, Rick Ryan, went through the same thought process Mike had just engaged in, probably with some sputtering and expletives, Lenore imagined. At no point did it leave Lenore's mind that they were also sizing up the possibility of prizes, because prizes drove readership, which drove advertising, as well as assessing the danger of lawsuits against the paper, if any part of this story could be constituted as slander, or made them appear to be idiots.

Lenore and Mike then waited together while Ryan called Chief Spats and got confirmation that the story was on the level and Bill Rittenhouse was legit. It was a move Lenore thought intruded too far onto her turf, was unprofessional, and made her look as if she was incompetent. Ryan should trust her enough to believe that she would check it out. It was this kind of rinky-dink stuff that made her remember this was a two-bit newspaper, and it was time to move on.

After Ryan confirmed what she already knew, that Rittenhouse was for real, she and Mike were on a conference call with the publisher and the paper's attorney, who gave the usual advice about sources and the word alleged but didn't quash the story. They were set to go. Getting approval didn't take the edge off the way upper management treated her. Approval also didn't assuage the anxiety she had not conveyed to Mike, although she thought he was smart enough to pick up on it: her fear of being in deep water, in over her head, in fact.

"We'll break it in Tuesday's paper and online that morning," Mike said. "Will that give you enough time?"

"Yep, I think so. It's pretty straightforward from here. I'll let Rittenhouse know." Lenore got up to leave and then turned around again. "I'll work from home and email it in. That all right with you?"

"Fine," he said. "Make sure you email a copy to Ryan as well, just to be safe."

"No problem." Lenore chafed. Obviously, the piece was going to be gone over with a fine-tooth comb. *Okay, then, I'll give them a story that'll blow their socks off.*

Lenore packed up her bag, throwing in her laptop, her tape recorder, several pads and pens, her camera, and her cell phone. She looked around her cubicle. Had she forgotten anything she would need for a few days? The bag was heavy now, mostly from the laptop. She put on her jacket, and then threw the backpack over one shoulder and walked out of the office.

Outside, she paused and lit a cigarette, took a long drag, and exhaled into the chilling air. Clouds were coming in. It would snow. She was about to turn toward the garage when she changed her mind. Checking her watch, she turned in the opposite direction and swiftly walked the three blocks to the county courthouse. When she got inside the double glass doors, she was panting slightly. The officer on guard looked at her sternly. She put her pack down on the desk for him to rummage through and walked through the metal detector. She gave him one of her winning smiles.

She smiled at him again. "Too many cigarettes."

He grinned at her, immediately taken by the blonde with the hour-glass figure in a black leather jacket. "What are ya up to today?"

"Just checking some records." Lenore waved and moved quickly toward the land records office.

Inside the land records office, she stood at the long counter that separated county staff from the rest of the world. She hoped her contact would be here. She didn't have much time until they closed for the day. She spotted Helen's gaunt figure and waved. Helen grinned and came up to the counter. Lenore knew Helen enjoyed being part of a reporter's investigations. It made her feel she was doing something important, she had told Lenore, more important than keeping shelves of paper and rolls of maps in order.

"Hey, how are you?" Lenore was never too rushed to make people feel they were friends of hers.

"Oh, you know, doing okay, considering."

Helen pulled the sides of her baby blue cardigan together across her narrow chest as if she were suddenly cold. She had told Lenore about the long hassle of her divorce, a child with learning problems, the difficulty of living on a wage that should have qualified her and her child for anti-poverty support programs, and the pride that wouldn't let her apply for them. Lenore remembered her story well. It was one of those stories that was collecting in her head for a long piece on civil service at the local level where salaries for people who did the actual work were contrasted with the salaries and perks of the jerks who were elected to office. But she didn't really have time for another installment right now.

"We should go to lunch sometime soon," Lenore said. "Call me when you get a minute next week so we can set that up." She looked at the woman's narrow face with the huge brown eyes, dark rings beneath them, and hoped Helen didn't think she was giving her the brush off. It was okay, though. Helen was smiling as if Lenore had given her the one gift she had wanted all her life. Lenore would have to remember to make good on the lunch.

"What do you need today?"

"I want to see who owns the fairgrounds land."

"Oh, I can tell you that. It's owned by the fairgrounds board of directors."

"You mean completely, it's not city land?"

"No, it's in the city limits, but the fair board owns it, the way you own your house."

Lenore thought a minute. *That's why the mayor was taking this roundabout approach. He couldn't just get the council to cut off the flea market's access to the land. He was trying to marshal public opinion to influence the fairground directors.*

"Who owns the land around the fairground?"

Helen went to a large map, identified a land parcel number, wrote it down on a piece of paper, went to a ledger on a table behind her, and looked up another number. She wrote the book and chapter number down on a piece of paper for Lenore, walked around the counter, and led Lenore to the stacks of maps and record books. They walked down the rows until they came to the right set of numbers on the binder. Helen pulled down the ledger and flipped it open to the correct page.

Lenore saw a drawing of parcels already subdivided around the fairgrounds, each identified as five- to ten-acre lots, all with the same heading: Consolidated Partnership LLC. Consolidated owned about one hundred acres, right around the fairgrounds. She took some notes about the date of purchase, which was 1994, the number and size of the lots, and their relationship to the fairgrounds, and found a reference to the cost. Only twenty thousand dollars to one Sam Greene, who, Helen said, had been a fourth generation farmer before he gave up the land to pay his debts.

"Any chance I could get a photocopy of this plat map?" Lenore knew she was pushing it a little, and she didn't have time to wait.

"Not today." Helen looked around over her shoulder and began to wring her hands.

Lenore put her hand on top of Helen's. "No problem. I probably don't need it. How do I find out who the partners in Consolidated are? Oh, and do you know if there's a road going back to all this on the county master plan map?"

Helen looked at the watch on her thin wrist. Pulled to the tightest hole, it still hung a little bit from her arm. "Come back to the counter," she whispered conspiratorially. "I can make some calls for you."

They walked back to the counter, and Helen called friends in two other offices. She came back to the counter looking as if she'd conquered the world. "Angela's going to fax over the list of partners to me in a second. And Fairgrounds Lane, the little spur off Patrick that's there now, was supposed to be extended in 2012 and then delayed, but there's been a rapid request application put in from the mayor's office that the county planning commission has already approved, so they're now scheduled to begin construction in a few months."

"Wow, you're good." Lenore admired the woman's connections.

Helen glowed. She walked over to the fax machine and was back immediately with two pages. She handed the papers to Lenore as if she was enjoying a moment of wicked glee she hadn't felt in a long time. Lenore looked down the list, using her finger to help her scan quickly. Her finger stopped at Jimmy Jones' name.

"Holy shit."

Helen laughed out loud and nodded.

"That explains a lot, don't you think?" Lenore asked, mostly to herself but including Helen.

Helen nodded.

Lenore put the list in her backpack, held out her hand to shake Helen's. "Thanks so much, Helen. I couldn't have done it without you. Don't forget to call me about lunch."

She strode out of the office, through the lobby, waved and grinned at the officer on guard, who took the time to admire the view of her walking out the door, and went outside. Now she had an idea of what the mayor was up to, and it was predictably simple. He was looking for a way to open up access to land he owned and had already subdivided for development so that he and his buddies could make a few million more dollars.

She stopped in the courtyard, put her pack down on one of the stone benches, and lit a cigarette. She would need to identify the other partners on the list, not just by name but by what else they owned and what other partnerships they were part of. At least one other name had leaped out at her, the district's congressman, Mr. Holier Than Thou, who had made the leap from a nobody Dartmouth graduate to state senator in one try. *And then* he had gone on to the House of Representatives when the old man who had held the seat for years retired.

It was all done with other people's money, donations from around the country, unprecedented for a local state race and much increased when he ran for Congress. She grudgingly admired the guy, even if she couldn't stand his politics. He knew what he wanted, and he went after it. She'd have to check if there was anything illegal about him being in a local partnership that owned commercial development land. Probably wasn't as long as he didn't handle it directly.

Lenore tossed the cigarette in the nearby cement ashtray and walked down the steps to the sidewalk. She had five blocks to go to her car, and it was getting really cold. Her black leather jacket, chic as it was, didn't provide much protection against the elements. She chided herself. *It's still February, idiot. You should have worn your fleece jacket and not worried about how you looked.* The wind was picking up, blowing her blonde hair in sheaves back from her face and her cheeks glowed pink with the cold and her exertion. By the time she made it to her car, she could see her breath puffing out of her mouth, smoke from a feeble dragon. She unlocked the car, threw her bag in, lit another cigarette, and headed out of town.

From NPR's All Things Considered she heard that Turnbull had died. A slice of cold air froze her chest. She put her hand there. Although she had guessed it and then had it confirmed by Rittenhouse, somehow, peculiarly, hearing it on the news, on NPR, made it more real, or maybe made it real for the first time. *What have I gotten myself into?*

Lenore pulled into her driveway and noticed the quiet first. No dogs barking. No dogs greeted her when she opened the car door. She wondered if the doggie door was stuck again. But they should have been barking. They always waited for her. She unlocked the door to her house and listened. Nothing. She started calling them, looking first in the family room on the bottom level where the dogs were accustomed to lie on the sofa. They weren't there. She dropped her pack on the coffee table and went into the kitchen. Their bowls of food were untouched. Her heart was thudding hard. She wondered briefly if her ex had come by and taken them. That would be the kind of thing he might do, the bastard, since they'd bought the dogs together.

Calling, she walked into her bedroom. There they were, on her bed, side by side, not moving. "Gordo? Frodo?" She called softly, walking to the bed, touching them. She watched for the slight movement of their stomachs that would indicate they were breathing. Nothing. She said their names again, tears this time springing to her eyes. Their eyes were open. She dug her fingers into the soft fur around Gordo's neck.

"Gordo," she whispered, "what happened to you?"

Then it hit her. They'd been killed, deliberately, and placed on her bed. She ran her hands over their bodies looking for bullet holes or some kind of puncture. No sign of harm, just this death posed on her bed for her to find. They must have been poisoned. A fifty-foot wave of panic crested over her head. Saliva dried in her mouth. Her ears ached from straining to hear the slightest noise. Silence. She scanned the room—nothing out of place. Nothing.

Get out!

Lenore scrambled—slipping on the hall carpet, bumping into the wall—back down to the family room, grabbed her backpack and keys off the coffee table, and rushed to her car. Heart pounding, eyes darting, she quickly scanned in every direction. No one. The street was incredibly quiet, and snow was starting to fall. She felt a scream forming in the pit of her stomach and ordered it to stop. Flinging the bag to the passenger seat, she jumped in and backed out of the drive.

Where am I going to go?

She drove the half-mile to the quaint, small town near her, pulled into a metered parking space opposite the tiny sheriff's office, and sat for a minute, thinking she would go in and tell the sheriff someone had killed her dogs, gone into her house, and put them on her bed. He probably wouldn't believe her. She was still thinking about telling the sheriff when her cell phone rang. She jumped and hit her knee on the dashboard. While she rummaged through her pack, the cell phone rang insistently. Finding it finally, she pressed the button to receive the call.

"Yes?"

"Lenore, where are you?" It was Rittenhouse.

"I'm in Shepherdstown, opposite the sheriff's office. Someone killed my dogs." Lenore realized she was nearly screaming, and then she was sobbing. "They killed my dogs! Oh God, they killed my dogs!"

"Get a grip on yourself," Rittenhouse said. "Lenore. Get a grip. Listen to me. I'm going to come and get you. I can be there in forty minutes. Go into the Chinese restaurant on the corner and wait for me inside. Do you hear me? Don't—"

Lenore interrupted the string of orders. "What the hell's going on?" she gasped, now in rage.

"I'll tell you when I get there."

"Why can't I drive my own car to where you are?"

"It's not safe." His terseness unnerved her more than the words he was saying.

"Okay." She hung up.

Lenore took her backpack, got out of the car, and locked it, and walked across the small street to the China Kitchen. The last thing she wanted to do was eat, but she was a regular at the restaurant, and they might just let her sit at a corner table with a pot of tea. Her life had been commandeered. She hadn't agreed to have her dogs killed, just to write the damn story. *Wait a minute, how did Rittenhouse know there was a Chinese restaurant on the corner? Has he scoped-out my entire life—or is he the one who killed my dogs?* Her heart sank. "Don't let it be that," she said out loud and opened the door to the restaurant.

It was warm inside, and even mid-week they had a good group of customers all happily eating an early dinner and chatting. For a moment the Chinese scrolls on the walls looked hideous to her, the smell of something frying in peanut oil turned her stomach, but then it was suddenly familiar and comforting. Mrs. Ling came up to her and touched her arm. Lenore looked down at the tiny woman and asked if she could just have a pot of tea. Mrs. Ling scanned Lenore's face, took her by the hand, and led her to a table against the wall. Lenore fell into the chair with her back to the wall. From here, she could watch the room and who came in the door, as if that would do her any good.

"Be right back," Mrs. Ling said and bustled away.

In the kitchen, Mrs. Ling told Lenore's favorite waiter to bring the reporter a pot of tea and some bean curd and spinach soup. "She need food," she said, nodding more to herself than to him.

Just as Rittenhouse had said, he was there in half an hour. He let her finish the soup, which she had spooned gratefully into her mouth after recovering from her surprise. She acknowledged Mrs. Ling's wisdom with a smile at her across the room.

Rittenhouse paid her bill, took Lenore out to his car, and held the passenger door open for her. He smiled, but she could see that he was tense. She got into the car, thinking that all of this was way beyond the call of duty. In exchange for her dogs, she was going to get him to give her the whole story, names and all. That's the one she would pitch to AP, with her byline.

They pulled away from the curb and wound slowly through the town's streets. They crossed the bridge over the Potomac River. It was snowing harder. Rittenhouse turned on the windshield wipers and said nothing for a few miles. Cones of light from the car's headlights illuminated the snow so that it seemed as if they were heading into a vortex of white dots that spiraled into infinity. Lenore looked away from the road. She was beginning to be glad Rick Ryan had called the chief of police. At least she had that slim confirmation to hold onto, something to indicate that she wasn't being kidnapped by the man who had killed her animals.

"Okay, tell me what's happening?" She pulled a cigarette out of her pack and lit up.

"Things have gotten a little out of our control," Rittenhouse said. "We didn't anticipate the level of ruthlessness that's now being displayed."

"What the hell does that mean?" Lenore thought she would lose it if the guy didn't give her some straight answers soon. "Where are we going?"

"We're going to Camp David, you know, the president's retreat in Thurmont. He's not up there this week. There's a cabin where you can work. You won't go to the flea market tomorrow. I may not be able to protect you at the flea market, and my guess is there probably won't be anything to see now. If we have Vance, the local dealer, I'll arrange an interview for you."

Lenore's mouth felt frozen, her face numb. She shivered. The cigarette between her fingers grew an ash. She waited to see if there was more information that might thaw out her brain.

"The drug syndicate I told you about earlier?" Rittenhouse looked over at Lenore's face to see if she was taking in what he said. She was blinking. "They tried to kill Turnbull's wife and kid today. It's likely that same group are the ones who killed your dogs...as a warning. We've got the Turnbull women in protective custody now, so that shouldn't happen again. And there's one other thing that might upset you."

He paused and checked her face again. "I hope you are one tough woman. Colonel Bosner, who you talked with this morning, had a fatal car accident this afternoon. Lost control of his car and skidded into a Jersey barrier on Interstate Seventy. His car burst into flames."

Lenore sucked in her breath as if she'd been slapped. There was a long pause, her cigarette ash dropped on the car floor, and she absently rubbed it out with her foot. She was thinking about Bosner, how healthy he had looked with his broad shoulders and solid frame, his neat crew cut.

"How did you know I'd talked to Bosner?"

"He must have been coming back from the mall. The steering mechanism in his car was fouled. And I know you talked to him because I checked."

"With what? Who?"

"I had a colleague play the tapes from your phone calls this morning."

"My phone at work is tapped?" Lenore's voice squeaked. "When did you do that?"

"Before I called Mike with the tip."

"So you predicted he'd give me the story?"

"Who else is there?" Rittenhouse turned his face toward hers and smiled. He didn't tell her they'd tapped all the phones in the office.

Lenore put two and two together. She wasn't sure the answer was four. She flicked her unsmoked cigarette out the window. "So, because Bosner's dead, you think they'll come after me." She stopped, and added almost as an afterthought, "And they'll kill me." She lit another cigarette with some difficulty. Her hands were shaking.

"Yes." Rittenhouse paused again and looked at her quickly.

"His wife?"

"In the car with him."

She sucked in her breath. "Oh, God, that lovely woman."

Rittenhouse plunged ahead with his current analysis. "Our guess is the cartel doesn't know about our operation. But whether they do or not, they're attempting to clean house, to get rid of anyone who could give evidence or testify against them. They've realized that taking Turnbull out was too big. It hadn't occurred to them before that it would arouse suspicion because they were blinded by their own arrogance."

Lenore blinked a few times, took a drag and blew smoke out the window.

"They found out about you because of Bosner, and they found Bosner because, well, Perkins already knew him and Turnbull interviewed him. They have nothing to lose now. Killing your dogs was just a warning to you because you weren't there when they expected you to be, and they just wanted to hurt something. What's driving me crazy is that we should have been ahead of them, and we're behind. Our team is working now to get innocents out of harm's way. Our local law enforcement partners are picking up the low-level drug dealers like Vance, hopefully before they're dead."

"And this, all this killing, it's all about money, about keeping their hold on their business?" She might scream her head off in another minute.

"Yes, it's about money, but it's also about power, about who holds the levers of power, and what they do with it."

"Fucking bastards." Lenore was furious, rage rising in her with every breath. She clamped down hard on the little voice that was still saying, *Gordo, Frodo*, the little voice that was still weeping, and said through clenched teeth, "I want the whole story. I want to be the one to break it, with everything, names, places, operations, financials, you name it."

"That's a lot to ask."

"Not as much as putting my life on the line, which is what you did." She was now fully thawed by the heat surging to her face.

Rittenhouse looked as if he was considering her demand. "I'll have to make some calls, get approval from higher up, but I think it will be okay. Our plans have changed anyway. The whole story could break by Sunday, if that is how the timing works out. Having the story out will give Senator Archer some red meat for his hearings." He looked over at her. "I think that'll be fine." He put his hand on her shoulder.

She looked down at his hand. "Oh, and who the hell are you? And what about my dogs?"

Bill Rittenhouse passed her his wallet with his national security agency ID. "I'm the intelligence analyst in charge of the task force. NSA and US Secret Service are two agencies the cartel didn't infiltrate. And I'll take care of your dogs."

Lenore stared at him. He turned away from watching the road for a minute and returned her look. Both felt a jolt of electricity run through their bodies, shaking them into silence.

Chapter 35

Three thousand miles away from his daughter Cheryl, whose name he read in the newspaper from time to time, Larry Roland sat in an interrogation room in the Los Angeles Police Department, talking to Peter Smith, US Attorney for the federal district court in California. He had been there for three hours. He was doing his best imitation of a broken record. "I'll give you what I know for complete immunity from prosecution, plus protection, an identity change, and relocation to the place I say. Otherwise, you've got nothing on me except gun possession, and I'll walk," Roland said to Smith.

The way Roland figured it, he owed Perkins nothing. The guy would as soon see him dead, had, in fact, planned to have him dead. He was pretty sure they would have killed him at the next pick up spot out in the woods. Left him there in the outhouse to rot until some hiker found the body. When the state police had picked him up just outside the rental car place in Azusa, Larry had been glad.

They had done it quietly, no rough stuff. Just gotten out of their car, walked up to him as he was about to open the door of the rental car, and asked him to come with them. He'd asked for ID, even though their car was marked, and the ID could be phony. But he risked going with them anyway. It was the best bet for staying alive. Besides, he was suddenly tired, way too old for this shit. He had decided this going about eighty miles an hour on the winding State Road 39 back into the town. His bandana had been soaked with sweat that wasn't caused by heat.

In some ways, this was safer than making it to Bimini by himself, although it would probably take a lot longer. Lots longer. They'd have to dress him up in a monkey suit and put him on a witness stand. *Man, I'd hate that. There has to be a way out of that.*

"I want anonymity, too, no public witnessing in any courtroom." He could try. Then he had another thought. "And I want money, one percent of what you confiscate, in cash, just the way you do for other confidential informants."

Smith had his marching orders from people much higher up the US Attorney General's Office food chain than he was. What the brass wanted was a clear picture of how the drug operation worked, the list of bank numbers where money was sent, who had recruited Roland, who was his contact person, and any other names and faces he could provide. They only needed Roland's information, not him. Roland was small potatoes. There was no reason not to save the taxpayers ten thousand dollars a year for his keep in some federal penitentiary. As far as Smith was concerned, as soon as they had that information, Roland could go get killed in any country he wanted.

"Deal," Smith said. "Tell me what you know from the beginning." He turned on the video recorder.

"Deal in writing," Roland said, "signed by someone with the clout to make it stick. Then I'll tell you what I know. Oh, and I get the original of this video you're making. You make the copy while I watch you."

Smith didn't flinch. He left Roland in the locked room and came back an hour later with a formal looking piece of paper stipulating the agreement. He brought a witness to the agreement with him, no less than the US Attorney General himself.

చుచుచు

Larry Roland looked at the AG and realized they had expected to get him, or this guy wouldn't have made the four-hour flight across the country. This wasn't a nickel and dime operation. Clayton Turnbull, may he rest in peace, was still scoring. Somehow Turnbull must have tipped someone off before Perkins had him taken out. Larry was glad he had asked for the money. He read the agreement over, and all three signed it.

Larry leaned back in the chair and started to talk.

Chapter 36

Bob Rosen stood in front of what had once been Margaret's house. It was now a collection of pickup sticks swarming with firemen in yellow coats. Very little was salvageable. *All those years,* Bob thought, *all that value, blown away in an instant.* He was waiting for the captain to tell him whether there were bodies inside, waiting with a sob held in his chest as if it was a child he might clutch in his arms to keep from danger.

He had arrived at the scene just as the fire department, called by a neighbor stunned by the explosion rattling her windows, got there. Several women stood together nearby, talking in low voices to each other, their faces scraped clean by fear. Two hugged themselves and shivered. Two others had their arms around each other.

It was getting colder, Bob noticed. He looked around. The gray Chevy was gone. He shuddered. In an hour, it would be dark. He wondered how long the neighbor women would stand watch. This was now personal. Their own safety was suddenly in question.

Captain John Fenwick walked out of what had been the house and over to Bob. He watched the tall man make his way across the rubble toward him. He tried to quell his shaking. Fenwick leaned down and put his hand on Bob's shoulder.

"No one was in the house," the fire captain said slowly and distinctly. "There are no bodies." He kept eye contact with Bob. "You may be in shock, sir. Let me know if you think you won't make it."

"No one was in the house," Bob repeated. "No one was in the house." Then he got it. "No one was in the house!" He was suddenly elated.

"That's right, sir," Fenwick confirmed. "There are no victims."

Bob almost laughed. *No victims? Hardly. But Margaret and Melissa are alive, somewhere. Where the hell are they? Margaret is in no shape to have gone shopping, and she wouldn't have let Melissa out of her sight. Her car, now charred, was still in the driveway. The gray Chevy was gone. That's it! Margaret and Melissa are in that agency vehicle.* He had to find them.

"Thank you, Captain. You've made my day." Bob shook Fenwick's hand, grinning at him, then walked to his car and got in it.

Fenwick looked after him, shaking his head. He'd never seen a reaction quite like that one. He walked over to the group of women who had been staring at him while he talked to Bob and told them the news. Their reaction was more what he expected.

Bob called his office. He had come straight to Margaret's from his visit with Clay's boss in the city. He was bringing good news. Not only would the agency pay for the funeral, they were going to give Margaret her widow's benefits from Clay's pension. He had thought the news would give her some relief. Everything combined, she would be financially comfortable. Not, he expected, that being wealthy mattered to her, but later the idea might provide some comfort. She wouldn't have to work. The value of the property was recoverable. She had insurance. The lot alone was probably worth a quarter of a million because of its location. She'd be okay. She'd have the luxury of having time to grieve.

"Becky," he said into his cell phone when his secretary answered, "I'm at what's left of the Turnbull's residence."

"Bob." Becky sounded exasperated. "I've been trying to find you. Your cell phone's been off."

"Oh, yeah, right," Bob said. "I'm sorry. I didn't want it to go off during my meeting, and I forgot about turning it on again."

"Well, Margaret Turnbull called you and said the men in the gray Chevy were there." Becky read from the message she had written down for her boss.

"Did she say anything else?"

"No, that was it, except to say she needed you. She sounded pretty desperate."

"Do you know where she went?"

"No. Did you say 'what was left of Margaret Turnbull's house'?"

"I'm coming back to the office now." Bob disconnected.

Bob checked his cell phone messages, something that hadn't occurred to him before now. There was Becky's message. A later message from Margaret said they were safe, and they would be at the funeral tomorrow. "Thank you for everything," she said. Her voice sounded thick, as if she'd been crying, but she didn't sound scared. Bob relaxed a little and noticed that his chest felt empty now. His pregnant grief had been delivered.

Chapter 37

Secretary of State David Campbell's richly appointed office displayed original works of art and crafts from all the countries he had lived in during the last ten years in various important ambassadorships. Long white linen drapes pulled back from the two huge windows in the corner office gave him a spectacular view of the city at night. It was at that view that Campbell stared while Lawrence Blackwell, National Security Adviser to President Werner, talked to him.

Campbell couldn't bear to watch the man talk. In too short a time he had developed the kind of revulsion for the way Blackwell's lips moved while speaking that made him want to retch. It may have had to do with what Blackwell said, but Campbell didn't think so. Most of the time they operated from the same set of ideas, if not principles. He had simply developed a severe case of animosity against the man, and there was nothing he could do about it.

After rambling through the history of the entire Cold War, its aftermath, the breakup of the Soviet Union, and the ensuing economic and political chaos in its previous

so-called republics, and the rise of the KGB thug who ran
the country, Blackwell had finally gotten to the point.

"So you're saying that Hopkins, the CEO of a giant
multinational oil company, a friend of the president's, has
been using field personnel in our embassies, our international education Internet server, and our military to fun-
nel heroin out of the former Soviet-bloc countries and
Afghanistan to sell in the United States in order to fund
his company's public relations campaign?" Campbell ran
a hand over his head. "That's quite an accusation. How
was a private individual able to set up such an operation,
commandeer our troops, and deploy field agents? And he
was able to set this whole mess up in just two years'
time? I think you might be misinformed, Larry."

"Unfortunately," Blackwell said, leaning forward in
the comfortable chair, "there are members of our own
armed forces and security agencies involved in this, for
their own personal gain."

Campbell looked skeptical.

"You don't need to believe me, David," Blackwell
said. "I am fulfilling my duty to inform you. But you really should consider these facts. You can't say I didn't
keep you in the loop."

Campbell shrugged. His dislike of Blackwell and
what he was saying was too intense to speak.

Blackwell continued, "I have the best possible intelligence on this, although we both know that facts on the
ground are often different, but I'm on top of the matter.
I'm handling it. There's no need for you to get involved."

"Who are you talking about?" Campbell was edgy.
He didn't trust this guy. Blackwell had not been his
choice for the position—too ambitious, too academic, too
unseasoned, too power-hungry—but Campbell had been
out gunned in the selection process by the president's

ambitious chief of staff, who had old prep school ties with Blackwell.

Blackwell named names that cut a wide swath through top echelons of the military, intelligence, and enforcement communities. Campbell listened.

"Who else knows this?"

"I'm on my way to inform Senator Archer now. I've already talked to the chief."

"I don't want to be part of this," Campbell said slowly, looking into Blackwell's small blue eyes. "State has nothing to do with this. Thank you for informing me." He stood up, signaling that the meeting was over.

Blackwell nodded. Campbell noted he seemed satisfied with the result of his visit. Blackwell's satisfaction made him uneasy. He would make some calls himself.

అచఁ

Blackwell left the secretary of state's office and walked slowly down the corridor ignoring everyone he passed along the way. His own staff, a gaggle of goslings honking in concert, followed behind him. It didn't matter that he was not, in fact, going directly to Senator Archer's office or that he planned to wait to inform the senator at an evening reception the next day. He would get around to dotting that 'i' in his own sweet time, and in the environment where he could casually mention it rather than have the information exchanged in a formal setting where Archer would feel he had to do something about it.

That, at least, was Blackwell's reasoning for failing to inform the head of the Senate Intelligence Committee about Hopkins, the oil pipeline, and the drug money for counter-terrorism efforts he had overseen without congressional approval. At that moment, Blackwell was still sure that he held all the winning cards.

DAY THREE

Chapter 38

Margaret sat up in bed, gasping for air, her heart thudding. Perspiration soaked her sweatshirt. Wet hair clung to her neck. She put her hand on her heart and stared around her, dazed, unsure about where she was. She looked at the clock on the bed stand next to the twin bed she had been sleeping in. Three a.m. The day of Clay's funeral. She had been dreaming something strange, something about water and the moon.

She looked over at the next bed. Melissa was sleeping soundly, her hair a red velvet drape fanned out across the pillow. They were not at home. They were in a cottage somewhere along the Potomac River in Virginia south of Mount Vernon. There were men in the cottage to protect them. Her house was destroyed. Clay was dead.

These were the facts of her life, now. This was all she had. She reached for her purse on the nightstand and pulled it onto the bed. She shook out its contents on the blanket. There was enough moonlight flooding in the window to see each packet of paper distinctly. One by one she picked up the documents that had verified her life, substantiated it, given it legitimacy. Her fingers traced the little footprint on Melissa's birth certificate from Alexandria hospital. She unfolded Clay's birth certificate. Born to Alma Lewis and Harry Turnbull in Carbondale, Illinois. A small-town boy, once a hero, now dead. Margaret was glad his parents had died so that she wouldn't have to break the news of Clay's death to them.

Then she noticed the envelope. Her name was printed on the front in Clay's handwriting. Her heart jolted. She slipped one finger under the flap and jerked upward, tearing the flap. Margaret pulled out the letter inside and stared at it without unfolding it. There were two pieces of paper. Slowly she opened it and read the first page in the moonlight coming in from the window.

My dearest, darling Margaret, Clay had written. *You are the love of my life. Without you and Melissa, there would be no meaning to anything I have done or do now. I cannot express to you how much the little things you do without thinking make my life worth living. I love watching you in the morning when you sit across from me drinking your weird tea, even after you've gone to the bother to make coffee for me. I love watching you sleeping, your dreams seeping out from your lips in small sounds. I love knowing that when I come home, you will be there, near me, breathing the same air.*

If you are reading this, Margaret, it's because something has happened to me. Perhaps we are very old, and I have died in my sleep. Perhaps something else has happened. But whatever it is, I didn't want to go away from you without your knowing how deeply I love you both, how much I'm sure the world is a better place because you are in it, and how well I know that you love me in return. I have been the very lucky recipient of your love for twenty-five years, as of this writing, and if we are very old when you read this, I will have been luckier still.

We have done everything we were supposed to do, my darling. You are with me always. Love, Clay.

The date on the letter was two months ago. Margaret put her fingertips on her mouth. Clay had known something was going to happen, and he had left the note to say goodbye so that nothing would be left undone. Even dead, he was trying to make her feel secure.

Margaret tossed off the covers and got out of the bed. She walked over to the window and looked out the second floor dormer. Snow covered the ground and gloved tree branches. There was no wind, no sound except Melissa's steady breathing. As far as Margaret could see, trees were covered with snow, their branches making strange white marks on the black paper of the night sky. A light flickered in the distance. She watched it. It came closer, two lights now. *The headlights of a car moving toward this house.* Her breath came faster. Margaret felt her brain shift into a gear she didn't know she had, some kind of primal, instinctive place where the word "go" inspired instant movement.

"Melissa," she said, standing rooted to the spot. "Melissa, wake up. Get your shoes on. Your jacket. Melissa," she was almost shouting now, if you could shout when all you could do was barely whisper.

The car pulled up to the house, practically under the window where she was standing. Two men got out. They were carrying guns. Big guns. Margaret whirled around, took three long strides to her child in bed, and shook her.

"Melissa, get up now."

Melissa opened her green eyes and looked at her mother. She was instantly awake.

"Shoes," Margaret said as she heard the first shot. "Jacket," she said as she heard the solid front door of the house slam back against the wall downstairs. She heard running and another shot. She went back to the window and cranked open both sides of the casement. This bedroom was on the second floor. Her fear of heights hit her hard. Just thinking of what she was going to do, she could hardly breathe.

"Go out the window," Margaret ordered Melissa. "Climb up onto the hip of the roof and then up to the top. Lie flat. Wait for me there."

Melissa had slipped on her backpack. Whatever was in there, the kid thought it was worth her life. For a second, Margaret thought she should do the same, gather those precious documents together and keep them with her. But there wasn't time. Clay's letter was in her hand. She stuffed it into her pants pocket. Shots downstairs reverberated in her ears. She locked the bedroom door, pulled the sheet off the bed Melissa had been sleeping in, tied it to the foot of the bed, dragged the bed toward the window, and threw the sheet out the window. She grabbed the jacket Agent Erol had loaned her, threw her arms into it, and climbed out the window after her daughter.

Margaret scrambled along the slippery roof, getting snow in her mouth and eyes, scraping her chin, holding onto each shingled edge of the old slate tiled roof that she could find with her freezing fingers. Her toes clutched the edges of roof tiles beneath her. She saw Melissa above her, lying flat along the roofline, holding her hand out for her mother, her eyes encouraging. Margaret panted, trying not to sob. Finally, she reached Melissa's hand and scrambled up onto the rim of the roof. They heard more shots.

Margaret closed her eyes for a minute. *Those poor men.*

Below her, a man stood at the window where she had just been minutes ago, saying, "What the fuck?"

Her heart pounded.

They would think she and Melissa had climbed down and were running away from the house toward the road. At least that's what she hoped. She waited. She heard heavy footsteps pounding out of the house, across the porch, down the steps, and then the sound of two car doors slamming. A car engine revved and tires whirred against the snow as they sped away. She waited until it was quiet. She looked around. There wasn't another house for miles. Two hundred yards away, Margaret saw the river glimmering slightly in the light of the crescent moon. She hoped for a boat. It wouldn't take the men long to figure out she and Melissa weren't running toward the main road. There was a river in her dream.

"Now," Margaret said, and let herself slip feet first down the snow covered roof toward the back of the house. When her feet touched the gutter that ran around the edge of the roof, she grabbed the roof tiles above her head. The slate cut into her fingers. One of the tiles dislodged and fell, clattering against the house. Margaret shuddered and held her breath. Melissa easily let herself down the slope of the roof and stopped on the gutter next to her mother. She watched her mother carefully. Margaret seemed to be out of ideas.

"Edge over to the column over there, Mom and wrap your legs around it then slide down to the railing on the back porch. We can jump from there."

Margaret was considering whether she could do it.

"You can do it, Mom. Go on. I'll be right behind you."

Her fear ensnared her. She could barely think. Melissa might be able to jump from the gutter, without harm, by rolling on impact, but Margaret could never do that, and they had to get down. The men would be back.

Slowly Margaret did as her daughter instructed. She kept her eyes on the spot where column met roof. She closed in on her target inch-by-inch. Her breath came in short, hard spurts, each one seeming to sear her chest. Her hands ached. Panic about how high she was off the ground, panic about slipping, panic about men with guns coming back all gathered in her stomach and rose up in waves, making her dizzy and her mouth dry.

She made it to the column, wrapped her legs around the slippery post, and let herself down from the roof one tile at a time, her hands slipping a little more each time until they clung to the edge of the gutter. *I have to be brave. I can't let Melissa down, can't let her die here.* She slid the rest of the way to the railing, her feet slipped out beneath her, her head hit the railing, and she crumbled to the ground, groaning softly.

Melissa looked down at her mother from her perch on the gutter, simply turned away from the house and leaped, hitting the snow-covered ground and rolling. She jumped up and ran to her mother.

"Get up, get up." Melissa put her hands under her mother's arms, trying to drag her to a standing position.

Margaret could hear the sob in her daughter's throat waiting to be released and marveled at her control. She wanted them to just be able to sit there, to wrap her arms around her daughter. She wanted Melissa to crawl into her lap the way she did when she was five and bury her face in her chest. She wanted to stroke her child's hair, reassure her, and tell her everything was going to be alright. But that wasn't going to happen now, and if they didn't move soon, that was never going to happen again. She had to get on her feet and moving.

"Mom," Melissa said in her most commanding voice, "*get up.*"

Margaret shook herself. Dazed, she looked around. Her right ankle was burning, her left leg was throbbing, her hands were numb. Something wet trickled down her forehead. She didn't have time for this inventory of injuries. She had to move. She could hear the whir of tires on the snow again, racing back to the house, close now.

"To the river," Margaret whispered.

Melissa dragged Margaret to her feet, wrapped her arm around her, and the two women ran through the small woods, Melissa almost carrying her mother, straight to the water's edge. They stopped and looked around. In the moonlight, they saw a dock and, at the end of the dock, a boat, a good sized one. It rocked gently in the tide. Their escape was only thirty feet away. They ran through the frozen shoreline brush that crackled under their feet, ran down the dock, and threw themselves over the side of the boat. Margaret looked around for controls, saw a metal ladder, and dragged herself up the steps to the command center. The key was in the ignition. She didn't think about what to do, she just turned the key. She wished for gasoline. The engine started immediately.

"Get it untied," she called to Melissa. The boat had a steering wheel. It would steer the way a car did. There was something that seemed to be a gearshift. She threw the lever into the top position. Nothing happened. There was something else to press or hit or move. Her eyes scanned the controls again.

"Mom, they're coming," Melissa yelled from below.

Margaret heard footsteps pounding up the dock toward them. She found another lever and moved it to the first notch. The boat lurched forward. She spun the wheel to the right, out toward the middle of the river and the boat started to move slowly, too slowly, in that direction.

On deck, Melissa watched two men in dark jackets running down the ramp toward the boat. Their feet pounded on the wood like a train coming right at her, almost in the same rhythm. Their jackets blew open from the speed of their pace. Guns drawn, they pointed straight at the boat as they ran. Melissa crouched down until only her eyes and forehead were exposed, enough of a target, she supposed, for men who were trained to kill people.

Without taking her eyes off them, she rummaged in her backpack and pulled out the small semi-automatic pistol and the extra magazine loaded with bullets she found in the drawer of the nightstand on her father's side of the bed. She'd known it was there. He had told her about it, shown her where it was, and told her to make sure she grabbed it if they were ever in trouble and he wasn't with them. She could still hear his instructions, on how to use it, in her head. "Aim for the chest, Melissa, aim for the chest." It was almost as if he had known something bad was going to happen to them. But she didn't have time to think about that now.

Melissa looked at the gun quickly to find the safety and turned it off. She held the gun in her right hand with her left hand cupping and supporting the right. She supported her arms on the side of the boat and waited until the men were in range—the range where she could actually hit them with a bullet—and fired.

The man closest to her reeled backward. She had caught him in the shoulder. She fired again, this time aiming, hearing her father say, "Keep your eyes open, Melissa," and caught him in the throat. He went down in a heap on the dock. The other man increased his speed. Melissa shot twice more and watched as the second man crumpled. She waited, her hands ready to squeeze off more bullets, her eyes scanning the dark for more men. In the space of a breath, she had become someone else.

Margaret heard two shots. Then two more. Then silence, the sound of nothing stretching out across the water, expanding these few seconds as if time were something freeze dried that could be dissolved in the right medium to fill any size container.

"Melissa!" Margaret screamed and left the controls, sliding down the ladder toward her daughter.

Melissa was crouched on the floor of the boat. Her arms were extended out over the railing. Clutched in her shaking hands was a short, silver gun.

"Are you shot? Are you hurt?" Margaret screamed and ran to her daughter.

"I'm okay, Mom," Melissa said in a choked voice. "I think I got them. I shot first."

Margaret looked over at the dock they were moving away from and saw the bodies of two men sprawled across its planks. She looked at her daughter. Melissa looked back at her. The girl's eyes were steady.

"Come up there and help me figure out how the boat works." Margaret had a new respect for her daughter's abilities. She didn't ask where Melissa had gotten the gun or how she had learned to use it. She didn't care. All she cared about was that they were alive, and the men were dead. About that, she was very glad.

They climbed back up the ladder to the controls and stared at them. Melissa looked at her mother. Her father had shown her how to manage a boat this size when they were on vacation in the islands. "Sit down, Mom, I can handle this."

Margaret wearily sank down on the floor, her legs out in front of her, her back against the railing. Her ankle was already swollen. Her head was aching. She pulled Agent Erol's jacket, which came down to her knees, close around her. Melissa tossed her backpack to her mother.

"My phone's inside it. Call Bob Rosen." Margaret's daughter was now completely comfortable with command.

Margaret nodded and pulled the phone out of the pack. Melissa put the gun on a shelf just above the wheel, pushed the throttle higher, and took them out to the middle of the river, headed, she hoped, toward Alexandria.

 භ

Inside the house, Agent Erol groaned and rolled over onto his back. He pulled his cell phone off its clip, hit one number, and, when Bill Rittenhouse answered, he said, "They got us. They may have gotten the women. Get the bastards." He dropped the phone.

Chapter 39

It was dark in the room, except for the small nightlight on the wall by the door. The room, Keith remembered, was done in the usual hospital lime green, a revolting color. But in the dark, it took on the shade of sludge moving slowly down the Potomac from water treatment plants. *Not a good metaphor.* He looked over at the bed, the white sheets folded down neatly under Cheryl's arms, her bandaged shoulder, her head on the white pillow. A line of light ran along the intravenous tubing in her arm. The sight tugged at his heart. She looked more vulnerable now than she ever had. *That's because she is more vulnerable*, he reminded himself. *Don't get carried away with the romance of the moment.*

Her heart monitor showed a reassuring pattern of blips. Keith had been there for the duration, sitting in the chair beside the bed. He leaned forward and put his head down on his arms on the bed. His dark brown hair was disheveled from having run his hands through it repeatedly while he was waiting for Cheryl to come out of surgery, and the gray eyes she had fallen in love with had dark circles under them. His skin was pale, his cheeks budding a two-day growth.

Archer would have to have his hearing on his own, Keith had decided instantly when he saw Cheryl hit the ground. He had decided it again when he looked at the blood on his hands, her blood. And again when the hospital orderly wheeled the gurney away from him through the double-swinging doors. When he had finally checked into the office, the senator himself had gotten on the phone, inquired about what had happened, and told him not to worry about anything but getting Cheryl back in one piece.

"There will be life-long jobs in my office for both of you, as long as I'm here," Senator Archer told Keith.

Keith was grateful, but he had a feeling Cheryl had no intention of staying in politics. It was clear to him also that he would go wherever Cheryl wanted to go, that much of his future had been revealed as he waited for her to come out of surgery. She was more important to him than his career, which, as he looked at it now, was so much meringue on the pie, whipped up and decorative. Yet you couldn't make a lifetime of meals out of it.

Running for office himself wasn't his cup of tea. He had no tolerance for small talk and pressing the flesh. The events he was forced to attend made him break out in a cold sweat. Other options—think tanks, professorships—seemed trivial now. Maybe they had always seemed trivial. He had gotten into this business because he had wanted to solve big problems. That notion seemed more naïve now than any other idea he had had about serving his country. Somehow he had thought that at the seat of power he could find a way to do good on a large scale—actually change the way government business was done.

What was it I'd ideally sought to accomplish? He had lost the pathway to those thoughts and memories that galvanized him when he first came to work on the Hill. Instead, he had been absorbed by the glamour of closed-door meetings, surreptitious telephone conferences, elevator intrigues, and meetings in the White House. The sense of having infiltrated the old boys club was seductive. Simply saying you had a meeting at the White House raised the value of your personal currency, at least for that moment, in the constant exchange of power that went on in the halls of Congress. He could remember how his heart had beat a little faster the first time Archer had said, "Walk with me," as he hurried to the floor of the Senate for a vote. That jolt of pride came with a long, lingering after-taste of arrogance. He hadn't been immune. Until now, he had thought he was fighting the good fight.

But what, in fact, had he accomplished in all this time? It seemed to him they were on a merry-go-round in Asbury Park, the one he loved to ride when he was growing up. The horse, painted with wild eyes and black mane flowing back from its long chestnut face as if lifted by the wind from its swift gallop forward, went up and down in place. The platform went around and around, and he would lean out as far as he could, trying to reach that brass ring that dangled from a long metal arm projecting from the post. Rarely as a child had he been able to grab that ring.

It took him years to realize the horse never went anywhere. There was, of course, the thrill of getting the ring the first time, but once he had figured out the timing—and his arm had grown longer—the thrill was gone. Other children, younger than he, took his place, excited at the opportunity.

I'm replaceable, he thought sitting next to Cheryl's hospital bed, *we're all replaceable, even the old man.* Beyond understanding that, he had no idea what he would do, what Cheryl would *want* to do. *Something simple*, he hoped wearily. *Something that mattered.*

"You look like something the cat dragged in."
Cheryl's voice was hoarse.

Keith looked up at her tired face and smiled and immediately took her hand. It seemed to him that the light had just come on. She, at least, couldn't be replaced, not in his lifetime.

Chapter 40

From the sitting room in the moldy cabin, Bill Rittenhouse could hear Lenore tapping hard on the keys of the laptop he'd had set up in the small bedroom. He had more to worry about now than her story. She had demanded a conversation with Archer, which he'd arranged. He'd also noticed that she double-checked the senator's phone number, calling back for confirmation. Temporarily, if how fast the keys were being hit was any indication, she had enough to write the story.

He paced the cabin. *We didn't move fast enough.* The bad guys knew what he knew before he did. He should have acted months ago, instead of playing this cagey game of chess with men who knew all the strategies cold. Somewhere in the back of his mind that DEA gun sting that went bad was shaking its finger at him. They had been thinking, if they let it play out, they would gather up more bad guys. *Shit. What a mistake.*

Rittenhouse sat, leaned forward in the chair, put his elbows on his knees and his head in his hands. They had been arrogant in their assessment of how fast the drug ring could move, how many men they had to do their dirty work. It wasn't a handful of corrupt men they were dealing with; it was an entire damn army. He had been too complacent, too sure that they had the time to set up, observe, gather evidence, and make arrests before the shit hit the fan. But he had been too late. It was too late the minute Perkins's goons had picked up Turnbull. Shit was flying everywhere.

He didn't have time for recriminations. He had to act. He had already dispatched two men to the house on the river. They had reported back: Agents Erol and O'Brien were dead. Two men, previously unknown to them, had been shot on the dock and were dead. Identification on them said the men were CIA. He had a man checking on that. Their guns had been fired. The bullets in their guns matched the caliber of the bullets in Erol and O'Brien. The Turnbull women were missing. He had no idea who shot the assailants. His agents were cleaning up the location. Rittenhouse shook his head. He had issued orders for everyone who was involved in the drug ring to be picked up, now. At least he had the warrants, although he didn't feel as if he'd won a pat on the back. He'd gotten the warrants as soon as he had confirmation from California that Larry Roland had talked and named names.

He personally would be knocking on Paul Perkins' door. Rittenhouse couldn't wait to see the surprise on the man's face, to hear his first reactions to the fact that they had him cold. He wondered if Perkins would reflect for a second on how Turnbull had felt when they picked him up in that phony arrest. Rittenhouse wondered how Perkins had managed to do it all. *How could he have managed the operation all these years or imagined he would get away with it?* There had to be somebody above him who was really in charge, but they didn't have a clue who that was. That's what they were hoping to get out of Perkins. Somewhere deep in Rittenhouse's mind was a feeling of impending dread, a fear of finding out that the real chief of this international drug ring held a higher office than just a deputy level posting in the FBI.

He looked up. Lenore was standing there, watching him. She walked over and put a hand on his shoulder, squatted down next to him, and looked into his face. "Rough night, huh?"

"Yeah."

"It's not over, is it?"

"No, it's not over. We lost the Turnbull women. We have no idea where they are. Cheryl Roland's been shot. She's in the hospital. Who knows how many of their low-level operatives are dead? And we're doing the arrests before we're really ready, so these jerks just might slip through the legal cracks in the final analysis."

"Cheryl *Roland?*" Lenore put the emphasis on the last name.

"Yeah, Congresswoman Hannah Gittleson's director of communications."

"Is she Larry Roland's daughter?" Lenore asked the question calmly enough.

Rittenhouse had already put her in touch with Larry Roland by phone. He was an unnamed source for her story and had detailed the flea market operation, as well as how he had been recruited by Perkins, and some of his background. Rittenhouse, listening to the interview on the speaker, thought Roland was candid enough. Roland hadn't mentioned he had a daughter. It took Rittenhouse a few seconds to hear Lenore's question. Then he groaned and put his head back in his hands. *How could I not have known about the connection?*

"That must be why Turnbull had called Cheryl. He was looking for more information about Larry Roland, who he'd been observing." It should have been obvious, but they had been blinded by her position. "I missed it entirely. I thought she'd been targeted because of her connection to Keith Hamilton, chief of staff of the committee running the hearing, as a warning to Senator Archer."

He and his team had thought they were so smart that nothing got by them. They had been so busy trading mental high fives and back slaps about figuring out the whole drug operation that they had stopped thinking. But Perkins' group had known about the connection between Larry and Cheryl and they were trying to keep her quiet, on the off chance she knew anything about her father and what he had been up to all these years. This was too involved, even for Rittenhouse. *Shit. I need to get someone over to the hospital to guard Cheryl.*

Rittenhouse looked around the room, his mind wandering as if desperate to get away from what he was supposed to be doing. He wondered what the high and mighty who stayed in these cabins thought about their surroundings. He guessed that being invited, or ordered, to come along was enough sugar with the pill. This kind of proximity, of access to the most powerful man in the world—to even be able to say you'd spent the weekend at Camp David—was enough incentive to pack your own anti-allergy nose spray and eye drops and put on a happy face.

Lenore broke into his thoughts. "I want to talk to FBI Director John Reese. I want to get his reaction to what Perkins was doing, maybe see if he had any involvement in all of this."

Rittenhouse looked at her. *Man, this woman never has enough. Does she not get it that this story is no longer important?* They would be making the arrests before the story hit the papers. From her point of view, that made it a stronger story. From his point of view, that made the story irrelevant. He sighed. He had been using her, now she was using him.

"Not yet, not till we pick up Perkins and see what he has to say. I'm going to have to leave you here. There are plenty of young, strong Marines around to guard you." It was almost a joke, and he smiled at her, wanly.

She smiled back. "I'll get some sleep, then. Let me know when you have him so I can call Reese before anyone else does."

Rittenhouse shook his head, almost in disbelief at her persistence. *Does she not understand that my world—the orderly gathering, deciphering, interpreting, and presentation of information—has been blown apart, that I have lost control of the operation, or that her story is now the very last thing on my mind, or that, frankly, I don't give a rat's ass?*

His thought must have been evident on his face. Lenore seemed to relent, her blue eyes losing their edge. She gave him another pat on the shoulder, stood up, walked to the bedroom door, and shut it.

℘✺℘

There are things even he doesn't know, Lenore thought. *Right now, he's knee deep in the big muddy.*

She threw herself down on the bed. The springs squealed. She put her arms up under her head and planned to think this through as well as what to do with the little juicy tidbit Chief of Police Spats had given her about the mayor. Within a minute, she was asleep, dreaming at first about playing Frisbee with Gordo and Frodo, watching their ears flap as they bounded across a grassy field and jumped up to catch the spinning yellow disk. Later, the dream turned ugly.

Chapter 41

Margaret apologized to Bob for calling him in the middle of the night. She said she didn't really have anyone else to call. Bob, awakened from a deep sleep, struggled to consciousness, listening to the sound of her voice crackling in the bad connection without making sense out of the words.

Abruptly, the words "boat" and "river" startled him wide awake. He sat up on the side of the bed and rubbed at his scalp with one hand trying to get the blood flowing to his brain.

"What? Where are you?"

"We're on someone's boat out on the Potomac," Margaret shouted into the cell phone. Her voice, straining against her fatigue, sounded eerie floating out beyond the boat into the wide black expanse around them.

Melissa had headed the vessel toward the lights that sparkled as if they were a gathering of fallen stars on the horizon, assuming that, where there was a massing of lights, there was a city, perhaps Alexandria but maybe DC. But really she had no idea where they were going. Out on the water alone, with only the night as a guardian, they felt temporarily safe.

It was amazing to Margaret how quickly the notion of safety returned. The sense that they had control of their lives was innate. The notion that they could make decisions that would work to their own benefit, that they could figure a way out of this mess and survive it, was still working. Good thing, too. Otherwise, they'd be dead already.

She couldn't convey all that to Bob. She wasn't sure why she was calling him. Rescues didn't seem to work anymore, and the people who rescued them got killed. She didn't want Bob to die. She and Melissa really had to rely on themselves. At least, that way, they were the only ones whose lives they were risking. Maybe she was calling Bob just to confirm that they were alive, as if telling him made it real. They weren't dreaming this. They were not hallucinating these two days of horror from which they would somehow wake up safe in their own home with Clay alive and making jokes over a pancake breakfast.

On his side of the phone connection, Rosen started talking quickly. "Two women out on a boat in the middle of the river make an easy target, too easy. These guys seem to know everything. You need some protection, even if it turns out to be ineffective. And with this call, the bad guys might be able to pinpoint your location from this connection."

"What are you saying? That being on the river is dangerous also?" Margaret sighed.

"Look, I don't know anything about the equipment available to the intelligence community," Bob said, "but I do know that satellites allow NSA to listen in on just about any conversation they want to. And these bastards seem to have all the newest gadgets at their disposal. And they seem to be everywhere. There has to be some law enforcement agency they haven't infiltrated."

Margaret could almost hear him thinking through the options.

"I'm going to call the Coast Guard," he said. "You hang up and stay off the phone. Head to a shoreline. Don't stay out in the middle of the river. You can be spotted too easily."

Margaret groaned. It hadn't even occurred to her that those monsters would have reinforcements out looking for her. It reminded her of a game she and her sister used to play with their father when they were little. He bought them rubber broad swords with silver-painted hilts and taught them a few fencing moves, plus the basic French of fencing—*en garde* and *touche*. They would put their feet in the correct stance, only momentarily in proper form because as soon as they were engaged in the fight, sparing and thrusting and jabbing their father, all instructions went out the door as they jumped and screamed and giggled with delight. Finally, one of them would put the point of a sword to his stomach. He would fall down, writhing and grimacing, and pretend to be dead for a minute. Then he would jump up and say, "The uncle is coming to avenge his brother!" and once more begin parrying with them. They dissolved again into delighted screams and giggles, disarmed by his ploy, no matter how many times he did it.

This time it wasn't a game, though, and she wasn't laughing. There would be more uncles coming to revenge their brothers. Margaret no longer thought of this as unfair, no longer thought about how she and Melissa were innocent victims, because they were *no longer* innocent. They had stolen a boat and killed two men, even if it was in self-defense. The bad guys should be on their guard: she and Melissa had uncles in their family also.

"Okay," she said to Bob and clicked off. She put the phone back in Melissa's pack and sat there for a minute thinking. Her daughter looked at her. It was Margaret's turn to lead.

"Steer the boat over toward the shore opposite the one we came from." Margaret was unsure what was east or west, north or south. "Keep as close to the shore as you can. When we spot a dock, we're pulling up to it and getting out. That is, if the Coast Guard doesn't find us first."

"The Coast Guard?" Melissa was astounded. "Do they patrol rivers, too?"

"I think they might be part of the good guys, honey. At least I hope they are." Margaret paused. "And if they're not, we'll get out of that jam, too. We're getting good at this."

Melissa looked at her mother, who was nearly crumbled up on the deck. Margaret watched her daughter's face and the revelation dawning there.

"I'm proud of you, Mom," Melissa said, "and Dad, too. I'm proud that I'm your daughter." Melissa nodded, as if she were confirming her own thought. "I love you, Mom."

"Me, too, sweetheart."

These were the words Melissa's father used to say to her on the telephone every night when he would call from wherever he was just before Melissa went to sleep. Melissa turned back to her steering, tears held tightly in her throat.

Margaret shifted her weight to ease the pain in her leg and felt the two pieces of paper she had shoved into her pocket. She pulled them out and smoothed them on her thigh.

She thought she might show Clay's letter to Melissa. It would comfort her.

She pulled the second piece of paper on top thinking it might be a letter specifically for her daughter and read it.

1: the letter started, *I know there's a syndicate distributing Southeast Asian heroin nationwide in the US. I think it's coming primarily from Afghanistan and Uzbekistan.*

Clay had been writing quickly, Margaret could tell by the handwriting. It slanted sharply to the right as if it were running pell-mell off the edge of the paper. In the moonlight, Margaret read.

2: At least two of the guys involved in the syndicate were in Vietnam at the rank of lieutenant or higher, one of them stationed in Cambodia, the other in Okinawa. That's where the plan started, when they successfully shipped dope back to the states in dead servicemen's coffins. They were in charge of loading C-130 transports back to the States. With buddies on the other end in Pendleton, they could move a lot of stuff, make a lot of money.

3: One of those lieutenants, Jawarski, made it to the top of the CIA over the last 30 years, and the other, Perkins, climbed the career ladder at the Bureau and was head of the drug interdiction unit. They're still in business. Nobody knows this, anyway I don't think so. Except the guys they're working with. I don't know how high up this goes, but I think it goes up pretty high. That reporter in California who broke the story about the CIA deliberately selling dope in black neighborhoods to keep them subdued, impoverished, dead, or locked up had missed the point. These guys didn't care if the population was subdued or not. Or what race they are. It's about the money, not the politics. And they are playing a long-term game, for the deep rewards, not the instant payoff.

4: The drugs are still coming in from Asia on US military planes and they've got guys on the ground supervising departure and arrival. These are guys they can trust, who'd rather die than give up information. Or maybe it's that they know they'd be dead, fast, if they did.

5: They're using some elaborate Internet connection through the US State Department under the aegis of an education—meaning propaganda—program to send emails that let the players know where to go, and when.

6: There's a connection to non-Arab oil fields and pipelines—

The writing stopped, as if Clay had been interrupted and had rushed to hide the piece of paper. Margaret's heart was pounding, her mouth felt dry. She put her hand to her cheek, to see if she was still there, still real. He had been investigating something big. He would never have left this information where she could find it if he hadn't thought it was important, and that he might die because he knew it. She and Melissa might die. That's why these shitheads were trying so hard to kill them. They thought she knew what Clay knew. She almost giggled. She was tempted to let the piece of paper float over the side of the boat into the water and be washed away. But Clay had died for these few words, this secret. They were his legacy. They were his vindication.

Now she felt a kind of anger she had never felt before. It shook her as if she were a flag whipped by the wind. Fury burned in her heart, made her breath come faster. There had to be someone she could give these notes to who could take the monsters down, who would clean up that foul nest of killers and soul polluters.

Hands shaking, Margaret folded the two pieces of paper together again and pushed them back into her pants pocket. At least her rage meant that her physical pain diminished. She could do anything necessary to keep them alive. Her daughter, it suddenly occurred to Margaret, had already proven that she would.

Chapter 42

Paul Perkins wasn't asleep. Still in his suit pants and white shirt, sleeves rolled up, tie loosened, he had been packing. He was getting ready for a trip out of the country that would look as if he were on Bureau business from the multitudinous forms he had filled out and filed. But as the time strung out and they had no reports, his absence would be taken as AWOL. Eventually, they would figure out that he wasn't coming back to the Bureau. They would realize in their own slow, Neanderthal way that he was done with their work.

At no time did Perkins imagine that any government group had been keeping tabs on his clandestine organization within the FBI. Turnbull had been the exception, and he had dealt with Turnbull. He would have been surprised to learn that Lessing had given the order to deal with anyone else even remotely connected to Turnbull. He didn't imagine Lessing had that kind of imagination or authority, at least without consulting him. He was pretty sure he had control of Lessing. And Lessing had the director wrapped around his little finger.

The next level of manpower down from him and his long-time counterpart in the CIA, Arnold Jawarski, were

busily removing those free agents on the street who had
been recruited by them directly more than two decades
ago. Those deaths would look the same as drug culture
drive-bys. Apparently, they had lost Roland. Perkins got
a call from inside the AG's office saying Roland had
been picked up by California State Troopers and charged
with carrying a weapon without a permit. Perkins
laughed. Roland would get himself out of that jam, and if
it looked like he was going to talk, Jawarski himself
would turn off that spigot.

Perkins stopped in his tracks for a minute considering whether Jawarski would take him, Perkins, out. Jawarski didn't know he was getting out. It was safer that
way. But once Jawarski had figured out that Perkins was
leaving the operation, he would also get around to the
idea that it didn't make sense to pursue him. After all,
Perkins wouldn't be taking a cut anymore. The take could
all be divided between Jawarski and Lessing. The extra
dough should ease the blow of his defection, as long as
they understood he wasn't going to give them away.

Perkins had everything set up for this escape: a lovely villa on the southern coast of France and another on
the island nation of Mauritius, each with the right accou-
trements, including the right women for each culture and
climate. He would divide his time between these two
places, flying in his private Lear jet, purchased so easily
in a sealed bid from the IRS's confiscated property web
site that he had to chuckle. He even had a pilot on retain-
er to fly the jet for him and, of course, a ground crew stationed at the private hangar at the regional airport where
he kept the jet. Money made the world go 'round and he
was finally going to take his spin.

The only thing Perkins didn't understand about himself is why he had waited so long to get out. He could
have left years ago, and without the hassle they'd been

through in the last few days. He could have quietly slipped away, even retired, and no one would have been the wiser. He couldn't remember now why he had wanted to bring Lessing in, why he had wanted to expand the operation. That had been a mistake. He had gotten caught up in making the organization survive, in making it bigger, more profitable, as if it were an organism that had a life of its own and that his purpose in life was to serve that organism. It was laughable how easily the operation had run him, instead of the other way around. He had somehow gotten confused, thinking he was the CEO of some legitimate enterprise. It had taken the Turnbull episode to remind him that what they had all been doing was illegal. But he was aware now, and this was the time to get out. He was a young sixty-three and had some juice left. He would enjoy himself.

Perkins walked down the flight of stairs from the spacious, nearly empty bedroom in his Reston townhouse, purchased for a quarter of a million dollars more than two decades ago when he still had a wife and kids. He was in the old part of Reston, the part that had been built on the revolutionary social concept of equality and community. Perkins snorted. Not that he'd ever bought into those ideas, but the area around Lake Anne, at the time, had been the most desirable, the most highly marketable. Nevertheless, at that time, Reston had still been remote, an outpost of suburban homes and almost too cute village centers in the middle of Virginia farmland. Now it was the center of the e-universe on the East Coast. His real estate agent would have no trouble selling the townhouse, complete with its tiny dock from which one of the new yuppies could launch a small sailboat out into the recurrently dried up lake. He would be far away, soaking in the sun, wearing white linen and no socks, letting his hair grow, drinking water with lemon slices, completely engaged by the millionaire life he had planned.

Perkins stood at the sliding glass doors of his living room, looking out onto the patch of snow-covered woods that led to his share of lake glittering in the shaft of moonlight that had broken through the clouds. Banging and loud voices suddenly yammered at his front door. He turned around slowly, coolly, as if he had been prepared, reached for his gun on the dusty, rosewood, built-in side-board, and backed into his study. Another sliding glass door led out to his deck from there. He was calculating the odds of running, hearing them shooting the lock and breaking down the door.

Jawarski would have come quietly, taken him by surprise. These had to be government stiffs at his door. By the sound, there were several of them. He could take out a few, but if he failed to get them all, then at the very least he'd be charged with killing an officer or agent, or they'd just shoot him in retaliation. If they were here, they had enough for a warrant, so they had enough for a grand jury indictment with the cash in his home, the passport with a fake ID, and the ghost trail of his emails on his computer.

If the feds—among whom he had not counted him-self for eons—had Jawarski, or any of his troops and they talked, then they had Perkins. Someone had talked. Someone they hadn't gotten to soon enough. It had to be Roland. Perkins could almost see that stupid son-of-a-bitch giving him the finger. And that damn lone eagle Turnbull. Without Turnbull, and the whole mob of people that had somehow been attached to him, Perkins would be home free by now. If they hadn't had to clean up that mess, their activity would have gone undetected for an-other decade.

He knew arresting and terminating Turnbull was a mistake. He had known it would go sour. Lessing had been so sure of himself. *Is there a way to take Lessing out?* That was a very tempting thought.

His mind was a tourist in the country of his real feelings, as if he wandered through a landscape of fear and fury in a little Fiat of reasoning, just put-putting along, unaware that the motor could die at any moment, spending a colorful currency that had no real value to him. Yes, and there in a narrow back alley, was the little shop where weapons and equipment to eliminate anyone who annoyed him could be obtained without remorse. It was an easy purchase. He shook himself. If only reality were vaguely similar to this sudden hallucination he seemed to be experiencing.

Watching the door to his study and the large window, he sat crouched against the wall of a study that had no books and from which anything he'd ever cared about had already been shipped to his real homes. He thought about what would happen to him after he was arrested. He thought about living the rest of his life in a five-by-ten-foot cell. He thought about the company he would keep. He couldn't kill himself. He didn't have the guts, just as he didn't have the guts to spend the rest of his life in jail. But he could get them to do it for him. He waited until he saw the shadow of a man's arm extend out into his view in the window. Of course, they were trying to surround him. Then he stood, aimed, and fired. He watched as the guy's arm jerked and his body dropped back behind his house. Perkins stood with his gun leveled. If necessary, he would take another shot, and then another. He had a full clip, and he had as much time as they would give him.

The study door flew open. Bill Rittenhouse stood in the doorway with his weapon aimed at Perkins. Perkins, without any change in expression, took aim to squeeze off a bullet in Rittenhouse's direction, but Rittenhouse wasn't taking any chances. In quick succession, he shot Perkins's shoulder and both legs, taking him down but leaving him alive. Perkins's bullet hit Rittenhouse in the shoulder, making him gasp and reel backward even with the protective vest. But Rittenhouse didn't drop, instead watching Perkins fall onto the parquet floor of his study. Rittenhouse walked over and kicked his gun away. Quickly, he patted Perkins down, searching for other weapons. Nothing.

The man was quiet: no weeping, no whining, no groaning, no speaking. Perkins lay on the floor and observed. He was too cool for Rittenhouse's money, but they had him. That, after all, was the point of this exercise: to arrest the man, to question him. Rittenhouse didn't want any of his young, gung-ho colleagues to make the mistake of eliminating their best potential witness.

"Stop," Rittenhouse ordered his team through the microphone connected to the ear pieces each man wore. "Search the house for material evidence. Don't screw it up."

Rittenhouse told a team member on the other end of his wireless connection to send an ambulance. He had his man. In a few hours, he would know what Paul Perkins knew about everything. Right now, he wanted to know where the Turnbull women were, if they were alive.

"Where are Margaret and Melissa Turnbull?"

"Dead, I expect," Perkins said calmly. "Frankly, I don't know." Obviously, Perkins wasn't going to take the Fifth. "But I can give you Lessing." He smiled.

Bill Rittenhouse shook his head. "We'll talk soon."

⌇⌇⌇

On the other side of DC, Arnold Jawarski, having been tipped that Perkins was going to be arrested, was already in the car he had stashed in a warehouse. The car was pre-packed with everything he would need to get established in Venezuela, including documents that identified him as someone else entirely, someone who ran an import-export business, and, on further inspection, would appear to sympathize with the current Venezuelan government. He was driving to the Baltimore docks to load the car and himself on the freighter that would take him to the port of Alcasa. He would drive from there to Maracaibo on his own.

He pushed the call button on his phone and spoke. "Take a spin at Turnbull's funeral tomorrow, give 'em a little scare."

He hung up. He'd already had a less traceable conversation with someone else he knew would get the real job done. It was always good to have redundant plans.

Chapter 43

Margaret heard the sound of the helicopter before she saw a light out on the river coming toward them. She froze. She had no idea whether this was the Coast Guard or more men who were trying to kill them. They were fairly close to the shore. She considered whether she and Melissa should just leave the boat going and jump off the side, swim for the shore, and try to run. The water would be freezing. That thought held her in place.

The helicopter was closing, its sound deafening her. She dragged herself to her feet and stood next to Melissa, watching the spotlight that had captured their boat, seeing the way the wind from its propeller whipped up the water in the river. They were deer in the headlights, not knowing which way to turn for safety. She saw Melissa pick up the gun and hold it out from her body with two hands, raising it toward the helicopter.

"Wait, honey, we don't know, we just don't know."

Waiting could get them dead, but Melissa lowered the gun.

From the water, Margaret heard a man yelling her name on some kind of bull horn. "Margaret Turnbull," he was shouting, "this is the Coast Guard. Turn off your engine."

Margaret looked at Melissa. They had to trust someone, but they also needed an alternate plan.

"Melissa," Margaret yelled over the sound of the helicopter and the instructions from the man on the cutter, "if they aren't who they say they are, I want you to get off this boat and swim to shore. Don't worry about me. Just swim and, when you get your feet on land, start running. Run to the nearest house and say your boat capsized and you need to use the phone. Call Rosen and tell him to come and get you. You can do it."

"I'm not leaving you, Mom," Melissa yelled back.

"Yes, you are, if it means saving your life." Margaret took her daughter by the shoulders and stared into her eyes. "You are the most important thing in the world to me, and I won't have you killed. Do you understand?"

Melissa nodded. She cut the motor, and they went down the ladder to stand on the deck. The large boat pulled up alongside, a rope was thrown over, and Melissa tied it on to their boat. The men had uniforms on. *Coast Guard* was painted on the boat. Melissa guessed they were the real deal. She put the gun in her backpack and watched while the men boarded their boat.

"Mrs. Turnbull, ma'am, we got a call that you were in trouble," said the man who seemed to be in charge.

"Yes." Margaret was still waiting to see what would happen.

"We're going to tow your boat into Alexandria, ma'am, but first we're going to get you some warm things to wear and take a look at those injuries." He nodded toward her face and leg.

"Could I see your identification, please?"

The man pulled a badge out from under his windbreaker and showed her. He was Lieutenant Ron Milner,

US Coast Guard, according to his photo.

Good enough, Margaret thought and then swayed, her knees starting to buckle.

Melissa put her arm around her mother's shoulders and held her steady.

"Do you have any green tea?" Melissa asked the young lieutenant. "She needs some tea."

"We'll take care of you, Miss Turnbull. It's okay now." Lieutenant Milner regarded the young teenager who seemed way too competent for her age.

A single tear escaped from one of Melissa's briefly closed eyes and rolled slowly down her cheek. She wiped it away with the back of her hand and half-smiled at the man. "We can take care of ourselves, thank you," she said in a strangled voice but with her chin lifted. "We just need a little help right now." She paused and looked at her mother, who nodded in agreement.

"Yes, miss," Lieutenant Milner said and helped them board the cutter. Even if no one else had—and it sure looked as if no one else had—he would keep them safe, that was for sure.

Chapter 44

Lenore was typing as fast as her fingers could go.

At five a.m., two days after Clayton Turnbull was falsely arrested for espionage, abducted, and then killed by rogue FBI agents, a special, multi-agency, law enforcement and intelligence task force arrested Deputy FBI Director Harold Lessing at his Great Falls, Virginia, home. They charged him with ordering the murder of Turnbull and conspiring to distribute billions of dollars in heroin under the cover of the agency.

Lessing—informed that Assistant Deputy Director Paul Perkins, head of the FBI's drug interdiction unit, had linked him to the international heroin smuggling ring—turned state's evidence. For immunity from prosecution, he gave task force interviewers the name of National Security Adviser Lawrence Blackwell, who, Lessing said, was the mastermind of the entire operation and the one in contact with the Central Asian opium cartel.

Within two hours of Lessing's arrest, a team of black-trench-coated men knocked on the door of Blackwell's Georgetown, brick townhouse and respectfully re-

quested that he come with them. They had a warrant for his arrest.

Blackwell, who opened the door wearing a black and red satin bathrobe, made them wait until he had put on a gray silk and wool suit with a quilted, red velvet vest and gray, silk cravat before going with them quietly enough. But once the suddenly former White House adviser was fully acquainted with the charges, sources said he demanded to be released immediately.

His call to the president was not put through by order of the chief of staff, who told a reporter Blackwell was terminated. Blackwell's call to US Attorney General John Pitcairn was not accepted. His face turned purple, and he began to sweat profusely. Interviewers called for medical assistance, and Blackwell was taken to Georgetown University Medical Center where he is under observation.

Lenore stopped typing. This was her second-day story, a follow up to the breaking story she had filed early this morning about how Turnbull was framed by government agents who ran an international drug cartel. She was sitting in the back seat of Bill Rittenhouse's car parked in a reserved space next to the Justice Department building. Rittenhouse, no worse for wear other than a substantial bruise to his shoulder, was fifty paces away talking to a small group of men in trench coats. She was working on her laptop, and it was cold. She shivered slightly.

She still had no statement from FBI Director John Reese. She wanted his statement for the story, before whatever press conference he called. She wanted to hear the tone of his voice when she told him what she had. She hoped no one from the task force had informed him yet. Still early in the arrest cycle, they may have been waiting to see if he was involved. Lenore wanted the element of surprise.

She had nagged Rittenhouse into letting her tag along for the Blackwell arrest until he had her helicoptered into DC so that she could go with him. She knew the bit with the clothes would let her colleagues in the media know she was at the scene. But she needed Reese. That would be the capper, and then this story had to go out immediately. She had to be able to find a wireless connection and send it, and she would send it simultaneously, to her editor, publisher, and AP. Let their fact checkers drive themselves crazy, she had nailed the story.

She thought about how to get Reese's home number. She was right here, at the Justice Department. She had her laptop, and her press badge, and a phone. There had to be a source, a contact here, as well as there was anywhere else, someone willing to tell her something they probably shouldn't for a brief moment of tabloid glory. Reese might even be here already, even without knowing about the arrests. She would bet he came in early every morning. And—*Wait a minute, he would have a space reserved for him right around here.*

She stopped rummaging in her backpack for her cigarettes and looked out the window. The spot right next to the car she was in was marked reserved for Reese, and it was empty. All she had to do was wait. Within minutes, a black SUV pulled up. Lenore jumped out of her car and watched to see what door Reese got out. The back right, she noted. *Of course, he's a big shot. He'll have a driver.*

She was there in a shot, even before his driver could come around the van, holding up her press badge and her phone, ready to record.

"Director Reese," Lenore faltered a little, not knowing how he was normally addressed. "Mr. Reese, did you know that one of your top agents and your deputy director have been arrested on drug conspiracy and murder charges?"

Reese stepped back, put his hand up, covering the microphone with his hand.

"Who are you?" Reese demanded. He looked around to see if this was just the most voracious of a shark party waiting to feed on him. She was alone.

Lenore held up her press badge for him to read. "Lenore Cavanaugh of the news," she said. Her voice was shaking, and so were her hands. She was alone with maybe the worst man in the world, and his bodyguard. She had no weapon, was not conversant with any fighting techniques, and might very well be out of her mind for lack of sleep. Hell, she could be shot, knocked out, canceled in a second, well before Rittenhouse even noticed. *What the fuck am I doing?*

Reese looked at her face, read novice, and shook his head no to the agent standing behind her ready to force her down onto the ground. "What is it you're asking me?" Reese asked calmly enough for a man whose stomach must have been feeling as if he had eaten rocks for breakfast.

"Paul Perkins and Harold Lessing have been arrested. Did you know that, sir?"

"No," Reese said. His voice was flat.

"They have implicated each other and the national security adviser to the president in a drug cartel operation that would have been going on under your nose for the last eight years, at least. Were you aware of their activities?"

"No." Reese appeared to be on automatic.

Lenore thought his brain must be whizzing through past conversations, observations, putting information together in a new way that made his blood run cold. He would be realizing, right about now, that that bastard Lessing had played him.

"Were you aware that the arrest of Clayton Turnbull, which you ordered, was based on deliberately falsified information, sir? That he had discovered at least some information about the drug operation?"

Reese didn't answer. He had closed his eyes.

"Sir? The Turnbull arrest?" Lenore pushed.

"That's enough, young woman. No comment." John Reese turned stiffly away from Lenore and walked with his bodyguard toward the Justice Department building. He was intercepted by Rittenhouse and his crew before he got to the door.

Left alone in the small parking lot, with the morning sun just beginning to take the chill out of the air, Lenore did a brief version of a touchdown dance.

Chapter 45

The funeral was at eleven a.m. They would go in the funeral home's limousine first to the chapel at Fort Myer and then to the grave in Arlington Cemetery. This was a change from their initial plans. Bob Rosen had somehow gotten the cemetery's bureaucracy to bend the rules and move more quickly than their usual pace, which was usually the speed at which the molecules moved in the bronze statues on the mall.

The last time Margaret and Melissa had been to Arlington Cemetery, they were tourists going to see the eternal flame burning in memory of slain President John F. Kennedy. Melissa had been three and had no memory of the trip. For Margaret, the place then was just part of the area's history, the civilization in which they lived, and she had wanted Melissa to see where brave men and women who had served their country were buried. Only in the back of her mind was the idea that someday Clay would be laid to rest here. She herself had been too young to think of death as a possibility. It had been so long ago, another century it seemed, when they had toured the landmark, walking by row after perfectly aligned row of

white grave markers standing as much at attention as sol-
diers waiting for marching orders.

The thought of going back now, of standing at the
edge of a grave where the earth had been ripped open
over a wound, made her gasp for breath. They would
cover the dirt, she knew, they would do everything to
keep her from realizing that the body of her beloved was
going to be put in the ground, covered with dirt. The
problem was she couldn't avoid thinking of it that way.
Covered with dirt. It was the last insult. The thought
made her furious, angrier than she had ever been in her
life. It wasn't enough that they had killed him, taken him
away from her. Now they were going to dump him into
the ground. *Really, cemeteries were nothing but elegant
euphemisms for human landfills.*

Margaret fought to control herself, the effort making
her shake. She had to remember Melissa. She had to think
of a way to help her child make her peace with this, if
that was possible. Across the room was her Melissa,
standing by the tall window of the funeral home's reception area. Margaret guessed that Melissa was seeing the
inner pictures of their night of horror together—a night
which now seemed a million miles away in this sanctum
of middle class etiquette. At any rate, Melissa looked as if
she belonged here, Margaret's mother had seen to that,
even though the child still clung to her backpack. Margaret, for her part, had held onto Clay's letter. *I will discover today who I should give it to.*

ℰ∾ℰ∾

They were both wearing the clothes and shoes Margaret's mother had purchased for them after unknown,
but kind, agents had picked her up at the airport. Sally
had taken the agents in stride. She asked only where her

daughter Margaret was. When the agents said Margaret had been forced to leave her house without any preparation, Sally had—in her own style—insisted on going to a mall. She insisted enough that they acquiesced, shrugging. Their job was to protect her, so they went along. Sally bought Margaret and Melissa matching black suits, pumps, and stockings. She guessed about the sizes. She bought underwear also, speculating that the girls wouldn't have had time to grab anything clean.

She went about her shopping as if everything was normal, succumbing to a moment of grief only as she was examining the soft, silky texture of the black slips she bought to go under the suits. She had remembered briefly, and then shoved it to the back of her mind, the joy she had in carefully selecting Margaret's trousseau just before her wedding to Clay. She had remembered, and then put out of her mind, how delighted she had been at the way the young man had gazed at her daughter from across her living room. She remembered and tried to forget how she had expected that marriage to go on for her daughter's lifetime.

But she couldn't think about that now. She also had to get to Liz, her other daughter coming in from New Jersey. The agents had said they would have adjoining rooms in the hotel.

She wasn't allowed to call or text Liz because the GPS on her cell phone might alert the bad guys to where they were.

It seemed, to Sally, that the agents were speaking a completely different language from English. Sally finished her shopping and went on to the next thing, as she put it to herself, being there for her daughters, whatever that took.

e/oe/o

Margaret looked at her mother, sitting quietly next to her on the dove gray velvet sofa, her hands folded neatly in her lap. *Mother always knows what to wear*. Sally was wearing gray because, Margaret guessed, she was not a principal mourner, although her grief glowed in her gray eyes whenever she looked into Margaret's face. That morning was a blur. Margaret wasn't sure how the communications had gone that brought them to the hotel where her mother was staying.

There had been a series of handoffs, she and Melissa getting into one car after another. They had been exhausted and dazed. But when her mother opened the door of her hotel room, Margaret simply walked into the older woman's arms. Sally said nothing but, "I'm so sorry, my darling," and held her as long as Margaret wanted. And then Sally had turned to Melissa, who, finally, in her grandmother's safe embrace had let go of her long-held sobs.

Liz stood next to Melissa at the window, stroking her hair, saying nothing. Margaret wondered how her family got to be so good at funerals. It's not as if they had a lot of training, just the usual number of deaths. Perhaps it was innate, not wanting to pry into someone else's feelings, not having any facility with small talk and clichés. Silence was really what she wanted from them, and their presence, and they were delivering. She would have to remember this, for when it was her turn to simply stand and wait.

She looked over at Bob Rosen, who was quietly talking with the funeral director. The plan now was to wait here for a while to see if anyone else would come to the funeral, and then anyone who arrived, after greeting Margaret, would follow the hearse and the limo in their own cars out to Arlington. Their limo would be manned by the two bodyguards who stood to either side of Margaret in the reception area. It seemed to be such a sane little plan, Margaret couldn't help wondering if something was missing, had been left out. Life just wasn't that simple. Not anymore.

The sound of mingled low voices in the hall area caught her ear. Then people from Melissa's school entered the room together—teachers, the dean, and Melissa's friend Katie and her parents. Margaret was too stunned to move. She felt as if she were watching a movie of a funeral: the concerned, consoling friends turning up unexpectedly, pressing hands, leaning in to whisper condolences. *What's my line in that play? Oh yes, "Thank you, you're so kind." Thank God I remembered it.*

Margaret watched their visitors with Melissa first. Girded by her aunt, the girl politely shook hands, turned her face up and at an angle to look at them, nodding, her beautiful pink lips framing words quietly, softly, as if she were taking great care with the formation of syllables. At the end of that line was Katie, the true friend. The two girls simply embraced and then went to sit on a sofa by themselves, heads down, whispering to each other.

Then there were others, Clay's colleagues at the Bureau lined up to pay their respects, some of them looking gray with grief, some angry, all of them trying to be comforting. Then neighbors arrived. After they greeted Margaret, they went into the quiet room where Clay's casket lay waiting to be removed for burial. Margaret wondered how all these people had learned when the funeral would be. She looked around for Bob Rosen and found him watching her, the lines of his face seeming to be folded into a fabric of kindness. She smiled over the visitors' heads at him. He smiled back, gently, so he would not overwhelm her with his sense of pride that she was pleased.

She was talking with Clay's boss when she heard...or was that sensed?...a collective intake of breath and a sudden silence of the steady murmur of sound people had been making. She looked up and saw Senator Ted Archer stride into the room, look around, and then walk directly over to her, bend slightly at the waist, take her hand, and look deeply into her eyes.

"Mrs. Turnbull," the senator said, "your husband was a patriot and a hero. It is a great loss to the country that he has died in this dreadful way. If there is anything I can do to assist you, please do me the honor of letting me know directly."

Before Margaret could say anything, the senator had placed his card with his home telephone number on it in the hand he had just been holding. She was stunned. She didn't know this man, except from seeing him on television. As far as she knew, Clay didn't know him. She couldn't even speculate about what would have brought him to Clay's funeral.

"Senator, I don't understand, but thank you," Margaret said. "I appreciate the time you've taken to come here." She stopped. There was really nothing else to say. She looked at him, mute, desperately hoping she wouldn't cry.

"Anything," the senator said again, "your husband was a hero." He stood up, pressed her hand once more, and then walked out of the room with his aide and a US Secret Service detail on either side of him to wait in the vestibule for the procession to assemble.

Sally looked at her daughter. The question was obvious. Margaret shrugged. "You know what I know, Mother, which is nothing," she said flatly, a little smile tweaking the corners of her mouth upward.

Sally patted Margaret's hand. "The man did the right thing," she said, "the right thing." She took a tissue out of her small purse and blotted the corners of her eyes.

Margaret turned her attention back to the room. A tall, slender couple was approaching her. The woman's arm was in a sling, and she was very pale. The man had his arm around her waist. He looked weary but calm. Another two people she didn't know from Adam, Margaret thought. *How did Bob find these two?*

"Mrs. Turnbull, I'm Cheryl Roland. I just wanted to say how sorry I am that this happened to you." The woman stopped. Her grief was palpable.

Margaret touched her hand and felt the woman's sorrow move up into her arm and wrap itself around her heart. It was genuine. Margaret knew this name. Where did she know it from? But without thinking, she stood up, wincing a little from the sharp pain in her ankle, and wrapped her arms around the woman, taking care not to jostle the wrapped arm. They stood there, faces buried in each other's shoulders, wordless, somehow drawing comfort from each other.

ᴇ⁄ᴏᴇ⁄ᴐ

Keith watched, amazed. On some level, he understood. Cheryl was apologizing for her father's actions. This morning, he had filled her in on Larry Roland's part in this whole mess, telling her what he had learned from Rittenhouse.

She had said, "Oh, that's what it was," and was more determined than ever to go to the funeral, despite the doctor's warning about opening the wound. She had promised to come back to the hospital afterward and get back in the bed. But she had to do this. Nothing would stop her.

He had worried that Margaret Turnbull would be cold, or worse, furious at the intrusion. He had been completely wrong. He would never understand women. He looked over at the woman who had been sitting with Margaret Turnbull. She was watching him.

"I'm Keith Hamilton," he said, "from Senator Archer's office," he offered to try and explain his presence at the funeral of a man he didn't know. "I am so sorry we weren't able to stop this." He swept his hand lamely toward the room that held Clayton Turnbull's coffin, hoping the woman would understand he meant Turnbull's death.

Sally nodded politely, now predisposed to appreciate anyone from Archer's office. It seemed only right that if the head man came, the people who worked for him would pay their respects as well. "Sally Barton," she said, holding her hand out as if she were the Queen Mother. "Margaret's mother."

Keith smiled and shook her hand. Then he stood there, at a loss until Cheryl took his arm. She seemed to be calmer now, as if the internal storm she had been going through had passed. She was no longer shaking. He had gone to her apartment in the morning and gotten her clean clothes and picked up her mail. A bulky envelope mailed from California had no return address on it. He had been curious but in too much of a hurry to open it. They would get to it later when they packed everything up.

Somehow, he hadn't been surprised to see Senator Archer outside the funeral home. It was as if their own lives had been bumped out of their normal orbit and into alignment with the Turnbull's, however briefly. He had talked to Archer as the senator was standing in the lobby of the funeral home and told him that he would be leaving his office as soon as Cheryl was able to travel. Archer nodded, expressed regret, but understood. It occurred to Keith, talking to the old man, that he still admired him.

But his work with Archer was done. He had turned the wheel as much as he could. It was someone else's turn to burn their shoulder at that job. It was amazing that the old man never gave up.

Cheryl guided Keith over to a corner of the room, rummaged for a tissue in her bag, wiped her eyes and cheeks. "That's what I needed. Thank you. I also want to go to the cemetery."

Keith didn't bother to ask if she could manage it. She would manage it. He did get her to sit down.

The last two people to walk in were Bill Rittenhouse and a blonde woman Keith guessed was the reporter Rittenhouse had hooked up with and couldn't shake, according to Archer. Keith had gotten hold of Rittenhouse by phone early in the morning and told him they were going to Turnbull's funeral. Somebody needed to know, he had reasoned, in case those thugs came after Cheryl again.

It seemed Keith's call was Rittenhouse's first news that the Turnbull women had survived the night. On the phone, Rittenhouse had seemed palpably relieved. It seemed odd to Keith that Rittenhouse didn't know where they were. It made him worry they'd put the wrong man in charge of the inter-agency team. Later, when he'd talked to Archer, Keith realized the women had been missing since the middle of the night. Keith had been the one out of the loop. And they did have a protection detail today. Someone besides Rittenhouse must be managing the operation.

Lenore's blue eyes scanned the room as if she were taking notes. She walked with an assured stride up to Margaret Turnbull. Something about that walk really irked Keith. He watched her squat down in front of Margaret and felt immediately protective of the new widow. Margaret Turnbull had been through enough. Cheryl's hand on his arm restrained him from carrying out his impulse to go over and intervene.

"I think she can take care of herself, Keith," Cheryl said, her voice low.

They watched a polite mask come over Margaret's face, the open grief suppressed, her posture, arms folded over her chest, protective. She nodded at the woman but said nothing. Lenore stood up, looking somewhat frustrated. She looked at Rittenhouse then spotted Cheryl and started walking toward them.

Keith figured the reporter thought if she couldn't get the human interest angle for a sidebar, maybe she'd be able to get something more on Larry Roland.

"I know who this is," Keith said to Cheryl, turning his body so that he was shielding her from Lenore's insistent gaze. "It's that reporter who's been driving Rittenhouse crazy. She talked to the senator. Her story ran this morning. She's looking for a follow up. Somehow she got Rittenhouse to bring her here."

"My guess is she would have come with or without him. He's here to prevent her from doing anything outrageous. Don't worry, Keith, I'm a pro."

Lenore was now within earshot, and then she was on them, hand extended to Cheryl along with her introduction. Cheryl took her hand firmly, gave her own name in exchange, and then dropped the reporter's hand and waited.

"Terrible tragedy," Lenore said, gesturing toward Margaret.

So it would be indirect, leading, attempting to get her trust. Cheryl said nothing.

"You know the background..." Lenore suggested. It was neither question nor statement.

Cheryl didn't bite.

Keith glowered at Lenore but followed Cheryl's

lead: no words said, no quotes out of context in the news-paper.

Lenore's blue eyes flared, as if she had increased the wattage deliberately. "You're in Ted Archer's office, aren't you, been doing the research and preparation for the hearings about the drug cartel being run by top White House officials?"

Keith nodded. Cheryl squeezed his arm in warning.

"So you know the whole story, how Turnbull got fingered by Cheryl's father?"

Had Rittenhouse not stepped up at that moment, gripped Lenore's arm firmly, and led her away, Keith thought he might have punched the woman in the face. Cheryl swayed against Keith as if from a blow.

"This whole mess started with my father?" she whispered.

A short, balding man walked up to Rittenhouse, who still had a grip on the reporter, and talked to him briefly but sternly. Then Rittenhouse led the woman out of the room and presumably out of the building.

Keith sighed with relief. His fists unclenched. *How could Rittenhouse have such bad judgment?* It made Keith worry about the investigation. Then he remembered that the investigation wasn't his problem. The hearing wasn't his problem. Whatever was uncovered wasn't his problem, at least personally. They were going far away. Montana, Cheryl had said, where they would make their own electricity and never read another paper or watch another news report again. It couldn't be too soon. He was over his romance with doing the right thing, making a contribution or a difference or whatever the lingo was these days to get you to commit yourself to a life of service for nothing but the notion that you were satisfied with yourself.

ᑫᔆᕮᔆ

Margaret looked for Bob Rosen and caught his eye. She nodded. It was time. The few minutes with Lenore Cavanaugh had restored her fury. It would be enough fuel to get her through the rest of this ritual.

Bob seemed to understand without words passing between them. He walked around to each group of people and said, "We're going now. If you would return to your cars and follow the hearse, we're going to Arlington Cemetery. The service will be held at the gravesite."

There was a general murmur in the room, the swish of fabric against fabric as people put their coats on, moved closer to each other to leave the room. Margaret listened for a minute, knowing that sound would now forever be associated with Clay's funeral. Her throat constricted. She looked for Melissa, who was watching from another sofa, still clutching Katie's hand.

You don't recover from this, Margaret thought suddenly. *Maybe the edges blur into the background, but the central fact of your father's death at an early age, the destruction of your security, remains in the foreground of the painting of your life.* Margaret stood up and went to her daughter. She put her hand on her head and stroked the child's beautiful hair.

"Come on, my darling girl, there's just a little bit left to do. We can get through this."

She took her daughter's hand and then turned to Katie. "Do you want to ride in the limo with us?"

Katie nodded. "I have to tell my folks." The girl put on her coat, squeezed Melissa's hand and said, "I'll be right back," and went out of the room.

Only Margaret, Melissa, Sally, Liz, and Bob Rosen were left in the room. Bob was reluctant to push Margaret in the direction of the door. He didn't want to seem as if he were hurrying her or just trying to get this over with. Everything had to be in her time. He stood near her with his coat on until she started to move toward the door. He held out their black coats for them to slip into. He didn't want them to be cold standing in the wind at the cemetery. They both murmured thank you. Melissa slung her backpack over her shoulder. Margaret took her mother's arm and then Melissa's. Her sister, Liz, took Melissa's other arm.

"Okay," Margaret said and the four of them, linked together, walked out of the room to the double front doors of the funeral home, which stood propped open. Their security detail stepped out in front of them, one stair below them. They walked out onto the veranda and looked at the hearse with the limo parked behind it, doors open, men in black suits and sunglasses on either side. Margaret and Melissa gasped and stopped. This was real. They were going to the cemetery. They were going to bury their husband and father, and they would never see him again.

Sally and Liz waited, saying nothing. Bob Rosen followed their lead. *Who could rush a woman to the edge of her husband's grave?* He watched. In these few moments, he realized that he would be happy spending the rest of his life watching Margaret Turnbull, even if it was from this distance. It was then, as if the sound were coming from a car radio parked on the next block, that they heard a car careening around the corner toward them.

Perched on the roof of a building facing the funeral home, the sniper Jawarski hired waited for a large enough distraction as he found Senator Archer in his sights.

Chapter 46

Mayor Jimmy Jones paced the six feet across the cell they had placed him in overnight and then paced in the other direction. He had been doing this for several hours, and his legs were tired. He knew he would get charley horses in both of them. But he couldn't bring himself to sit down on that cot they called a bed. He thought about bed bugs and other assorted cooties that must be just waiting for his ass to hit the surface. He couldn't reconcile himself to the idea that he was still here, in the local Frederick jail, as if he were some common criminal who the police picked up for some misdemeanor possession of narcotics and whose parents were too damned mad at to bail him out.

"I'm the damn mayor," Jimmy Jones bellowed to anyone who might be in earshot. His face turned nearly purple, and his breath came in short bursts. "I'm gonna embarrass you by having a fucking heart attack right here in a jail cell that my budget pays for every damn year," he yelled.

At this point, after hours of such verbal castigations, nobody bothered to answer him.

Jimmy went over in his mind exactly what had happened just as he had gotten comfortable at the Spa. The door had burst open, a dozen men in uniform had rushed in and grabbed him right out of the chair. He hadn't even had time to zip up before he was shouldered into the back of the black and white and driven away. They said they were charging him with soliciting a minor. "God's grace," he had spluttered, "she's no minor. She's been running that business for five years." Then he stopped, realizing that he had just sort of confessed to whatever it was they were seeking to charge him with.

He had made his one call to Doc, and it had rung through to the vet's answering machine. He had expected that—at any moment of his being picked up so unceremoniously, stripped of his belongings, photographed, fingerprinted, and tossed into this cell—he would have been released without further embarrassment. He had anticipated a full on-his-knees apology from the police chief. He planned to have a good breakfast and laugh about this little snafu with Doc, chalk it up to overzealous law enforcement and the young officers just not knowing who he was.

That was twelve hours ago, and, still, no one had come to talk to him or bail him out. He hadn't even seen the night arraignment judge. There was surely something fishy about this whole episode, and he was making a list of whose heads would roll when the guard slipped the morning newspaper through the bars of his cell.

There he was, on page one, as he often was, but this time it was that awful perp walk shot and a story with what the newspapers called a seventy-two-point headline: "MAYOR NABBED IN LOCAL WHOREHOUSE BUST."

Are they allowed to use the word whorehouse in a newspaper? Aren't there any standards anymore about what they can print? He was going to have to teach those morons at the news their business when he got out of there. He didn't bother to read the short article that filled two columns below the headline. *What's the point?*

He was, slowly, beginning to put two and two together. Doc didn't show, his wife didn't show, none of his so-called staff showed. Forget his friends. Clearly, he was done with politics in this town. *Screw them! Just screw them! I'll be back on top before they can say who's your daddy? And then I'll get them all good.*

To help calm his nerves, Jimmy Jones picked up the newspaper again to scan the ads and read the Sports section. As he turned the pages, his attention was drawn to a story on page three, top left by a headline that made him sit down on the cot.

MAYOR STANDS TO MAKE MILLIONS ON LAND DEAL

The byline was Lenore Cavanaugh. Jones put his hand over his heart. That woman was going to kill him.

Consolidated Partnership LLC, of which Mayor Jimmy Jones is a principal, owns 100 acres immediately adjacent to the county fairgrounds and stands to make millions on its $20,000 1984 purchase of the land, if the Mayor's plan to remove the Sunday flea market and build a road through the parcel receives final approval by the County.

The mayor could feel himself trembling. He gripped the edge of the cot to try and control the shaking of every limb, his head, his stomach. He read more.

Fairgrounds Lane was supposed to have been extended in 2002 but had been delayed until a rapid request application put in from the mayor's office and already approved by the county planning commission expedited construction. A hearing, to rezone the property from farmland to residential, is already in the pipeline.

"How the fuck does she get this stuff? Something has to be done about her."

The mayor only this week suggested to the city council that something be done about the flea market at the fairgrounds, which is owned by a private foundation. The mayor could not be reached for comment at the time the newspaper went to press.

That was it, the end of his career, the likelihood of retiring a very rich man, all sewn up in a three paragraph story by a blonde bimbo. Jimmy Jones leaned over his knees to stop his head from spinning. He was found an hour later by the guard on his regular walk through. The mayor had had a massive stroke that left him unable to speak.

Chapter 47

Keith was the first of the funeral party to see two black mini-vans careen around the corner toward the funeral home. He thought at first that some late arriving VIP funeral guests were simply getting in line for the procession to the cemetery in Arlington. He watched as the front passenger windows on the vehicles slid down slowly.

He saw a flash of light off the sight of one of the guns. It took him a second to register what he was seeing, and then he yelled, "Get down, get down!" and wrapped his body around Cheryl, bending her knees from the back so that she fell onto the steps with his arm under her. He looked around desperately to see where Senator Archer was, hoping his driver and guards were alert enough to protect him.

Margaret, her mother, sister, and Melissa were still standing arm in arm, now closer to the limousine behind the hearse. The urgent sound of Keith's voice had made them all turn to look at him. They looked in the direction of the shooters. Margaret dropped to the sidewalk as if she had been shot, pulling her mother down with her. Melissa did the same with her aunt Liz. She then reached up and grabbed her friend Katie. The women did not scream.

Keith could feel anguish building in his chest. This could not be happening. *Doesn't the government have any protective detail on these people who were able to do their jobs? And who was left from that gang, who hadn't been picked up in the raids that were supposed to have gone down last night?*

The sound of shots reverberated off the buildings around them, making the strafing doubly terrifying. It seemed to continue forever and then it was over, the vehicles gone.

ↇↄↇↄ

Bob Rosen had not dropped and covered. He had run toward Margaret with the intention of throwing his body over hers. Even as he ran, he knew it was a hopelessly heroic gesture that was doomed to failure. He grimaced as he held the palm of his hand to his shoulder from which blood was seeping. *It could have been worse*—the only thought that flew through his head.

Before he let himself collapse on the pavement, though, he had to check on Margaret to make sure those monsters didn't succeed in killing her. Bob staggered toward the women, who were still prostrate on the ground by the limo. He saw Melissa put her hand on her mother's arm and squeeze it. He saw Margaret lift her head and smile in a wistful way at her daughter. He heard Melissa say to Margaret, "God, Mom, there's just no end of bad."

Liz sat up. "What the hell just happened?" Melissa's friend Katie giggled a little hysterically. "Wow."

They're fine. Bob sat down on the cement, his head lowered, tears streaming down his face, blood pouring from between his fingers. *Thank God, they are fine.*

Margaret crawled forward and caught Bob's head before it hit the sidewalk. She moved closer to him and cradled him.

"Mom, put your hand down hard on his wound," Melissa ordered.

Margaret did as she was told, no longer wondering how her daughter knew such things.

"Katie, do you have your phone?" Melissa asked. Katie nodded. "Then dial nine-one-one and get the police and ambulance here."

Melissa looked around, trying to assess the damage from her cover behind the limo. And then she saw it: Senator Archer was on the ground. And although she still couldn't hear anything but the breathing of the people closest to her, she could see his aide's mouth open in a scream.

Chapter 48

Larry Roland leaned back in his rattan chair, looking out over the sparkling blue bay where his boat was safely tucked into its slip in the marina. He smiled, lit a cigarette, and lifted the cold beer, still slick with water from the ice in the cooler.

South Bimini was the right place for him. He had made it. Fooled those damn government goons, fooled even the good guys, among whom he counted his daughter, Cheryl, and gotten away clean with enough money for two princes to live comfortably for the rest of his life. He hoped Cheryl accepted her share and that she wasn't too much of a goody-goody to keep it. He owed her, for all those years he wasn't around, even if he wouldn't have been much of a role model. In fact, he had to admit that she'd done better without him.

The winter sun was kind. He closed his eyes and leaned his head against the cushion. He needed a tan. He read on the front page of today's paper that the national security adviser to the US President had died of a heart attack after being arrested in connection with the round-up of an international drug cartel. Roland noted that the president was not expected to go to the funeral. *No love lost there*, he guessed. The media would be calling this drugs-for-oil scheme "Kazakhstan-gate" for a long time.

Also on the front page was a story about a foiled bomb plot at the Baltimore port. Roland thought it was an odd story that was probably planted to head off any attempts to dig any deeper into connections between the national security apparatus and affiliated bad guys in other countries. In the back pages, a week ago, he read that Turnbull's funeral got shot up by some renegade CIA agents on a secret payroll. At least, that was the official whitewash of the assassination that had made the papers. Senator Archer died in that attack. Archer's death, of course, just made the white hats even angrier.

Undoubtedly, Perkins's couriers and pickup guys were falling all over the continent. He doubted any of them would ever make it to trial. Roland was very glad he'd gotten his 'get out of jail free card' from the US Attorney General himself.

He might, after all, count himself as one of the good guys, after a fashion. He did point them in the right direction in exchange for his freedom, even if that happened after he fingered Turnbull for his rabid overseers. They really lost control on that maneuver, totally overplayed their hand. They could have just quietly removed Turnbull, given him an early retirement with lots of glory, and then knocked him off with that same heart attack bit without making a big to do. That would never have made the papers or stirred up all that fuss. There was just no accounting for the mess that people's egos made.

Even without Archer, the paper said, there would be a full congressional investigation of the FBI and CIA, their abuse of power and their narcotics dealings. Some female member of Congress, a Hannah Gittleson, had sworn to get to "the bottom of the corruption," as she called it. She said Senator Archer had asked her to do it before he died. She had no clue. She had better be careful, or she might find herself lying in some ditch off the jogging path along the Potomac River, a seeming suicide.

Roland took a swig of his beer. He heard a click, something that might be described as a whoosh, and stopped thinking entirely. His head, with a small hole at the back of his shaved skull, fell forward. The bottle dropped from his hand and smashed on the blue and white tile floor of his patio.

എ⁊ഐ

A few days later, a man calling himself John Keating took his fishing boat out of its slip and sailed off into the sunset. No one ever came in to Alice Town to claim the supplies Keating had ordered. Eventually, the locals broke open the crates and took what interested them.

Chapter 49

They made a small squad of women, standing shoulder to shoulder by the grave, standing sturdily as if each served as the foundation for the other. They held hands, examining the mound of raw dirt. They looked out over the vast Arlington Cemetery, watching the many small American flags planted by the headstones wave in the breeze. It was one of those February days when winter is on hold for a minute, the sky wide and blue with only wisps of white clouds. It was a fine day, as Clayton Turnbull used to call them.

Margaret and Melissa Turnbull were again in funeral dress, unharmed by bullets or bombs, survivors of a war they didn't seek. They were resolved to honor Clay's memory, to salute him, to say goodbye, even if no one else was there. Maybe it was better that they were alone, except, of course, for the large contingent of silent protectors standing in a circle around them at a respectful distance. They didn't need anyone else to say goodbye to Clay.

Margaret's thoughts went to Bob Rosen. He was resting quietly in a suburban Virginia hospital far off the radar. It had been a week since the attack at the Alexandria funeral home. Bob would live, such a relief. She could not bear to have another death chalked up to this horror. But she did not want to visit him. She thought maybe she never wanted to see anyone she had ever known again, except her small family. *Whatever's* left *of my family*, she reminded herself.

What she wanted was to live as quietly as possible. She and Melissa were searching Google maps for places they had never even heard of. They found a small town on the Potomac River, a historic place, worth exploring, and close enough to the East Coast to drive to the Atlantic Ocean if they wanted a long walk on the beach. They planned on renting a house to start with, to see if they were comfortable there. Large enough to have a university, the town they'd checked out on the web had a bookstore, a small theater, some restaurants, a bakery, and an art supply store—everything anyone would ever want in a town with fewer than two-thousand people in it, none of whom knew them or cared anything about them.

Just over the river, in Maryland, there was a private school, St. James, which Melissa might attend. She could be a day student. Margaret would drive her there in the morning and pick her up in the afternoon. Being a chauffeur would give her focus, purpose.

The idea for a life was taking form in Margaret's mind in the same way that paintings began. It was a problem she wanted to solve, pieces that needed to go together, a pattern to be discerned, colors that needed to be laid down next to each other, and she knew her mind would work on it, even if she wasn't paying any apparent attention to it.

What she wanted was a clean slate, where they could work out how to live without Clay, to make a new home. She had to inhabit the idea, furnish it, nourish it, a place Melissa would be willing to come back to when she went away to college, got married. *That's my job now.* She could not, for Melissa's sake, wander from her mother's house to her sister's house like a nomad trailing her tent behind her. Creating a place was what she was good at.

Margaret looked at her daughter's beautiful face. She thought she saw a flash of Clay in one of his moods of quiet contemplation, then Melissa lifted her head and began to sing.

"Amazing grace," the young woman sang out at first softly, choking back a sob, "how sweet the sound, that saved a wretch like me..."

It was Clay's favorite hymn. He used to hum it when he did chores around the house. Margaret put her hand over her mouth to suppress her sob and then found the voice to join her daughter. "I once was lost but now am found..." they sang in homage to their dead warrior.

THE END

About the Author

Ginny Fite is the author of the dark mystery/thrillers *Cromwell's Folly*, *No Good Deed Left Undone*, and *Lying, Cheating, and Occasionally Murder*, a funny self-help book on aging, *I Should Be Dead by Now*, a collection of short stories, *What Goes Around*, and three books of poetry. She resides in Harpers Ferry, WV.